LOVING JOE GALLUCCI

KATE GENOVESE

PUBLISHED BY FIDELI PUBLISHING INC.

ISBN:978-1-60414-664-6

CHAPTER ONE

April — 1970

Meg bounded from her 1968 yellow Volkswagen as it continued to jump and lurch forward in the parking spot — even once she had shut it off, an ongoing problem that, as usual, she tried to ignore. "I need to get this damn car fixed," Meg said to her friend Trisha as she pushed the buzzer to get into her sister Lizzy's place at the Cedar Hill Apartments. "I can't afford shit; I should never have bought that car in the first place."

Meg and Trisha were in nursing school, a hospital-accelerated program that would give them the title of Registered Nurse after three years; but they had to go through the program with little time off: a week here, a few days there, a total of four weeks vacation in three years. It was a tiring course of events for girls who were barely eighteen.

The elevator door opened and Meg and Trisha got on. Meg hit the button for the ninth floor. With their student uniforms on and curlers in their hair, the two looked more like Ethel Mertz and Lucy Ricardo than the potheads they really were.

"Lizzy said she was saving a half ounce of really good pot for us," Meg told Trisha. "I hope she follows through." Both girls were looking forward to a frolicking night in Boston after a long, grueling week of school. In the first year of their nursing program they couldn't wait for the weekend! Bar hopping at K-K-K-Katie's and Lucifer's in Kenmore Square was something the two of them did every Friday night; smoke a joint, have a couple of drinks, find some guys to dance with and occasionally go out to breakfast in the wee hours of the morning. That was how the girls made it through school; it helped them cope with their rigorous schedules during the week.

The elevator ascended, heading for Lizzy's apartment, but was interrupted on the seventh floor. As the door opened, Gwen, a friend of Lizzy's, entered with her brother Jimmy, and their dad. Gwen was a petite, adorable brunette, who was a nurse.

"Hi, Meggie!" she said excitedly. "God, do you look tired. I remember those days from school; so exhausting." Gwen checked Meg from head to toe, wondering why she was here with her uniform on, hair in rollers and looking as stoned as Janis Joplin.

Meg wasn't focusing on Gwen or her comments. Her eyes were glued to Gwen's brother. Jimmy was a tall, six-foot, lean hunk, with beautiful brown eyes, long black hair pulled back in a ponytail, and a construction worker's body. As Meg stood staring at Jimmy, Trisha kept nudging her, hoping Meg would snap out of her present mental state and introduce her to Gwen. Finally, after a sharp poke in her left side, Meg stepped out of the fog. Bright-eyed, suddenly aware of her surroundings, Meg said,

"This is my roommate, Trisha. We're going to pick up something at Lizzy's apartment."

"We're going up there, too," Gwen said. "Timmy's there. Liz has been babysitting for me all afternoon." Timmy was Gwen's two-year-old son, the same age as Paul, Lizzy's little boy. They had met two years before at the park on the grounds of the apartment building. Gwen proceeded to introduce her brother, Jimmy, and her dad, Ed Romano, to Meg and Trisha.

As the apartment door opened, Meg grabbed Trisha's arm and whispered, "Jimmy is beyond cute, and here I am with rollers in my hair, stoned, and fumbling all my words!"

"Forget about it," Trisha said. "He doesn't even look like someone you would date. Since when do you like guys with ponytails? Furthermore, he didn't give you a second glance." But as they all entered Lizzy's apartment, Meg noticed Jimmy looking at her when he thought she was busy with something else. He would glance, peek from the corner of his eye at Meg, and of course Meg's heart was pounding; in love with Jimmy Romano at first sight! The chemistry was definitely there.

Lizzy had opened the door to let the group in, unaware that Meg and Trisha were with them. Ed Romano rushed through the doorway and grabbed his grandson, throwing him in the air and giving him great big hugs as the two-year-old landed in his arms. While everyone focused on Mr. Romano and Timmy, Meg dragged Lizzy into the bedroom. There was a frantic look on her face.

"What is wrong with you, you mental case!" exclaimed Lizzy.

"God, Jimmy is adorable," said Meg. "I'm acting like such an idiot; I have rollers in my hair, my uniform on! What a geek I must look like to him!" Meg sat on Lizzy's bed, in her own little world, fantasizing about kissing him, maybe having him barge in the room and ask her for a date.

"Hello in there," said Lizzy, "dreaming up another one of your romances in your head, little sister?"

"Put a good word in for me, Lizzy, tell Jimmy what a great sister, what a fun person I am," smiled Megan.

"Meg," said Lizzy, "you are going nowhere with that guy! He's not your type. I wouldn't ever allow you to see him or fix you up."

"Oh, come on, Liz. My heart is pounding, I'm sweating … I've never felt this way about anyone at first glance!"

Lizzy shook her head. "Meg, Jimmy's a nice guy, but he's into stuff way over your head. Don't get mixed up with him."

At that moment, Trisha burst into the room. "Come on Meg, we gotta get back to the dorm, get ready for tonight."

Lizzy reached over into the silk pouch and handed Meg a half-ounce of the best Colombian dope around.

"Thanks, sis," said Meg.

"This is as far as it goes, Meg. Nothing stronger. I don't want to hear of you doing downs or speed or any smack," said Lizzy.

"Oh, for Christ's sake," said Meg, "I'm in nursing school. I wouldn't do anything to hurt myself. I only want to have a good time."

"Good times can get out of control, Meggie and bad times can sneak up on you real fast. I'm serious, nothing more then pot or you'll get a good kick in the ass from me!"

As Meg was leaving the apartment, she went over and shook hands with Mr. Romano. "Nice to meet you, sir; hope I see you again."

The middle-aged man with a sad face and even sadder eyes stood up as Meg and Trisha were leaving. "Good luck in school," he said. "I remember Gwen doing what you're doing not long ago. Nursing is tough, but a great profession."

Jimmy, with his brown deep-set eyes, high cheekbones, and angry expression, simply waved good-bye with a uncomplicated gesture. Meg wondered if he was just playing tough, pretending he didn't care, so as not to show his real feelings.

When Trisha and Meg reached the Volkswagen, Meg collapsed against the driver's side door. Two rollers fell out of her hair and she was perspiring. "What the Jesus is the matter with me? He's just a guy. I've never felt so attracted to anyone in my life," she said.

"Yeah, and you better get over it. You have a boyfriend in Vietnam, and he's depending on you being there for him when he gets home in a few months," Trisha reminded her. The thought of having feelings for any guy other than her boyfriend, Steve, made Meg feel temporarily guilty. Although she knew the relationship with Steve wouldn't last, she was uneasy; him fighting the war while she was stateside, partying, smoking pot, drinking, even flirting … "Oh, the hell with it!" said Meg. "I'm eighteen-years-old! What am I supposed to do? Stop living?"

At that moment she saw Jimmy exiting the apartment building, his ponytail going from side to side as he grabbed his baseball cap and placed it on his head, pushing the visor down as if he were hiding from someone, or something. He caught a glimpse of Meg looking at him and nodded his head; a shy nod; a gesture that kept the image of Jimmy Romano in her thoughts for many months to come.

CHAPTER TWO

November — 1972

Twenty-one-year-old Jimmy Romano was desperately trying to get his girlfriend, Amy, to go to bed with him. It was one o'clock in the morning. The Johnny Carson Show had just ended, and Jimmy was making his move, inching his hand up Amy's blouse, trying to undo her bra.

"Get lost," said Amy. "I'm not sleeping with you anymore. No sex until you make a commitment. I won't be strung along by anyone."

Jimmy rolled his eyes as if to say, "not this subject again." He sat on the edge of the bed, put his face in his hands, and thought about his relationship with Amy. Five years they'd been dating; high school sweethearts since their junior year. Jimmy, the star quarterback of Newport High, and Amy, the head cheerleader were expected to get married. Their friends just assumed they'd be hitched in another year.

But Jimmy wasn't ready. He had dropped out of Northeastern University after two years. His athletic ability had earned him a football scholarship; a full boat for his high school heroics; but, in the second season he had a severe knee injury, preventing him from continuing to play football at the college level. After surgery and a fairly long recovery he faced reality; no football, no college. He didn't even like studying; why stay? So, Jimmy quit and started working in his father's family furniture business, Romano & Sons.

Ed Romano was second-generation Italian. His grandfather, Adolpho, came to America from Rome in the early 1900s when he was only eighteen-years-old. Adolpho and a friend, Antonio Figorillo, also from Italy, came to Boston and started the F&G Furniture Company. The two had a blooming business by the time both were twenty-five, making custom furniture for affluent people in wealthy towns such as Newton, Marblehead, and Weston, towns north and west of Boston, Massachusetts.

Adolpho married Angelina Caruso soon after arriving in Massachusetts. They met at a dance in East Boston around 1915. Together they had six children, Eddie being the oldest. Eddie and his brother Vinny started working with their dad when they were barely school age. Mr. Romano would pick them up after school, take them to his shop and start preparing them for furniture makers, first sweeping floors, then learning to cut wood, to use the machinery and form designs.

Eddie was a natural and was passionate about his work. When he met his wife, Anna, in 1945, and then had three children, he expected his two sons to follow suit. Both boys rebelled. Jimmy, at age ten, was a promising athlete and wanted nothing to do with the family business. His love for football was equal to his father's passion for furniture making. Joey, the oldest son, just didn't care, refusing to ever work in the shop. But Ed didn't give up hope. When his father and Antonio both died, Ed and his brother changed the company name to Romano & Sons in hopes of his two sons seeing the light and joining the business.

When Jimmy damaged his knee and could no longer play football, his dad welcomed him into the business with open arms. His Uncle Vinny, still single but hoping to have sons himself, took pride in the family business and welcomed Jimmy right along with Eddie, hoping this was a new start for his nephew.

But Jimmy was an angry and resentful kid at age twenty. He felt victimized because of the injury that prevented him from playing football and it was well over a year before he got off the "pity pot" and started to put his heart and soul into Romano & Sons.

Jimmy knew he wasn't ready to commit to Amy. Oh, the sex had been good. Amy was fun, reliable and dependable. She had put up with his bad moods after the injury, even nursed him back to health, but he wasn't in love; and when he was honest about their relationship, he admitted that he hadn't been faithful. There were other girls in college, high school even on the side, without Amy knowing. He never felt he was totally committed to her, even though there were feelings … He rose from the bed, shaking his head.

"I can't make promises, Amy. It's not fair to give ultimatums like that. I need more time."

Amy wouldn't back down, even though she wanted to. She loved Jimmy; hadn't seen him since the beginning of school that semester — almost three months. She was looking forward to a nice Thanksgiving weekend, but she wanted that ring on her finger! That commitment! Amy came close to relenting. Sometimes she was desperate to have Romano as her last name. She was tired of being poor.

Her mother, a single parent, had brought up Amy. Her dad took off when she was a baby, and the two of them spent years in a tiny, run-down apartment in Newport, depending on welfare for practically her whole life. Amy now had the opportunity to possibly marry into a fairly wealthy family. She would graduate in another year, yet she knew her teacher's salary wouldn't be enough for the lifestyle she wanted.

She sighed. All she had to do now was reach over, touch Jimmy, and the conversation would end and their intimacy would begin. As she was contemplating this, the telephone rang.

"Who the hell is this at this hour?" Jimmy asked. He slowly lifted the receiver. It was his father. His dad seldom called his apartment; he knew something was wrong, especially at this time of night.

"Okay, okay, I'll be right there," Jimmy, replied. He looked at Amy, concern and worry in his eyes.

"That was my dad. There's been an accident at the shop; he said nothing serious, but he needs my help. I gotta go."

"I'll go with you!" Amy announced, picking up her coat. "You need someone with you."

"No," said Jimmy, quickly and emphatically. The last thing he needed was another person to worry about if something was wrong. But he felt bad about being so abrupt with Amy, and of course for ending their conversation and whatever else may have happened … "I need to do this alone, Amy. Thanks for offering, but just go home, I'll call you tomorrow."

Jimmy grabbed his leather jacket and ran out into the frigid night. As he was starting up his sixty-nine Ford pick-up, he wondered why his dad was at work at this hour. He knew his parents' relationship was rocky and his dad was a workaholic but this was going way overboard! He had left his father at six o'clock that night, his father telling him he would be leaving soon himself, and here it was, way past midnight and his dad was still working!

Jimmy drove all the back roads to Cambridge where the building was located. Stopping for traffic lights on the empty streets of Brighton and Allston, his thoughts went to Amy. He knew he cared about her, but he also knew that to him their relationship was a convenience; someone to be with, talk to, go to a movie with. And the spark was dying out. The fiery lust he had felt for her as a seventeen-year-old was fading. He remembered the feelings he had when he ran into that chick, Meg, at his sister's apartment building; chemistry, something happened in his psyche and his loins. He couldn't get her green eyes, those cat eyes out of his head for weeks after. No way could he marry Amy, if he could have feelings like that for someone else.

Jimmy thought of his recent drug use, too. He had been dabbling in smoking pot, taking Seconals — better known as downs — sometimes. Although it was fun and he only did it at parties, he realized he needed to watch himself. Using drugs was an easy escape from his problems: pop a couple of reds and your misery was gone, even if it was only temporary. Drug use was the climate of the sixties, all his friends smoked weed; it was a way of life. Some of his high school buddies that went over to Viet Nam, straight-laced and patriotic when they left, started using pot, smoking opium over there. And a lot of them continued to do so, even to use heroin, when they returned to the States. Everyone dismissed it as just the hippie way of life; and it seemed natural to Jimmy, no big deal. But he knew he should only stick with the pot, the escape was too available and too easy and he had to watch himself, especially working with his father and being around all that machinery …

What was wrong with his father now?

A gentle snow was falling as he passed Simeone's Restaurant and drove onto Tudor Street, where the family business was located. As he pulled into the driveway he smelled smoke and looked up to the workshop area where smoke was exiting one window and flames were shooting out the opposite side. "What the fuck!" yelled Jimmy. "My dad is in there!"

Jimmy jumped out of his truck, desperately looking from side to side — a phone booth! A person! Anybody! But the streets were deserted and bare. He ran to the door to get in and find his father, but it was locked.

"Dad! Dad!" he screamed at the top of his lungs. "Open the door!"

Nothing. Silence. The fire escape! Jimmy furiously started to climb the metal stairs, calling for his father the whole time. Suddenly a Cambridge Police cruiser drove by and Jimmy waved it down.

"Help! Please help! My dad is in there!"

Within minutes, fire trucks and police cruisers were surrounding the building. A veteran fireman broke through a third story window and made entrance for the rest of the workers to put out the fire. They found Ed Romano on the fifth floor, next to a woodcutting machine that had caught on fire. He was in shock but still able to speak.

"I put it out, I got the fire out myself" Ed Romano announced proudly to a fireman.

An ambulance was called and took Eddie to Massachusetts General Hospital. Jimmy met them in the emergency room. After a three-hour wait, the ER doctor finally came out, looking sadly at Jimmy.

"Are you the only next of kin?" he asked.

"No … my mom," Jimmy replied.

"Call her," said the young resident. "She needs to be here. We have been working on your father, trying to stabilize him, but his burns are serious." Jimmy was in shock as he made his way out the emergency room door to the phone booth. He knew already that this would be the worst conversation of his life.

CHAPTER THREE

December — 1972

Christmas bulbs were hanging from Five Central at Massachusetts General Hospital. Ed Romano finally made it onto a regular floor after two weeks in Intensive Care. The accident that had left his upper body with third degree burns brought him to the Emergency Room, the Burn Unit, ICU, and finally Five Central.

Jimmy had stood vigil that entire first night. He called his mother at five in the morning, right after he talked to his sister, Gwen, who would go and fetch Anna Romano. Anna, hysterical, needed to be treated in the ER and given a mild sedative. Her husband wasn't even forty-nine-years-old and she couldn't believe this had happened to him, to them! They were starting to build on their relationship again after a few troubled years in their marriage.

It had been a fluke that Eddie had been at the shop so late. He had come home that night for supper, told her he needed to go back to the shop to finish a piece of furniture he was working on so they could try to get away for the weekend to talk, sort some things out.

"We're both so young. How could Eddie have done this? Why was he at work so late?" Anna mumbled through her tears to the emergency room nurse. "I told him to call my son Jimmy for help with the furniture tonight, so he wouldn't be alone and he would get done quicker, instead he went by himself and look what happened! He was too tired, he shouldn't have been alone."

Gwen and Jimmy tried unsuccessfully throughout the next day to reach their brother, Joey, in Colorado. His girlfriend Sandy kept telling them Joey would be home in a few hours. But there was no Joey.

"What the hell?" said Jimmy. "It's his father. Why would he be avoiding our calls?"

The fact was that Joey had gotten the message and didn't want to deal with this tragedy. He felt that he had enough on his mind. He had never been close to his dad, anyway; and now the family wanted him to rally; be there for Eddie? "No way, I'm not going!" he said to Sandy. "I spent half my life trying to please that guy and I was never good enough. Suddenly I need to be there for him? To hell with that."

Sandy begged and pleaded with him to get a plane back to Boston; and finally, reluctantly, Joey got a flight out of Denver the following day to Logan Airport in Boston; Jimmy would pick him up around six that night.

In the meantime, Eddy's physical condition worsened. His kidneys started to fail and his temperature rose. The doctor told the family they would have to pump him intravenously with antibiotics to fight the infection and possibly put him on dialysis. Jimmy was nauseous. This couldn't be happening to his family, his father.

"He's not even fifty-years-old!" Jimmy said to one of the nurses, a twenty-six-year-old woman named Patty who was sympathetic to him. She consoled Jimmy, brought him coffee. What she really wanted to do was hug this guy, tell him how sorry she was for his situation. After four more days with the Romano family, after getting to know all of them, she felt a kinship, as if she could really help; but she felt it mostly toward Jimmy.

Gwen, with her husband at her side, couldn't stop crying; wailing hysterically that her father would surely die. Anna, helped by her tranquilizers, seemed okay, and Joey, full of anger and rage, didn't want anyone near him. Jimmy, although furious about the accident, let Patty help him through his darkest hours. He needed to talk, vent, and Patty was there for him.

"Do you have a girlfriend?" she asked one afternoon. Jimmy thought of Amy, away at the University of Massachusetts in Amherst, totally out of the present picture.

"Not really," he said.

So, it was Patty, with her empathetic ways, who helped Jimmy face his dad's illness. After her eleven-thirty shift ended, he sought solace in her apartment on Newbury Street, a relationship that would go nowhere, but which was something for the time being, something to help him through this tragedy. Patty fell in love.

Jimmy didn't. He was too angry, filled with hate toward God, toward the universe, for letting this happen to his father. He had finally begun a relationship with Ed Romano. His dad had become a teacher, friend, confidant; and a stupid, uncalled for accident with one of the machines, took all this away. Jimmy's Uncle Vinny kept encouraging him to work, to pick up where his father left off. But every time he went to work he saw his father's face when he had found him in the fire, looking at his burnt hands and remembering his father's words that night "I put out the fire, the machines are okay, none of the furniture was burnt, I saved the furniture."

One night, standing outside the hospital with Patty, Jimmy screamed, "God, I hate you! Why my family? Why my dad? He's burnt on his whole upper body! How is he supposed to work again, use his hands?"

The next day Eddie was told that his hands were so badly burned that he needed skin grafts and that he would never have full use of his upper extremities. His kidneys had also failed and he was receiving dialysis three times a week; and the dialysis was barely keeping him alive.

Jimmy was with him when the doctors gave him the devastating news and he saw the exact point where his dad gave up physically, emotionally, and spiritually. Ed became depressed, started refusing dialysis, and — although in pain — he left the morphine at his bedside, refusing to take it either.

Gwen begged her father to cooperate. A nurse herself, she knew he needed dialysis for his kidney failure. The Romano's could only watch their husband and father decline physically each day, become confused, think he was at work, making another masterpiece. It was unbearable for them to see this man decompensate, this artist who had been so full of life and energy, a man who could build, design, and create the most intricate pieces of furniture for celebrities and other people of importance and affluence. They were helpless as they watched him try and cope with a world he couldn't relate to, a world filled with IV lines, medication, doctors and nurses, people helping him when it had always been the other way around.

Jimmy, Joey, Gwen, and their mother watched their dad slowly slip away from this earthly place to another dimension. And they could do nothing about it.

CHAPTER FOUR

January — 1973

Eddie Romano died of kidney failure caused by his burns on January 17, 1973, his forty-ninth birthday. His wake was for two days; Monday night and the following Tuesday afternoon and night. Giovanni's Funeral Home in the North End of Boston was packed. Eddie's three kids and wife never stopped shaking hands. People they had never met before told stories of Eddie in his younger days. Eddie, The Furniture Maker let people pay on time: "Pay me when you can," he'd say to his *paisano* friends; and with his generosity, he had built a legacy of friendship, the most important thing in his life. Men who had worked for him in the past came to give their last respects with tears in their eyes. Men who Eddie gave jobs to when no one else would because they couldn't speak English.

At his funeral Mass in the church, Jimmy delivered the eulogy. "I never got to tell my dad how much I loved him, how much I respected him. I never knew he had so many friends. I'm so proud to have had a dad who was so loved, and now we all have wonderful memories of this remarkable man, a man whose life and legacy will live on."

But Jimmy was hurting. Amy came for the wake and funeral but he wouldn't go near her. He told her to leave; he didn't need anyone and didn't want anyone. Amy was crushed; beyond hurt. *What will happen to us now? She wondered.*

Patty, the nurse from the hospital, couldn't reach Jimmy either. He was a stone; someone made of steel, who no one could hurt emotionally.

Gwen's best friend, Lizzy, came with her sister, Meg. *God, no! … Not Meg,* Jimmy thought. *Why is she here? I'm screwed up enough.* But Meg belonged there. She was also Gwen's friend and was feeling bad. *God, does she look beautiful!* Jimmy mused. *Long black hair … those green eyes … tall and slim. But I can't … I won't! I won't let anyone near me.*

Meg approached him, leaned over and kissed his cheek. "I'm so sorry about your dad, Jimmy."

He breathed in her fragrances: her shampoo, perfume, deodorant … and something there brought him back to reality.

"Thanks," was all he could say. He needed to mourn, mourn a death, the death of a father/son relationship. He needed to mourn the death of a man who had brought nothing but goodness into the world.

Hundreds of friends and workers gathered outside the funeral home for one last goodbye to Eddie Romano. Joey, Jimmy and Gwen surrounded their mother as a priest said one last farewell inside. Eddie was buried in Newport Cemetery next to his parents amidst the lilacs, evergreens, and azalea bushes that would bloom in the spring. A party of sorts was held afterwards at the Romano home with plenty of Italian food, pastry and wine.

Later that night, one of Jimmy's friends found him in the backyard smoking dope with some hippie looking people who weren't really friends.

"Come on, Jimmy. Let's go for a walk," said George.

"No, it's cool here, George," Jimmy said, lighting up the bone, pretending nothing was wrong.

"You don't want to do this to yourself, Jimmy," said George. "Please come for a ride." But he couldn't get through. Jimmy refused to leave because he didn't care what he did to himself; he was made of stone and wouldn't let anyone break through his exterior to find out what he was really feeling.

A few hours later, Amy found Jimmy in the TV room at his mother's house. She sat next to him, wrapped her arms around him.

"I'm so sorry," she said.

"Back off, Amy. I told you to leave me alone. I don't want you and I don't need you. I don't need anybody!" With that, Jimmy stood up, walked angrily to the front door, out to his truck and left. He left Amy crying in the doorway, left his mother, flabbergasted at his behavior ... left both of them emotionally spent, wondering what would happen next.

As Jimmy was leaving, he saw his dog, Rita, a little mutt he had loved since he was a little boy. He heard her crying, but he couldn't let her get to him. He was never, ever going to feel this sad again in his life. He was so full of hatred and anger that he no longer wanted to have any relationship ever ... no way!

As he neared his apartment, he realized he couldn't bear to be alone. A gut-wrenching loneliness and sadness enveloped him and surrounded him with feelings of death. He would go to Newport Center, try to buy some dope, something to help him through the night.

As he approached the center, he saw his Uncle Jimmy, for whom he was named. One of Newport's finest; he'd been a policeman for twenty-five-years. He was also one of the biggest assholes around. His uncle would know what he was up to, so Jimmy just waved, turned around, and headed back to his apartment. So many memories, Jimmy thought … So many sad, pitiful memories.

How will I deal with them all?

CHAPTER FIVE

May — 1974

Megan Bridget Flaherty graduated with all A's from Boston General Hospital, something she never thought she'd accomplish. Dressed in an A-line white uniform, white nylons and adorning nurse's cap, she graduated second in her class of 200 students. Proud of herself … by all means.

Astonished, as well.

Meg (or Meggie, as her dad liked to call her) was the sixth of eight children born to a very Irish second generation family on the paternal side, and a third generation Scottish family on her mother's side. John Flaherty's family was from County Kerry, Ireland. He was born in Cambridge, Massachusetts, in 1911. His parents, Megan Quigley and James Flaherty, came off the boat at Ellis Island in 1890, both of them ten years old. They met at a wild Irish dance years later in South Boston, married in 1908, and proceeded to have seven children. Their son John, Megan's father, was the first.

John Flaherty told Meg that the minute she was born he knew he had to name her after her grandmother. "You had a fiery spirit two minutes after you were born, just like your grandmother." Megan Quigley, or "Meg" to her family and friends, was a spitfire. She had long red flaming hair and a personality to match. She could dance the Irish jig like there was no tomorrow and always carried a harmonica to every affair. Meg talked her husband-to-be, James, into eloping at the age of 20, much to his parents' chagrin. But Meg Quigley had too much fire, was too high-spirited for James Flaherty to refuse. He was madly, deeply in love at first sight.

When John was five-years-old, his parents realized how smart he was for a child his age. John knew how to read third grade books in kindergarten and loved being around adults, listening to their conversations and commenting. What really astonished them was how at the age of ten John was reading the newspaper from front to back, especially political events happening locally and around the world. John would read to his six other siblings about Boston politics and how shabbily the Irish were treated when they first arrived in Boston in the mid 1800s; how the Irish worked hard in America, and through sheer numbers and political savvy were able to make Boston their own. The little Flaherty's would look at their brother in amazement when he told the story of Hugh O'Brien and Patrick Collins, the first immigrants to break the Brahmin hold on Boston City Hall. His brothers and sisters would sit cross-legged in a circle, listening, mesmerized by their brother and his ability to comprehend the Boston Globe and the Irish Times.

It was clearly politics that interested John. His father noticed how his son's eyes would light up when a friend of his parents would talk about the presidential election, or what the local politicians were doing for the homeless and needy; how his people, the Irish, were getting along in Boston, in America. John passionately wanted to improve life for his countrymen someday.

At age sixteen, John was not only very cerebral but a great athlete. His father was his biggest fan, pushing him forward, encouraging him to go to Harvard or Yale. John received an academic scholarship to Harvard University in 1927. Upon completion, he went directly to Harvard Law School and became a practicing family lawyer, during the Great Depression.

John met Megans's mother, Mary MacGory, in a downtown Boston restaurant in 1934. They were both sitting with dates but near one another at separate tables. John and Mary were bored to death with their companions, especially Mary, who was fixed up with a narcissistic businessman whose main topic of conversation was himself.

John was with Eleanor, his girlfriend of ten years, who was on the verge of tears because John hadn't proposed to her yet and seemed to have no intention of doing so. He had fallen out of love and was trying to tell her in a gentle way that he wasn't interested in pursuing the relationship any further. Eleanor was not going to let him off that easily, however. He was a Harvard graduate, an aspiring lawyer and climbing the political ladder.

"You can't do this to me!" Eleanor reacted strongly to the rejection. "I'm almost thirty-years-old. Who am I going to find now?" She was shouting in the quiet restaurant. "You're just a selfish mick!" And with that, she slammed her napkin down on the table and ran from the room.

Mary and her date, Bob, were leaving as this scene erupted, and Mary and John bumped into each other on the way out the door. "Excuse me … I'm so sorry," said John. He had stepped on her foot while hurrying to try and catch up with Eleanor.

Both of them felt an instant attraction toward the other, but for obvious reasons they were unable to communicate. Two days later Mary and John once again met in a downtown deli at lunch hour. They introduced themselves over turkey sandwiches and coffee. Two years later, in the midst of the Depression and feeling the effects of the stock market collapse, Mary MacGory married John James Flaherty with over four hundred guests in attendance at the Continental Hotel in Harvard Square in Cambridge, Massachusetts. John was on the city council in Cambridge and had half of the city there. Mary, from a large Scottish family from Nova Scotia, had her parents, twelve brothers and sisters, cousins, and aunts and uncles present at the wedding.

Most of Mary's family was blue collar, college never having been an option for them. So, when a MacGory was marrying a college man, and a Harvard man at that, it was quite a celebration for the relatives, especially the ones who traveled from far away. Money was no object. John paid for the wedding. Mary's father, an ice deliveryman, had no means to throw a big wedding for his eighth daughter. Despite that, and among politicians such as the Kennedy's, O'Neil's and the Curly's, John and Mary were wed in 1936.

And now, almost forty years later, their sixth child and fourth daughter became the first nurse in the family, and it was a very proud day for John and Mary Flaherty.

"You done good, Meggie," John said as he gave Meg a big bear hug. His favorite daughter never ceased to amaze him. She had become more like his mother as she matured and was as fiery and feisty as Meggie Quigley had been in her younger years. Meg had been a track star in high school; she had won trophies, medals, and had even gone on to state competitions. Her grades were excellent and she had entered the finest hospital school of nursing in the country.

Meg was going to start a fulltime job at Boston General Hospital on a surgical floor. She had found an apartment in Kenmore Square with two other nurses. John Flaherty handed her a $500.00 check that night for her first two months' rent. Money was no object where Meg was concerned. The other siblings, especially her sister Lizzy, felt the favoritism and lack of attention from their dad.

Lizzy was two years older than Meg, had gotten pregnant by her long-standing boyfriend when she was nineteen and had to drop out of college to marry Paul. He had been home on leave from Vietnam and became a twenty year-old dad after his tour of duty. John Flaherty was as angry as a father could be. His Lizzy was smart — no, in fact, she was brilliant! He felt she was wasting her life. Although he loved his grandson, Paul, he held some resentment towards Lizzy that he never quite got over.

Courtney was another story. Five years older than Megan, she craved her father's attention. She was a pleaser; she could never do enough for her parents. From an early age, Courtney saw the favoritism her dad gave Megan; and she had been jealous from then on. Oh, she knew her father loved her; but it wasn't the same as the love he had for Meggie. Her younger sister could do no wrong, and Courtney hated her for it. She was mean and cruel towards Meg, teasing her, making her life as miserable as she could. At twenty-seven, Courtney was a mother herself, yet was still vying for the attention of the powerful John Flaherty and never quite receiving it.

One day Courtney stormed into the house after seeing Meg at a party, smoking pot and drinking beer. She couldn't wait to relay the message to her father, and was already shouting as she opened the front door. "Dad, where are you?"

John Flaherty came running down the winding flight of stairs, thinking someone had been injured, the way Courtney was carrying on. "I saw Meg last night, high as a kite, smoking dope, embarrassing our family!"

John Flaherty wouldn't show his anger and hurt to Courtney. Instead, he replied, "Aren't you overreacting a bit, Court?"

"Ohhh … you frustrate me, Dad! Does Meg ever, ever do anything wrong in your eyes? She's your favorite. You've always stuck up for her, protected her. Now look at Meggie, the Senator's stoned daughter!"

John Flaherty, State Senator from Massachusetts, was aware of the problem; underneath he was worried about the political implications. He could just hear people talking, saying, "Oh, yeah! That Meg Flaherty. What a pothead hippie, with her long hair, love beads, and bell-bottoms."

The last thing John Flaherty needed was a scandal, not now, at a time in his life when he was thinking of running for Governor in a few years.

"I'll talk to her, Courtney. I will take care of this myself."

This incident had happened a week before Meg's graduation. He waited another week before he approached Megan. She had been staying at their house until her apartment was available on the first of July. One sunny afternoon he found Meg sitting in the backyard, "soaking up some rays," as she put it, in the vernacular of the times.

"Hi, kitten," he said, as he pulled a chair close to her. "What's going on?"

"Nothing, Dad, just relaxing, going out tonight with Steve."

Her father sighed. Steve, he thought. I hoped that would've ended after he came home from Vietnam. But it was lingering on. Oh, Steve was nice enough. His tour of duty had ended abruptly when he stepped on a mine. Next thing he knew he was at Philadelphia Naval Hospital with metal covering seventy-five percent of his body. He was discharged from the marines, angry at the world. A year later he was still angry, an alcoholic who treated John Flaherty's daughter poorly. Meg's father knew she was only staying with him out of pity.

"I know you're not crazy about him, Dad, but Steve is really okay. He does care about me deep down. He's just having a hard time getting over what happened to him."

John Flaherty sighed as he thought about how hard it was raising kids, especially in the seventies, and especially with daughters. "Meg," he said, "what I'm really concerned about are the rumors I hear of your pot smoking. Is this true?"

Meg flipped out. "Oh, for Chrissake! I suppose that goody-two-shoes Courtney came running to you with that little tidbit!"

"Stop that now, Megan Bridget! Is it true, then?"

"I dabble," said Meg. "And not often." The truth was, Meg was getting bored with marijuana, THC, bongs, rolling papers and the whole scene. It was simply an escape when things got tough emotionally. That's when she'd cop out, enter the world of disassociation and get stoned. "I'm turning over a new leaf, Dad. No pun intended," Meg chuckled. "No more pot when I move into Kenmore Square."

"And get rid of that boyfriend of yours. He has no ambition," added her father. Meg knew this to be true. Steve was collecting one hundred percent disability for his war-related injury, not even looking for another job, was partying hearty and treating her like dirt. She was slowly, ever so slowly ending the relationship.

The truth was that Meg was afraid of his violent temper. One evening they had quarreled and Steve came very close to hitting her. This was an awakening for Meg and a realization that Steve had so much pent-up anger that he could actually become abusive to her. Besides, the puppy love that had kept them together through high school was over. Their relationship was now one of convenience. They were used to each other. Steve, she knew, didn't love her anymore; but he was as much afraid to end the relationship as Meg was. Her father was right. She needed closure and knew the end was coming soon.

"Dad, don't worry. Steve and I aren't serious, the relationship is dwindling, and by the end of the summer we'll be history."

"Is that a promise?"

Meg smiled and told him to count on it. Laughingly, she said, "I'll have a new boyfriend by Christmas."

But John Flaherty wanted his daughter to have fun, travel, not always have a boyfriend in her life. He was worried she became too dependent on men, wasn't happy unless a guy was around. And Meg knew this to be true. She felt safer having male companionship, someone she could lean on.

Six months later, after Meg and Steve broke up, she immediately found another guy. "Another nowhere man," as her father, said. "You pick men that are going nowhere, Meggie. You're beautiful, smart, why in hell do you pick guys from the wrong side of the tracks, have no jobs and have no ambition?"

"Oh, Dad, you want me to find a Harvard football player and that isn't gonna happen. No one has ever been good enough for you, no matter who I date," sighed Meg.

John knew she was right. No one was good enough for his Meggie. "Couldn't you, for once, go out with a guy whose hair isn't longer than yours, doesn't drive a Volkswagen bus and wear love beads, or someone who isn't always flashing us the peace sign, Meg?"

"Not very nice coming from a state senator's mouth, Daddy," Meg said with a big grin on her face, "but someday I'll find someone you'll adore."

Meg was thinking about Jimmy Romano. After his dad's death and seeing him at the wake, Meg's feelings rekindled. Lizzy told her it was useless. Jimmy Romano was in his own world, full of hatred and bitterness. He was upset that his dad's business had been sold; he felt inept and confused and wouldn't let anyone help him. His Uncle Vinny had started out on his own after he sold the business. Kept most of the machinery that was half owned by his father too! His uncle told Jimmy to find another job elsewhere, he couldn't pay another worker, money wasn't coming in yet and he needed to work by himself. Plus Vinny became angry with Jimmy when he saw him smoking pot in his truck after work had ended a few months before. The two quarreled the next day and Vinny told him, at that point, to find work somewhere else because he was going to sell the business.

"I want my father's equipment, at least half of it," Jimmy had said angrily.

"It's my machinery, Jimmy. Your father owed me money, so count your blessings I'm not charging you or your mother for it!"

This did nothing but fuel Jimmy's anger. He knew his father owned most of it; Jimmy had seen checks written out to the company where his dad had purchased them.

Meg had seen Jimmy briefly right after the funeral, pulling away from his sister's apartment building. Meg was going inside when she spotted his white pickup truck. He looked so sad. "Jimmy!" she called. He either hadn't heard her, or pretended not to.

Still, she knew her father wouldn't like him either; he had all the characteristics that John Flaherty hated. Although she loved her dad, she hated the snobby, better-than-thou attitude … one that all politicians somehow develop over the years. Most people loved her father dearly, but with his children, he had way too many expectations and demands. An "A" wasn't good enough in school; she needed to get an A+. Coming in second in the cross-country races was not an option with her father: nothing short of a first place blue ribbon was good enough for his daughter — the Flaherty's had to come in first. Meg felt that she would never be able to please him, she wasn't ambitious enough, and her boyfriends definitely weren't. Even now, into her job as a staff nurse for only six months, her dad wanted her to apply for the head nurse position on her floor.

"I can pull a few strings," he said. "Being on the Board of Directors of the hospital carries quite a bit of weight."

"Don't you dare, Dad … I'm not ready for that position."

"Well, you're not going to be a staff nurse all your life, are you, Meg?"

And it would go on and on. He wanted her to climb and climb, to reach her potential; but Meg didn't even know what her potential was. She only knew she was happy living in Kenmore Square, taking care of sick people, making them well. That was all Megan wanted for now. She didn't need to be "in charge" of other nurses, she was content where she was.

And her mother! How Mary Flaherty was trying to find her a husband!

"Aren't there any nice doctors for you to date?" asked her mother one day when they had met for lunch in the hospital cafeteria. Mary had an appointment and met Meg on her lunch break. "Look at that adorable fellow over there," as Mary pointed to a dead ringer for Frankenstein. "He's so big and strong looking. I bet he played football."

"Yeah, and went to Harvard, too, I'll bet," Meg replied, as she rolled her eyes. "He's an intern, Ma, has no interest in me and he has a girlfriend! Besides, I hate doctors."

"Why, for the love of God?" her mother asked impatiently.

"Because," replied Meg, "they're snobs, have no social skills, and they're probably clueless when it comes to sex."

"Megan Bridget!" exclaimed her mother, taken aback by her daughter's language.

"You don't really think I'm a virgin, do you, Mom?" Meg asked casually as she continued to eat her roast beef sandwich.

"You're telling me way too much, Megan. I brought you up to be a good Catholic girl, and fornicating is a mortal sin! Look what this drug-filled hippie generation has done to you! The next thing you'll be telling me is you're pregnant!"

"Nope" said Meg, "I'm on the Pill." She knew she should stop. Getting a rise out of her mother, making her angry, was a game to Meg. She had done it her whole life. She hated her mother's holier-than-thou life, not the least; of which was Daily Mass. Meg had been forced to go to Mass every Sunday and Holy Days of Obligation. Confession every two weeks to confess her awful sins, saying the Rosary, making Novenas every Lent since she was ten years old … the Catholic religion was shoved down her throat, right along with the guilt that went with it. The priests and nuns made her feel ashamed for the tiniest moral infraction.

Meg had stopped going to church during nursing school. She figured she had committed too many mortal sins by the age of twenty and was going to hell anyway. So, why bother going to church? God didn't like sinners. That was the message she received growing up. She remembered when she was sixteen, sitting in

English class, day dreaming about Steve, picturing them making out, going almost all the way, then suddenly remembering she was having impure thoughts and that was totally against the Catholic faith, she would need to go to confession or else she would stay longer in purgatory when she died!

Meg spent most of her childhood and especially teenage years riddled with Catholic guilt. She had been caught once when she was a junior in high school skipping Mass on Sunday morning. Meg and her two girlfriends, Joy and Nancy, had gone for a ride through Harvard Square instead of going to church. They drove slowly through the streets of Cambridge, looking for cute boys and going out to breakfast at the Pancake House at the time the three should have been receiving communion. All three girls had gotten caught when Nancy's father walked into the restaurant and caught them red-handed. Meg was punished for four weeks but worse then that, her parents gave her "the silent treatment," and her sister Courtney delighted in the fact that Meg had gotten caught. Courtney was thrilled that for once, her father was paying more attention to her than to her sister; and she made life unbearable with her goody-two-shoes attitude.

"Okay, I'm sorry, Mom. It's just that you're always so perfect; everything in your life is so in order. Haven't you ever done anything wrong?"

"Do you think I've lived in a bubble, Megan? Of course, I've sinned! We all do. But I have also repented. I love God, I am faithful to my husband, and I live as a good Catholic." She crossed herself piously as she spoke.

Meg sighed. As she looked in her mother's beautiful cobalt blue eyes, she wondered if this good woman knew about her husband's infidelities.

When Meg was eighteen, she was taking the train from Boston back to her home in Westbridge. As the train was going back and forth, side-to-side, she started to drift off to sleep. Suddenly she was aware of voices near her.

"Guess who I saw going into a sleazy hotel today?" said a tall, thirtyish businessman to one of his colleagues. "John Flaherty, our popular state senator! He had this gorgeous blonde, a babe about twenty-years-old, on his arm, and they were kissing. I think she works at the Capitol Building. Maybe one of the secretaries."

It was the first time she heard something like that; but it was far from the last. So it went, over the years, rumors about her father and his peccadilloes. Did her mother really not know? Was she in denial, or just plain stupid?

Meg had confronted her dad two years earlier, after hearing that he was discreetly seeing the Governor of Connecticut, Mary Walsh. "Is it true, Dad?" asked Meg.

"Of course not, dear. People try to get politicians in trouble; people are resentful, unkind, mean-spirited. I wouldn't do that to your mother!"

Meg wanted to believe him, but knew he was guilty. She looked in his eyes and saw the darkness right clear to his soul. John Flaherty was a very handsome and charismatic man. Even at the age of sixty, women stared. He worked out, jogged, and maintained his college weight. He was definitely aging gracefully.

So was her mother, though, Meg thought. So, why was he cheating on her and if Mary Flaherty knew, then why was she accepting this lifestyle?

Her mother stood up to leave, scanning the cafeteria one more time for possible eligible bachelors for her daughter. "We'll see you Saturday night for dinner, Meg? And, please don't bring that dreadful new boyfriend of yours … you'll give your father a heart attack. Besides, I want you to set an example for your younger sisters."

Meg's younger twin sisters had been a huge surprise to the Flaherty's. Mary thought her family was complete after Meg. After all, she was forty-two. Who would expect to get pregnant? Especially with twins! Still, when Meg was four years old, little Shannon and Tara arrived, turning the Flaherty house into a nightmare for the other siblings.

Now, at age twenty, the girls were the total opposite of Meg; shy, quiet bookworms, both going to Ivy League schools, not the least interested in boys.

"They're lesbians," said Lizzy one day when they had gone shopping.

"So what if they are?" Courtney, always the rebel, replied.

"I don't think they know what a lesbian is," Meg said.

All three started laughing. The twins were so different from the rest of the Flaherty's.

"If I didn't know Ma better, I'd say she had an affair with the meat cutter at the A&P. They both look like him," said Jack Flaherty, the oldest child in the Flaherty clan. All the siblings really cracked up over that because they knew Mary MacGory Flaherty would never commit a mortal sin and risk the fires of hell.

"Don't worry, Ma, I won't bring Frankie," said Meg.

Frankie Colinari was her most recent fling. It was only platonic for her. He rode a Harley Davidson motorcycle, was a good dancer, and made her laugh. But he was not the type of guy to bring to a future governor's home. Besides, Meg was getting ready to ditch him. He wouldn't keep his hands off her and she wasn't physically attracted to him. Kissing him was bad enough!

Meg thought that maybe her mother was right when she told her not to go out with Italians. "Why, Ma?" Meg asked.

"They simply don't keep their hands off of you," replied Mrs. Flaherty.

Of course, her mother was referring to their long-time next-door neighbor, Phil Mastriani. Mr. Mastriani had a thing for Mrs. Flaherty. When there were neighborhood parties and Phil had too many drinks, he'd grab Mary's behind or start kissing her neck. "If you marry an Italian, you'll spend the whole time in the bedroom," Mrs. Flaherty told all her daughters. "Stick with your own kind!"

CHAPTER SIX

March — 1975

"Code ninety-nine! Code ninety-nine!"

The disembodied voice came over the loudspeaker at Boston General Hospital. Code ninety-nine was a cardiac or respiratory arrest; someone was dying. Meg pushed the code cart down the halls of Eight West, into room 822. It was her beloved Mr. Morgan, who had had surgery a week before. The doctors had repaired an abdominal aortic aneurysm, but he had not been doing well the last twenty-four hours. The nurses had administered oxygen when he complained of shortness of breath; but his blood pressure was dropping, he was developing chest pain, and they were preparing to transfer him to the Intensive Care Unit. In the midst of the preparations, his heart stopped. Matt Cleary, the doctor in charge of the code, yelled, "Megan, start compressions! Beverly, you give the medication! Veronica, get another intravenous line going! Where the hell is X-ray?"

As Meg started compressions, she realized her own heart was going a mile a minute. She hated codes, hated death and, worse of all, Mr. Morgan was one of her most favorite patients. He had been in and out of the hospital so frequently she had gotten to know him and his family. Loving, caring people, she thought as she pressed down harder on his chest, trying to get his heart to beat once again, bring life back to his limp body.

Meg knew it was hopeless; he was dead, gone, no color in his extremities. He was turning bluer by the minute and the cardiac monitor had been showing a straight line for over five minutes.

"Push down harder, Meg," shouted Dr. Cleary. "Get a stool to stand on, it will be easier to do the compressions."

"He's dead, for Chrissakes!" yelled the charge nurse, Cynthia. "Call the code off Dr. Cleary; we've been doing CPR for close to an hour."

They all stared at Cynthia, amazed at her boldness, her guts to speak up to the doctor like that. But she was right and Dr. Matt Cleary knew it.

"Okay, let's stop," he replied a few moments later. "Time of death is 6:58 pm."

The shift was ending in another hour but Meg knew that because of the code, they'd be behind schedule. Veronica and Meg cleaned up Mr. Morgan, did postmortem care. While Meg was attaching nametags to his left toe and left hand, a necessary task for identification purposes in the morgue, Matt Cleary walked in the room.

"This was a tough one," he said. "Especially for you, Meg, you knew him. Maybe we should all go for liver rounds to ease our troubled minds?" He was referring to a few beers at a local bar where one would frequently find doctors and nurses when their shifts ended.

"I don't know if I can go," said Meg. "I have to get up so early tomorrow."

"Just one beer, Meggie," Matt suggested.

Dr. Cleary had a brotherly affection for Meg. He was fifteen years older than she and always felt as if she needed protection. She seemed so vulnerable, fragile, at times. One time Matt confessed this to Meg.

"Vulnerable! Fragile! Me? You got the wrong chick," said Meg. But Matt knew better, could see through her tough act.

Megan ended up finishing her work quickly and was working on her second beer when the rest of the staff showed up. Matt saw her down one beer and start on another.

"Thought you were taking it easy. What was that about getting to work early, Meg?"

"Oh, what the hell," said Meg. "It's hard to stop at one. Besides, it's still early. And, you know, Mr. Morgan dying really got to me. I really got to know him well, saw his wife right before I left. That made it worse." With the next beer Meg ordered a shot of whisky to go with it.

"Meg, I'm taking you home now. You don't need all that." Matt said as he signaled the bartender not to pour the drink. Perhaps he was rethinking his invitation to her to join him at the bar.

"Leave me alone, Matt, it was your idea for liver rounds, I'm just following doctor's orders. Besides, Katie O'Toole's back."

"Who's Katie O'Toole?" asked Matt.

"Katie O'Toole is the name I give myself when I want to get messed up, y'know, drunk? I become a different person, so I named that person Katie O'Toole."

"Don't let the rest of the staff know that, or you'll never get the head nurse position on Seven Central and besides that, they'll get a psych evaluation on you!" he said, more serious than joking. Meg, although she really didn't want the job, had applied for the head nurse position that was opening up.

"I've got to prove to my father I can get this job and get it on my own," Meg told Matt.

"Tell me more about Katie O'Toole. Does she fool around with older doctors?" Matt asked jokingly.

Megan sipped her beer. "Katie goes inward, doesn't feel pain. Matter of fact, she feels nothing; she forgets who she really is, and what she's supposed to be doing in life."

The next day Meg wished she had just gone home when her shift ended. There was nothing worse than going to work with a hangover, accompanied by the shame that washed over her when she overindulged. Besides, she hated booze; she would have preferred a couple of Seconals instead, a mild hazy buzz instead of this intense pounding she was facing after a night of too much alcohol.

Two days later, Matt approached her. "Do you think you have a drinking problem, Meg?"

"You mean, like am I an alcoholic, Matt?" she said sarcastically.

"I didn't say that," Matt replied softly, looking at her with caring eyes.

"No, you implied it, Dr. Cleary." Megan stormed past him, regretting what she had done a few nights before and what she had told him. She planned to avoid Matt Cleary from now on at all costs.

Two weeks later Meg was called into the Director of Nurses' office. "Congratulations!" said Priscilla Jacobs. "You're the new head nurse on Seven Central! You're pretty young for the job, Meg, but your hard work has paid off. And, besides, everyone loves you! You're so easy to get along with. I do have to say that there was some opposition from the administration because of your age and lack of supervisory experience, so people will be watching you … and me, for that matter. What I'm really saying is that I'm counting on you to not let me down here."

Meg threw her heart and soul into her job. For the next six months, she lived and breathed nursing. She set up educational programs for the staff nurses, worked over twelve hours a day, and stayed straight as an arrow, making sure she was not part of the "liver rounds." She didn't want a reputation, nor did she want Dr. Cleary to think she had a drinking problem or that she couldn't handle her new position. Meg convinced herself that going out for drinks that one night, getting messed up was a one-time thing and that she was a responsible woman, nurse, head nurse at that! Why had she been so foolish to tell Matt Cleary that Katie O'Toole was back! Now she would really have to stay clean and sober, to prove she was responsible and not the airhead she sounded like that night. And for the following months, she showed everyone she was a leader, a professional.

Then one very hot and steamy night the following summer, Meg entered her stifling apartment, and as she opened all the windows and poured herself a Diet Coke, she realized how lonely she was. It was a Friday night and she was staying in. Just as she was digesting this sad state of affairs, the phone rang. Her high school friends, Carol and Frannie — her party animal friends — were going to the Grog in Brighton. The Grog was a sleazy bar but always had great bands, live music, good drugs, and hunky guys. And although Meg knew she should stay away, her friends convinced her to join them.

"We're picking you up in twenty minutes," said Frannie, "so put on some makeup and get into something sexy!" Meg's loneliness took over and she agreed to go.

She went through her wardrobe, wondering when the last time was she wore something sexy. That word was not in her vocabulary. She wasn't sexy, didn't know how to flirt like some of her friends. Meg was simply Meg … no superlatives to describe her. Furthermore, the Grog was really a dive. Jeans were what most people wore. Sure, a sexy blouse maybe.

"Oh, hell!" shouted Meg, "Like, who cares? Who am I going to meet, anyway?"

She thought of the last six months. Work was her life at this point. She was twenty-five years old, starting to move up the ladder in nursing, was becoming more politically involved in her nurses' union. Oh, how proud her father was!

"You're moving up, Meggie. This is making our family look good. You'll be on the committee to help change health care before you know it. The State House is waiting for you!"

But Meg also longed for her predictable old life. What was so wrong with drinking a beer, smoking a joint, going to peace rallies on the Common? When she and Steve had broken up, one of the things he was mad about was her stand against the war.

"For Chrissakes, you were on the six o'clock news, holding a sign that said 'No War!' I was there, Meg. I practically lost my leg! What did I get injured for? Nothing?"

Meg remembered not caring about his feelings, aware only of her passionate feeling about the futility of the war. Insensitive? Maybe. But she had been obsessed with getting her feelings out on the six o'clock news, and so what if her boyfriend was a marine and served in Vietnam! She wanted to make a statement!

Meg missed those days of not caring what other people thought, free spirited, having a voice! Now she was inhibited, trying to please everyone but herself. The Flaherty name came first, never her true feelings as before. She hated herself at times for buying into the political world, the world of her father, where people were not real, some phony, only focusing on climbing the ladder, getting ahead … Megan felt she was falling right into that trap. She missed the days of saying what she felt, shooting from the hip. Suddenly, her life was politically incorrect if she said what she felt.

Tonight would be good for her. Get out with her old friends. She had the weekend off; Monday was a long way away. The only thing she had that was sexy was a green tank top, so Meg slipped it on with a pair of tight bell-bottom jeans, knowing she would fit right in at the Grog.

He was there.

Meg saw him as she rose from her table to go to the ladies' room. They had arrived at the Grog at ten thirty. The place was hopping. A live rock n' roll band had most of the bar dancing, including Meg and her friends. The smell of marijuana filled the room as joints were passed around.

Jimmy Romano was there with his friends, sitting at a long triangular table with several girls and guys. One particular girl with long blond hair was sitting on Jimmy's lap, kissing his neck. Meg hoped he didn't see her as she went by his table, but as she glanced over their eyes met. She hadn't seen him in a while and wasn't sure how to react; so she just nodded her head, acknowledging that she had seen him. When she got to the line for the bathroom there was about a ten-minute wait. Oh shit, she thought. Now I'm really close to his table.

Meg's heart was pounding as she checked her watch. It was eleven-thirty by then. I'm leaving, she thought. I'll just go home, go to bed; I can pretend this night didn't happen. Why am I having this reaction, just seeing Jimmy Romano? Get a grip, Meg!

Suddenly a hand touched Meg's neck; a strong, large, warm hand that made her turn, wondering who this person was that was sending sparks of fire throughout her body. Of course, it was Jimmy.

"Meg, right?" he said. "Yeah, you're Lizzy's sister. I remember you from our sisters, our nephews. How are you doing?"

"I'm okay," Meg replied. She was filled with anxiety and a feeling she hadn't felt in a long time. Desire. She pulled herself together and spoke as evenly as she could. "How have you been, Jimmy, since your dad died?"

But the music started to blare even more loudly and he yelled in her ear, "I can't hear you!" With that, Jimmy grabbed Meg's hand and pulled her outdoors into the street and the warm, humid summer night. "That's better," he said. "That noise and all … what did you ask me?"

"Oh, I just asked how you were, how your mom is, your family, since your dad died."

"Hanging in there," said Jimmy. "Thank you for coming to the wake."

But it was clear he didn't want to talk about his family.

"I heard you graduated from nursing school. That's cool."

But Meg couldn't concentrate, couldn't carry on a conversation. Her heart was crashing against her chest and she wanted desperately to tell Jimmy how she felt about him, share her feelings. But she held back, tried to make small talk. For ten minutes they discussed their nephews, work, even the weather, inane things that occupied their words while their minds were elsewhere.

Finally Megan, building up her courage, decided to tell Jimmy how she felt the few times she had seen him. It was a crazy risk, but a risk she was willing to take so she could try and get to know

Jimmy Romano. She didn't care about the warnings Lizzy had given her, how Jimmy was into drugs, angry and unhappy. Meg was totally in the moment, wanting to wrap her arms around Jimmy, kiss him passionately, feel the desire she hadn't felt in so long. Remembering the first time she saw him and how the sparks flew she said, "Look, Jimmy, I'm going to be honest. I'm really, really attracted to you."

Jimmy stared at her for a few seconds, initially embarrassed and not knowing what to say. Suddenly he blurted out, "I thought you had an old man, a boyfriend that was in Nam."

"That ended," said Meg. "He was injured, came home, its over."

"So, one of those 'Dear John' stories," said Jimmy.

Meg was furious …furious at herself for opening her big mouth, and even more furious at Jimmy for his sarcastic response.

"No, asshole. It wasn't like that at all," Meg said tightly. She started to run away from him, toward her car. But with two giant steps he caught up to her, grabbed her hand, pulled her shaking body to his and gently leaned her against the car they had been sitting on and kissed her. Gently at first, then with a roughness that neither of them could control. Meg's stomach tightened as the kiss ended and he buried his face in the hollow of her neck, breathing in her fragrance. Destiny … a kiss that only happens once in a lifetime. A kiss you would remember, even when you were eighty-five years old, sitting in a rocking chair, remembering that kiss like it happened yesterday, the most desirous, sexual experience of a lifetime.

When it ended, and he stepped back, Jimmy stroked Meg's face with the back of his hand, looked into her eyes and simply said, "Good to see you, Meggie."

He left her leaning against the car, shivering with desire, wondering what the heck just happened and wondering why he left. But she didn't follow. He took off, around the corner, away from the Grog, his shadow disappearing, throwing Meg into a physical, mental, emotional, and sexual turmoil for months to come.

CHAPTER SEVEN

January — 1976

One of the worst snowstorms on record was pushing its way through Boston. The wind was blowing hard as Megan made her way into the lobby of Boston General Hospital. I'll be here all night, she thought. No nurses will make it in this snowstorm. The Blizzard of '76 is upon us.

After seeing Jimmy, Meg had realized two things. First, she was in love. Second, she didn't want to get hurt. She had never met anyone who moved her like Jimmy Romano. But he hadn't called, nor had she seen him after that night. She needed to protect herself, especially since he made that comment about her breaking up with Steve. What was that all about? So, she worked and worked and didn't allow time for intrusive thoughts, such as thoughts of Jimmy Romano. Her status as head nurse was ever changing with the political views on health care. She was even interviewed on television on the Governor's Council to protect the elderly and fight against the changing Medicare rules.

When the storm finally ended, three days had past and Meg had spent an entire seventy-two hours at the hospital, napping here and there, taking care of patients, washing them, feeding them, and administering medications. Now, as she walked down Brookline Ave. towards her apartment, the lethargy was overwhelming. A car pulled over and it was a maintenance worker from the hospital.

"Hi. You work at the hospital, don't you?" he asked.

"Yes," she replied. "You do too, right?"

"Yeah, in Maintenance. Want a ride?"

Meg hesitated because she really didn't know him. *What the hell?* she thought. *He's probably just getting off work, like me.* "Okay," Meg said. "I only live about two miles away, I generally walk but I am way too tired, so if you don't mind, I'll take you up on it!"

"Hop in," he said.

The fist to the side of her face was sudden and tremendously frightening. Meg knew immediately that she was in the car with a maniac, possibly a murderer.

"That's just to show you I'm in charge, bitch. Any wrong moves and I'll use this on you," and he flashed a switchblade in front of her face. "Now, tell me where you live because I'm going to fuck your brains out and probably kill you, Ms. Megan Flaherty."

"Who are you?" Meg could hardly get the words out. The fact that he knew exactly who she was didn't help. "Why are you doing this?" Her heart was hammering in her chest.

"I've been watching you for a long time, Ms. High and Mighty. You think you're so important — you know, head nurse, politician's daughter, all that crap. But you're really a stupid bitch just like all the rest of them."

Meg made a decision that overrode her fear. "Okay, listen. Just let me out of the car; let's forget this ever happened. If you get caught you'll go to jail, my father will make sure of it."

"I said shut up!" And he backhanded her in the face once again, leaving her with a huge hematoma near her eye and a broken nose. "Just take me to your apartment."

Meg had to think quickly. She was starting to panic, and she fought it. She had to get out of the car.

They were leaving Kenmore Square. Traffic was slow because of the snowstorm, and she thought maybe she could just jump out. But he had locked all the doors from the driver's side control panel. It was impossible to escape that way.

Please, please, God! Help me! It was all that she could think. She could not know that the man sitting next to her had been abused by his mother through his entire childhood, and had made it his mission to get back at her through other attractive women in authority.

His name was Ralph Jarad. He had been released from prison six months before on attempted rape for which he had served two years at Walpole State Prison. He had convinced the parole board that he was rehabilitated, had served his time, and was a good prisoner. He had even taken college classes. He promised to continue with school when he was released.

But this twenty-eight year-old psychopath had no intention of going straight. The hospital had employed him in maintenance for the last four months. He had followed Meg around at work, stalked her in the cafeteria. He even trailed her one night when she was out on a date. He investigated her background and knew her father was a politician. The thought of abducting a celebrity of sorts aroused Ralph. He hated how Meg walked around "bossing" people, telling other nurses what to do, just like his mother had.

As Ralph drove, his anger rose and he gripped the steering wheel with such rage that he didn't see the truck coming.

It was a moving van headed north on Brookline Ave. Ralph swerved to avoid hitting the van and skidded into a parked car. The impact caused Ralph to hit his head and become disoriented for a few seconds. As he gained his composure, he tried to back up, but the wheels kept turning. He was stuck on a huge patch of ice!

Meg screamed, "Let me out of this frigging car!"

Ralph was stunned. He saw people heading towards the car. *Oh, my God! I'll get caught, go back to jail!* He jumped out of the car, realizing it was useless to try and follow through with his plan. He ran as fast as he could. Meg saw him bolt onto a passing train on Commonwealth Ave. heading to Brighton. She started to climb out of the driver's side, feeling faint and dizzy. You'll be okay, she told herself. Take a few deep breaths.

As she stood up, the fuzziness started. She knew she was going to pass out. The last thing she remembered thinking was, *Oh, my God. What is my father going to say?*

Meg was in a coma for forty-eight hours. People had rushed to her aid, called an ambulance, and she was taken to New England Trauma Center. After two days, she woke up in her hospital room. Flowers surrounded her, as did her brothers, sisters, and parents. She had the worst headache of her life. She temporarily couldn't remember what had happened, but slowly the events unraveled and she became sick to her stomach.

"You all need to leave now," said the robust nurse as she entered the room. "The doctor needs to examine her."

John Flaherty knew the police were also waiting to get a statement and he wanted to talk to Meg first and find out what happened. The emergency room doctor had notified him that Meg had been attacked and he rushed over immediately. Over the following two days, he had heard terrible rumors that Meg had been hitchhiking and was raped in the car. According to her doctors, there was no reason to believe that, there had been no sexual assault. Other rumors said that she knew the assailant, had invited him back to her apartment to spend the day with her. By far the worst thing he had heard was that she had "asked for it," had led the guy on, luring him and then backing off.

The *Boston Globe* simply stated that Megan Flaherty, daughter of State Senator John Flaherty, had been attacked on her way home from work on January ninth. As terrible as the crime was, this was bad publicity for the senator. He had started his campaign for governor and although in its early stages, John Flaherty thought he had a good possibility of winning the election come November.

This juicy piece of gossip was not good for his chances. He needed to find out exactly what had happened and deal with it before it went any further. The public had no idea what actually happened and were clueless as to who the perpetrator was; Meg's father needed to know the truth before anyone else. He approached the nurse and asked her if he could be alone with his daughter for a few minutes after the doctor examined her, and to make sure he saw her before the police did. The nurse agreed. It was hard to say no to John Flaherty.

The family went to the cafeteria for coffee. Sitting around a long rectangular table, Mr. Flaherty said, "I want you all to go home, not talk to anyone about any of this."

Courtney, predictably, said, "Leave it to Megan to screw up. If this gets around any more you'll never be governor." All her siblings, even her parents, gave her the evil eye, staring at her in disbelief. They all knew the rivalry between the sisters, but Courtney was relentless, not a loving bone in her body for Meg.

Lizzy asked, "Why are you here, Courtney? We're all here, rooting for Meg, praying for her, she's done nothing wrong, she was attacked, this wasn't her fault, don't start blaming her!"

"We'll see," said Courtney. "She probably enticed the guy, teased him, and then wouldn't put out."

"Stop that!" shouted Mr. Flaherty.

Courtney's husband, Ray, even looked at her with disgust. He grabbed her hand and said, "Time to leave, Court. You've outdone yourself this time."

As the Flaherty children filtered out, Meg's parents went back upstairs to Meg's room.

"Mary, dear, why don't we each talk to Meg separately? Having both of us there might be too overwhelming at first," said John persuasively. So Mary Flaherty waited in the solarium, watching with worry as her husband walked into their daughter's room.

Meg was sitting up in bed, tears in her eyes. She had a severe concussion, a broken nose, and several bones in her face were fractured. "No permanent damage," said the doctor. "You look like you just went a round with George Forman, but you'll heal, Meg!" He was trying to make her laugh, feel something other than the misery, fright and loss of control that she was experiencing.

She saw her dad enter the room. "Meggie," he said, as he leaned over to kiss her cheek. "What in God's name happened?"

Meg slowly let the story unfold, how she thought she knew the guy, the snowstorm, being too tired to walk home, getting in his car, the first blow to her face, how he said he was going to rape her, had a knife, then finally the accident and his flight. … It had all come back to her, every detail.

"But he didn't touch you, right?" queried John Flaherty.

"Besides beating the shit out of me, Dad? No! But he would have if he hadn't hit that parked car."

"Why didn't you call me, Meg? I would have picked you up."

She replied, "It wasn't like that, Dad. I was so tired, I thought I knew him."

"Some people say you were hitchhiking, Meg."

"That's not true, Dad!" she said immediately.

"Yes, well, you know that people talk. They gossip."

"I can imagine," said Meg. A minute or so passed and she added, "You do believe me. Don't you, Dad?"

He hesitated. "Well, of course, Meg, but …"

Meg looked in her father's eyes, his worried, doubtful eyes.

"But you're afraid this will hurt your chance to be governor. Right? Like, people will listen to rumors and believe them."

"No, Meg, I didn't say that."

"But you thought it, Daddy. You thought it." The hurt she felt at that realization was overwhelming. She had nearly died, and her father was concerned about what it might do to his image. Worse still, for the first time in her life, he didn't believe her.

There was a knock at the door. It was the police, two detectives with questions. But Mr. Flaherty quickly whisked them out, stating that she needed to rest, had been in a coma for forty-eight hours. They'd have to come back in the morning. Such was the power of John Flaherty's requests.

Well, in a real sense, they worked for him, after all.

The police returned to the hospital at nine o'clock the next morning. Meg was finishing breakfast. Trying to finish was more like it; nothing appealed to her.

The two detectives were very nice, to the point, asking basic questions. At the end, they asked Meg if she could identify the assailant in a line-up or in a photo book of ex-convicts they had at the police station. Meg was too freaked out to even think she could face her attacker again. "I'll have to think about that one," she said. Couldn't this wait? Just a little while?"

So far, the police were clueless. Nobody around got a look at the man. As a matter of fact, several people said they didn't see anyone in the car except Meg. The car was stolen, traced to a family that lived in Belmont, and had been missing for twenty-four hours. There were fingerprints but only of the owners of the car and Meg's when she grabbed the steering wheel to get out of the car.

"He had gloves on," said Meg.

Both detectives looked at each other as if they didn't believe her.

"Are you doubting me? How do you think I got these bruises and broken nose?" she said angrily.

The older detective told Meg's father that if they could just find the guy it would be helpful. No one had even seen him.

Meg spent two weeks in the hospital recovering. She had a setback with some double vision and dizziness so she needed observation. On January twentieth, she was able to go home.

"I can't go back to my apartment," said Meg. "What if he's there, or near there? I'm too afraid."

So, Meg went back home with her parents to finish recovering at their house. She took two more weeks off from work. When she got home, she called the Assistant Nurse Manager on her floor.

Beverly was ecstatic. "Meggie, we miss you."

"Do you know what happened?" asked Meg.

"Well," Bev hesitated. "Your dad told me, but there are all sorts of rumors. Were you hitching?"

"No!" cried Meg. "I feel like everyone is turning this around, like I'm the bad guy. I was the one who was attacked!"

"Calm down," she said. "We're not listening to rumors."

The doctor had given Meg tranquilizers to take as needed during the day and Seconals to help her sleep at night. Meg was starting to have nightmares of the attack and welcomed the sleeping pills.

At the end of February, Meg went to the police station to see if she could identify the assailant through photos. She spotted him almost immediately.

"Ralph Jarad, ex-convict, still on probation, spent two years in Walpole for attempted rape" stated the younger of the two policemen.

God, what a sleazebag … beady little eyes, devil eyes! "Find my attacker!" she yelled, losing what fragile control she had regained. The policemen looked around at each other after Meg's outburst, thinking she was unstable, wondering if any of this was made up.

On the ride home, her father told her she needed to get a grip. "You have to get over this, Meg. Stop talking about it and get back to work, and back to your apartment, too. Your roommates are there; you'll be all right. Besides, you sounded out of control back there in the police station, screaming at the police! Megan, you're a Flaherty, you're supposed to be calm and composed. We have our reputation to think of! You're embarrassing me, girl!"

"But, Dad," she said, "what if he finds me in my apartment and kills me?"

"Megan, it's over. I need you to stop talking about this and get back to normal."

"Why, Dad? Am I interfering with your campaign? Is this nothing but a scandal for you? Am I damaging the family name and your possible governorship?"

She was right, of course. John Flaherty kept hearing rumors about his unstable daughter, that she had somehow caused this course of events by hitchhiking and coming on to the guy. He had to squash these rumors and pay off the paparazzi not to put anything else in the media about his daughter.

"Megan, I'm driving you back to your apartment and I expect you to move on, go back to work, back to your old life as if this never happened! Do you hear me, young lady?"

"Loud and clear, Dad! Loud and clear." But as she spoke, tears made their way down her still-swollen cheeks.

CHAPTER EIGHT

November — 1976

Jimmy Romano was reading the headlines of the *Boston Globe*: "Upset in the Governor's Race: John Flaherty Loses to Incumbent, Larry Hagopian."

So, he lost, Jimmy thought. *I'll bet he blames Meg.*

Jimmy had heard of Meg's attack earlier in the year and her father's reaction, about how John didn't really believe his daughter's account of the event, and how he was trying to squash any stories from getting into the local papers. Jimmy got his information from his sister, Gwen. She had remained very close to Lizzy and heard all the gossip about Meg and the Flaherty family.

When it first happened and Meg was hospitalized, Jimmy felt that he had to see her, just visit once. Right before her discharge, he showed up at the hospital a few minutes before visiting hours ended. He didn't want to run into any of the family. As he was about to enter the room, Mr. Flaherty came charging out.

"Who are you, young man?" staring at him disapprovingly, checking out his ponytail and beard.

"I'm a friend of Meg's. Actually, I'm Gwen's brother. You know, Gwen? Lizzy's friend."

"Yes, well, Meg isn't well enough for visitors. You'll have to leave."

"I just want to say 'hi'," said Jimmy.

"If you don't leave this minute, this second, I'll call security."

Jimmy stared into this man's eyes — mean-spirited, self-centered eyes that were turning evil.

"Just tell Meg that Jimmy came by, please," he said, and walked away.

And Mr. Flaherty, as far as Jimmy knew, never told Meg he had come to visit.

Serves him right to lose, Jimmy thought. *Maybe he'll learn to humble himself. And now that he lost and isn't a state senator anymore, he might have to go back to being a lowly lawyer!*

Jimmy was very intuitive. He knew a person, their intentions, just by looking them in the eyes. They were, as he knew, the window to the soul. His father had taught him that, to be able to look in someone's eyes and test their honesty. Eddie Romano had done that his whole life, making furniture, beautiful exquisite pieces for the middle and upper classes, rich and famous people. When he asked to get paid, he could tell whether or not they would send him a check. He learned the hard way and he learned to be honest himself. If a piece of furniture wouldn't be ready on time, he would say so, apologize and be respectful. He instilled this in his children as well.

And his father was so smart! He missed that. Eddie Romano spoke three languages fluently — Italian, Spanish and French. His customers and workers were from all these nationalities. He learned, respected their cultures and never let them down. God, did Jimmy miss his dad … The business had sold, he was out on his own, going from job to job; working for a moving company, a rent-a-car operation, and, most recently, bartending. Jimmy couldn't get it together and figure out what he wanted to do.

And Megan had been on his mind since their last meeting at the Grog.

He loved her. He knew it the minute he saw her that night: her green eyes, long silky black hair … that smile. But he had made a pact with himself. He would never love again, get hurt again, be left again like his father left him. Now he was alone and wanted to stay that way. He would become like a tombstone: no feelings, no communication.

Yet, he had cried when he heard of the attack on Megan. He had wanted to comfort her, touch her soft skin, kiss her again, the kiss of a lifetime; always, always something to remember and be grateful it happened.

Jimmy knew he had to straighten out his life. Many of his friends from high school and a few he met in college had started using heroin. A beautiful brown, cheap heroin had surfaced in Brighton, a suburb of Boston. When it first came out Jimmy snorted it a few times, got a buzz, used it recreationally, but after a few times the high wasn't so good.

One night a friend showed up with something called a point, a syringe, and that was the beginning of the end. Jimmy allowed himself to use intravenously every Saturday night, a reward after working all week. The high was good and instantaneous. He felt nothing … the memories of his father's death, the building burning, and the wake and funeral; even thoughts of Megan disappeared. It was only Jimmy and the drug for a precious few hours.

He was taught to use it correctly: a spoon, cotton balls, water, heroin, then heat it up. The flame under the spoon melted the heroin, and when it bubbled, he let it soak into the cotton and drew it up, getting rid of the impurities so he wouldn't get the "cottons" an overall systemic reaction to bad dope.

And so it started. Jimmy chipped at the heroin, didn't get addicted; just played with the drug. But slowly, heroin became his God, his reason for existing all week, to get high on Saturday night; and he thought he could control it. When it slipped into his conscious mind, he denied the emotional addiction. I'm in control, he thought. I won't let it get any worse. But he was in too much pain to be honest with himself; he needed the drug for the emotional release the heroin gave him, a feeling of ecstasy.

One Saturday evening Jimmy was going to Roxbury to meet his dealer and buy his heroin. He had stopped in a convenience store in West Roxbury to get a drink when he ran into a couple of guys he had played football with at Northeastern.

"Hey, Romano!"

Jimmy turned, and two big guys, still looking like football players, embraced him.

"Hey, buddy, tough break with your knee. We missed you after the second season. What are you doing now?"

Jimmy was embarrassed. "Well, kind of between jobs. Bartending. Y'know how it goes."

But each of these guys, his colleagues, had moved on, had homes, families starting, and were successful in the world. Jimmy knew he was stagnating.

"But the chicks are good, right? You were always top-shelf with the chicks!"

"Yeah, right," Jimmy said. And when they left, said their good-byes, Jimmy looked in the mirror of his car and faced reality for thirty seconds, "You're a drug addict, you stupid son-of-a-bitch! What would dad think?"

The next day Jimmy called his brother, Joey, where he was living in North Whitcomb, a beautiful little town in the Berkshires, the mountains of Massachusetts. Joey, who had dabbled in drugs, fought his way to sobriety and ended up with a religious cult in this peaceful area, told Jimmy to come visit.

"Get straight, find God," Joey said.

So, the week after Thanksgiving Jimmy left on an adventure that made him wonder if it might not be better to just use drugs.

The cult was called "The Children of the Virgin Mary." They had tents and trailers nestled into this cozy town, economically poor town of hippies and Jesus freaks.

Jimmy arrived and spotted his brother immediately. Joey, three years older, had hair braided down his back, his wife, Sandy, who had changed her name to Grace, and their two toddlers, embraced Jimmy as he jumped out of his truck.

"You're here to find the Lord, Jimmy, through His mother, Mary," said Grace. "Peace is with you."

Jimmy spent six weeks in the Berkshires. As unbelievable as it seemed, he stayed straight, away from any heroin and enjoyed his two nephews more than anything. Joe and Jimmy got to talk about their upbringing around campfires, bottles of wine and free love. There were lots of women who surrounded Jimmy, willing to give themselves unconditionally. After six weeks on a Sunday morning, Jimmy woke Joe up to tell him he was going to hit the road.

"I'm leaving, outta here, back to Newport, my apartment and see how Ma is doing."

Their mother, Anna, had never quite gotten over her husband's death. She was depressed. She worked, came home, and stared at the TV all night.

"Why are you leaving, Jimmy? Give it more time, stay straight here, get a relationship going, all the girls love you" said Joey.

"Times up, brother, I need to get going with my life, get a real job, and like I said, check on Mom." Jimmy really couldn't stop thinking of Megan, he knew that was the reason he was leaving, but didn't share that with his brother. The two men hugged, promising to keep in touch.

"Stay away from that brown heroin shit," said Joe.

There had been two overdoses over the preceding two weeks in Newport. Either the heroin was stronger or the two people who died did too much.

The weather was bad. As Jimmy started his truck, snow was falling and the roads were slick. But he made it home safely and swore off drugs. He'd turn over a new leaf, try to go back to school and get his life together.

Jimmy arrived home in time for a New Year's Eve party. He planned to start the evening having dinner with his mother and her side of the family, aunts and uncles from East Boston. His Aunt Josie pulled Jimmy aside after the big Italian meal of veal cutlets smothered in homemade sauce, antipasto, and plenty of wine. Jimmy was about to dive into the Italian pastry when his aunt signaled him to go into the den.

"I'm worried about your mother. She's too depressed. This has gone on too long. Your Dad's been dead for four years and she's no better." None of us are, Jimmy thought.

Jimmy was aware of his mother's decline but didn't know what to do. He was barely hanging in there himself!

"How can I help her, Josie?" Jimmy said.

"Call her doctor. Get her on an antidepressant. She won't listen to me but she will to you, Jimmy. Or tell Gwen what I said … your mother needs help."

And when he left and was kissing his Mom goodbye, he realized how emotionally sick she was. God! She was barely 50! She could remarry again! He'd talk to his sister tonight. He was going to Gwen's for the real New Year's Eve party at her apartment.

The sound of Neil Young's *Southern Man* was blasting from his sister's apartment. The smell of pot was seeping through the door. Although Gwen, straight as an arrow, didn't smoke pot, many of her friends did, especially her husband, Donny. As Jimmy walked in, Don waved him over to have a hit of pot from his bong.

"No, thanks. Better not," said Jimmy. "A beer would be okay, though," and he walked to the refrigerator. Lizzy spotted Jimmy and walked into the kitchen to greet him.

"Happy New Year, Jim. Heard you've been visiting Joey in those wild mountains! I spent an over night there with Gwen last summer camping. What a trip! Joey and Sandy — I mean Grace — are really Jesus freaks now. Did you find Jesus, Mr. Romano?" Lizzy asked teasingly.

Jimmy told her about his trip, which led them into a conversation about his brother's religious cult and different newly-formed religions springing up everywhere.

"I almost joined the Hare Krishna's in high school," laughed Lizzy, "but my Dad put a stop to it, and thank God he did!"

"Guess I'm sorry to hear about your dad's loss for governor … for your sake, anyway."

"Yeah, well," said Lizzy, "a lot has happened in the last year. Our name was in the newspaper way too often, most of it negative publicity, especially for Meg."

Jimmy hesitated, took a sip of his beer, thinking whether or not to venture onto the subject of Meggie. He finally said, "How is she? Is she okay? I did try to visit her in the hospital after the attack."

"Meg isn't well," said Lizzy. "Oh, she's working, getting through the day, but she keeps having flashbacks of the attack — really debilitating flashbacks — so she drinks to drown the memories and takes tranquilizers. None of us can reach her. Meg swears there's no problem. She thinks because she jogs six miles a day and works full- time, that she's fine, but she's an emotional mess. I'm afraid she's going to kill herself unintentionally with the booze and sleeping pills she's taking."

"What does your father say?" Jimmy asked.

"He pretends there's nothing wrong, he's in such denial half the time. Two weeks ago, Meg's picture was in the paper with a drink in one hand and a joint in the other, in a bar in Boston. The remarks under the picture were 'politician's daughter, Meg Flaherty, doesn't seem affected by her father's recent loss for governor.' My father, after my sister Courtney showed him the paper, said, 'They got it wrong. That's not Megan. It looks like her, but that's not Meg.' But then when I'm alone with my Dad, he'll admit to me he knows she's gone off the deep end. I guess he goes in and out of reality when it comes to his favorite daughter."

People started walking in the kitchen and their conversation was over; but before Lizzy left she found Jimmy by the record player, looking for the latest Van Morrison album. She timidly walked over and put her hand on his back. "I have a favor to ask you, Jimmy. Maybe you can talk to Megan. I mean, she still likes you, and she never knew you went to see her in the hospital. It's just possible she'll listen to you. Could you do that for her?"

"I don't know, Lizzy. How can I help? I'm just as bad. One of the reasons I went to see Joey was to clear my head and get away from town and drug friends. I just wouldn't know what to say to her without being somewhat of a hypocrite myself."

"Please think about it, Jim. We don't know what to do. She keeps doing such crazy things." She hesitated. "Last month she asked to borrow her girlfriend's car for the weekend to go to New Hampshire, to go skiing, you know? Sarah wasn't crazy about the idea, but she let her have the car while Meg's was being fixed. Two days later, Megan calls her from Maryland! Apparently, she decided at the last minute to give a ride to these two old friends from high school that needed transportation to Baltimore! It was so thoughtless of Meg … and, you know, so unlike my sister! She's sick Jimmy. We even had a family meeting, confronted her, all ten of us, but she laughed and walked out. We haven't heard from her since and it's been almost a month. My father says to leave her alone. Once his pride and joy, and now Meg is the biggest embarrassment for our whole family."

"Fuck your father, Lizzy. And to hell with all of you Flaherty's if you look at Meg as an embarrassment. Is that all he cares about, the family name? I bet he blames Meg for his loss for governor. No wonder she's all screwed up." Jimmy felt the anger on Megan's behalf rising inside him. "Hearing that story really pisses me off! I'll try to help her, see if she'll listen to me, but there's no guarantee. She might throw me out if she knows why I'm there."

Jimmy decided to show up at Meg's apartment one Saturday night around midnight, two weeks after he spoke with Lizzy. He had found out Meg was dating some loser he knew named Jake Walsh, a parasite who was living off Meg financially, borrowing her car, and supplying her with Seconals when she felt the need.

It was a balmy night for January. He parked his truck and waited for Meg on the stoop outside of her place. Around one o'clock in the morning, Meg pulled up with Jake. Neither of them noticed Jimmy right away. But Jimmy was on a mission, and stood up and wouldn't let them in the door.

"Beat it, Walsh. I want to talk to Meg alone."

"Yeah, right," said Jake, as he tried to push Jimmy out of the way. Jim didn't budge.

"Get lost, loser, and don't come back tonight," and he pushed Jake out on the sidewalk. "Oh, and leave her car, Walsh. It's hers, not yours."

He heard Jake mumble, "Moron," as he walked away, heading towards the T in Kenmore Square.

Meg's heart was pounding. Jimmy Romano, here, in person! Thoughts of him had filled her mind so many times, but why was he here now, barging back into her life! "Why are you here and why were you so rude to Jake?" she asked.

"Remember I said, get lost, loser? That's because he is," said Jimmy, "A big-time user and loser. And you deserve one hell of a lot better than that. What are you doing, Meg? I'm worried about you. I don't like what I'm hearing."

"All you're hearing are rumors," said Meg. "I'm fine. I work, I jog and I'm back in school."

Jimmy said, "Yeah, and you're using drugs like there's no tomorrow!"

"Not true!" she replied.

"Let's go inside," Jimmy said. "I need a cup of coffee. We can talk in there."

"Guess what! You get lost, Jimmy Romano! You think you can just walk in my life, screw up my head and walk out. No way, buddy. I told you last time I saw you I had feelings and you walked. You kissed me first … oh, wasn't I lucky! Then you walked and I never heard from you again."

"I tried to see you in the hospital, I told your father to tell you," said Jim angrily.

"Yeah, right!" shouted Megan. She pushed past him. "Now, you beat it, Romano. I'm not getting hurt and I'm fine. Go report back to Lizzy, or whoever your informant on me is, that her sister is alive and well and doesn't want any help from the Flahertys or you!"

"Come on Meg, that's not fair. People care. I care," said Jimmy. "At least let's be friends. Let me help you!"

"Friends, did you say? Friends? Jimmy, don't insult me! You walked away from me that night, this big important kiss, hurting me …" She was nearly incoherent. "You walked then, so walk now, buddy! I don't need you or anyone else!"

She let the door slam in Jimmy's face. She was shutting him out of her life, out of her drug world, the safe little place where nobody could get in. She didn't need anyone. She was sick and tired of being hurt, betrayed by family and friends. What the hell made Jimmy think she would trust him, let the likes of Jimmy Romano step into her world and help her, and then leave her again! No way!

Ten minutes later, there was a tap on her door. Meg ignored it.

"Open the door, Megan, or I'll break it down," Jimmy said through gritted teeth.

"Get lost, Jimmy, I don't need your help. Please, please leave," Meg said imploringly. She was tired, she was sad; she had tears streaming down her face.

"No, Meg. I won't leave until I see you face to face. At least let me know you're all right and then I'll go; we can part on good terms."

Meg, feeling defeated and not wanting Jimmy to make a scene, opened the door. She went and sat on her sofa where she was rolling a joint.

"Megan, honey, go to bed. You don't need more drugs tonight. You're high as a kite as it is," Jimmy said this as he grabbed the pot and rolling papers from Megan's grasp. She furiously charged at him and with her unsteady gait fell on the floor.

"Go to bed, Meg," Jimmy said calmly.

"Not until you leave. I'm staying right here until you get out of here."

"Do you hate me that much, Megan? Or do you hate yourself and are afraid to let me inside your brain to try and help you?"

"I hate men, Jimmy. And that includes you! So go!"

Jimmy lifted her up and walked her to the sofa. "I'll go, but you need help, Meg, and I do want to help you!"

Meg was too upset, too furious at his self-righteous attitude. "Help, Jimmy? Help me? You mean like how my father helps me? Maybe you two are alike after all! You both pretend to help and then you're out of my life again. Men just aren't there for the long haul."

Jimmy, hurt and furious, said, "Don't ever compare me to your father, Megan! You don't know me well enough to assume I would desert you." Angry and hurt, he turned and left Meg's apartment, left her sitting alone wondering why her life was turning into shambles, and why it simply kept getting worse as a feeling of impending doom crept into her soul.

CHAPTER NINE

April – 1977

Meg woke up screaming from yet another nightmare of the attack. A cold sweat broke out as she sat up in bed screaming. Beth, her roommate, ran to her side to calm her down. It was three o'clock in the morning, and she had to be at work at seven. She knew sleep was over for the night, unless, of course, she took a Seconal. But her body was getting used to them and she needed more and more of the little red pills to help her forget, help her to sleep.

Beth made her a cup of tea and Meg told her to go back to bed.

"You have to go to work, too, Beth. I'm sorry."

As Meg sipped her tea, she reflected on the past year, especially the fateful day when her life changed. Her assailant had never been found which kept Meg in fear. Many of her friends and colleagues believed her story; half didn't. She'd get comments like, "Well, why did you get in the car with him?" Even one nurse said, "You should have known better."

Meg had felt betrayed by her father, but also by her profession. As a nurse, she felt other nurses never stuck up for one another. They were more often then not back stabbers who offered no support to each other. Nurses are the biggest group of women in the world, collectively, and they simply turned their heads, became jealous at one another's good fortune. Meg realized her profession had let her down. And defending herself was getting real old, constantly trying to explain to her colleagues how tired she had been after working seventy-two hours straight, the snowstorm, how nice the guy initially appeared … they would look at her quizzically, wondering if she was telling the truth.

When Meg had taken her new position, she had been required to take some management classes that would teach her how to be a charge nurse while getting along with the staff so they could work as a cohesive unit. During the class, the instructor who was lecturing stated that eighty-five percent of nurses come from emotionally troubled families such as alcoholic households or abusive homes. They have learned behavior such as being caretakers and pleasers, and have low self-esteem. Frequently they go into care taking professions because that is what they were taught as children, and they feel comfortable caring for and pleasing others and in general not taking care of their own needs, leading to bitterness in their lives, wanting to find fault with others, especially those who have good fortune in their lives.

Now she realized this might be true of her staff. Dysfunctional nurses who still held anger and resentments from their childhoods; somehow, Meg could understand this, even forgive. But her father was not validating the worst, most horrible pain. She felt betrayed. And he wanted her to get on with her life, stop talking about it. He didn't believe her flashbacks. He said sarcastically, "So, what do you think, you were in a war, having flashbacks? Don't be so dramatic."

But the fact was, Meg felt as if she was in a war, an emotional battle that traumatized her indefinitely.

She had finally sought out a psychiatrist six months after the attack. He continued to talk to her, to give her tranquilizers and sleeping pills when her medical doctor would no longer supply them. Meg knew, as a nurse, that she needed to talk to someone about that day over a year ago, and it worked for a while, but the flashbacks would occur, even at work, and she would have anxiety attacks and have to go home. Maybe her father was right. Stop thinking about it … pretend it didn't happen.

Over the last two months the intrusive thoughts had gotten worse, even with counseling, so she stopped going and depended on her pills more. Then Jake came into the picture. He supplied her with Seconals so she could sleep. Meg didn't care if he was using her for her car and money. She was using him, too.

Who cares? she thought. *He meets my needs.*

Then Jimmy had to come back into the picture. Friggin' Jimmy Romano! And that night she felt strong, was not going to get hurt by him. She was starting to get him out of her mind when he appeared, so cool, calm, in control, and as handsome as ever.

It had taken a lot of strength to make him leave, to walk past him on that January night. Jimmy was right, though. She was depending on her pills to get her through the day, and she really didn't want to stop. And the way she acted when she let Jimmy into her apartment, falling down, telling him he was like her father. She was wrong to do that and embarrassed about it the next day.

She had become the embarrassment of the family as well, getting blamed for her father's election failure.

It was six o'clock when Meg roused herself from her thoughts and looked at the clock. She needed to get ready for work, and work was another story. She was still the charge nurse but was beginning not to care about her job anymore.

The Director of Nursing, Priscilla Jacobs, had even called Meg to her office, telling Meg she was aware of her apathy. "You have to put in a better performance, Meg. Your staff is not happy with you and you don't look well. Do you need another leave of absence?" That was the last thing Meg needed, a leave of absence. That would give her too much time on her hands.

"I'll liven up," Meg said, laughingly, to the director. "Give me a few months and my floor will be the best in the hospital. I owe it to you, Priscilla, you bent over backwards to get me this position. I don't want to let you down."

Meg knew this was a serious warning, and as nice as her boss was, she knew she meant business. Meg had to start improving her personal and professional life.

Meg rose slowly from the table, tears in her eyes. It had been one month since that conversation with Priscilla and not much had improved. As she got into the shower and let the steaming hot water waken her body, she knew it was only a matter of time before she lost her job. She felt it in her bones. Something was going to break. She couldn't go on like this. Only three hours of sleep, sometimes less, every night … taking sleeping pills that left her too groggy to function properly.

Megan hit bottom on the morning of April 30. Two weeks before that, her flashbacks of the attack started happening every day, debilitating her. She started taking her sleeping pills at any time of day or night. She took so many she started hallucinating.

She told her roommate, Beth, that her old boyfriend, Steve, was out in the parking lot waving at her. When Beth looked out the window, no one was there. Beth immediately called Lizzy and told her what was happening. Liz made a few phone calls to local drug rehabilitation centers and found one she thought would be appropriate for Meg. It was called The Way Back, and was mainly for professionals with substance abuse problems, located in Bath, Maine.

"She'll be far enough away from Boston, away from her connections," Lizzy told Beth.

Meg thought she was going out with Lizzy shopping for the day at the outlet stores in Maine. Once in the car, Meg fell asleep for the four-hour ride and she awoke in front of the rehab, Meg had no idea where they were and why she had to leave Lizzy. Her hallucinations were continuing and Meg wasn't caring why she was there.

The next morning Meg woke up to the sounds of the beach: waves, the cries of gulls, and the smell of salt air.

"Good morning," said Ann, the psychologist assigned to Megan.

"Where am I?" asked Meg.

"You're in a detoxification/ rehabilitation center in Maine. Your family and friends were worried about you, that your addiction has gotten way out of control. They're worried about your safety," said Ann, as she looked at Meg compassionately.

But Meg was angry. "I'm not a fucking addict and I'm signing myself out."

But as Meg stood, her head started to spin and she almost fainted. Then the tears came. Tears that she couldn't shed, hadn't allowed herself to for months, finally arrived and wouldn't stop.

Ann sat with Meg for over an hour, cradling her like a baby. When the tears stopped and Meg became more in control, Ann stated, "Time in this place is going to be hard work, Meg. You're going to have to face some tough issues in your life, mainly your addiction."

Meg was so spent she couldn't reply. Oh, her anger was there. She was furious with her sister, but she had no fight left … she wanted to give in, stop trying to pretend she was fine and just admit she had a problem with pills, that "Katie O'Toole", her make-believe drug-addict self, had taken over, was out of control. But Meg knew if she faced reality, she might go insane. She couldn't stand the flashbacks without drugs. She'd kill herself if she had to stay here clean and sober.

"How long am I here for?" asked Meg.

"As long as it takes," said Ann. "It's up to you. Probably three months."

"I need to call work," Meg said.

"Your sister's taking care of that," said Ann.

"I may lose my job," Meg said, on the verge of tears once again.

"You need to concentrate on one thing and one thing alone: your sobriety," Ann said convincingly.

Meg knew she had no choice. She was already here and would give it a shot.

"Try, even for one day," said Ann. "Everyone here is in the same boat, Meg. You're going to be okay, there are nurses here and some doctors as patients, they'll help you, too."

And so she started … structure, structure, structure … Alcoholic Anonymous meetings … Narcotic Anonymous meetings. Meg would sit there at first, not relating to any of the other inmates, her word for the other patients. She felt imprisoned, even without the bars. She could walk out the door any time. No one would make her stay. Yet for some reason she stayed, not knowing why. Several times she tried to sneak to the phone, call Jake to bring her drugs, but each time she got close enough to an office with a phone, someone from the staff would walk by and look at her suspiciously, so she gave up and ever so slowly she started to snap out of the fog she had been in and realize she was a little sick, needed help.

At one NA meeting, the head speaker decided the topic would be The Serenity Prayer, which states, "God, grant me the serenity to accept the things I cannot change; the courage to change the things I can; and the wisdom to know the difference."

Vinny, the leader, had been in the rehab for six months and was getting ready to leave. He told Meg he had been a heroin addict, overdosed, and ended up being admitted to the hospital. From there, he was sent to The Way Back. Meg approached Vinny after the meeting and took a risk, told him about her attacker. "Accept the things you cannot change," had made sense to Meg. She was trying to change what had happened that night, make things right, or pretend it didn't happen. What she hadn't been doing was accepting. Vinny put his arm around Meg.

"That's what it's all about, Meggie, accepting. Accepting what has happened, accepting the things you cannot change such as the attack, but courage to change the things you can, like your lifestyle. You can change that, Meg."

But as time went on, Meg never felt like she fit in at the meetings. People talked about drinking, doing drugs, not being able to stop when they started. Meg said she never really felt that way. She felt as if she escaped from problems. She drank and did drugs for a reason, didn't just sit there and get high for the sake of getting high. "I could always shut myself off, except for a few times," she said.

Raymond, a counselor there for twenty years, said to her one day in group counseling, "Tell us about those few times, Meg, the few times you couldn't stop."

Shit, Meg thought. *I don't want to go back there!*

But Ray persisted. Meg had been at the center now for two months and he felt she was ready for pressure.

"Well, after work, going for drinks, I'd let Katie O'Toole come out."

"Who?" Ray asked.

"Katie. The person I turned into when I decided to get fucked up, outta my head."

"Tell me about Katie," said Ray.

"Nothing to tell," Meg responded. "It was just me, feeling shitty about an event in my life, something I couldn't handle, so I'd drink, smoke pot, whatever."

"What were those things that were bothering you, Meg?" asked Ray.

"I never felt important in my house, growing up, and the importance to excel was too great at times. I was always somebody's daughter or sister or niece. I was never just Megan. So, I learned to escape those feeling as a little girl, pretend it didn't matter. But as an adult, it *did* matter. I finally wanted to be somebody … not somebody's relative."

"So, you drank, got high?" asked Ray.

"Yeah. Why not?"

"Because it showed you your addiction. You couldn't handle booze, pot, whatever."

"But the thing is, I can," said Meg. "I've been here two months. I'm sober; I'm not having flashbacks of being attacked. I'm okay. I don't need to escape!"

"Until the next time," said Ray.

"I don't think there'll be a next time," said Meg. "It doesn't matter to me. I'm really not an addict."

Two weeks later, Meg approached Ann. "I need to get out of here," she said. "I've been here over two months and there's nothing more I can get out of this place."

"Do you exercise, Meg?" Ann asked.

"I used to run," Meg said forlornly, "about six miles a day."

"Well, that's what we're going to do, then," said Ann. "There are some extra running shoes around somewhere. We're going for a jog."

Fifteen minutes later, the two women were jogging in unison on the beach, slow easy strides. Meg hadn't run in over two months. The fresh air and ocean smell made Meg feel alive as she kept pace with Ann, slow easy strides. She was starting to feel the endorphin rush she loved during a run, as if you were invincible, could run forever.

"So, you don't think you need to be here, Meg?" asked Ann.

"No, I'm ready to leave, had enough. I need to get on with my life. Go back to nursing. I'm almost twenty-seven, you know."

"Nursing, Meg? What about drugs? You administer drugs. How do you feel being around narcotics, sleeping pills?"

"What are you getting at?" asked Meg. "Are you telling me to quit being a nurse? If you are, that's not going to happen. I wanted to be a nurse since I was five years old. I won't stop nursing. Besides, I'm going back to school to get my degree. I'm going to teach in a nursing program. That's always been my dream."

They had run about two miles. Meg, out of shape, tired, needed to rest. They leaned on a rock, catching their breath.

"Listen," Ann said, "give this place a few more weeks. Regroup, and think about your priorities, what you need to do to not use drugs again."

"I'm homesick," Meg said, afraid that Ann would make some calls home and she would have to stay there.

"Don't panic, Meg. I can't make you stay, none of the staff here can. I just want you to make the right decisions before you get discharged. I want to be sure you're leaving for the right reasons, and that you're ready! You can have visitors, Meg. Call your sister. I'm sure she'll visit."

"I know my parents won't. In Lizzy's letters she said they were extremely disappointed in me. They keep saying I had once been my father's favorite; the one he thought would go places. I've disappointed him, and he'll hold it against me, and that this place is costing him thousands of dollars. He'll never let me forget it."

"Sounds like he had too many expectations of you, Meg. Maybe it's your dad who should be disappointed in himself."

"I don't care anymore. I probably won't even contact him when I leave. And my mother's useless. You'd think she would have called, written. My father probably gave her orders not to! I'll make my decision in a few days. I actually have no place to go to. My roommate had to replace me, find some other roommate, so I'm virtually homeless. I'll call Lizzy. You're right, she'll help."

But Lizzy didn't return her phone calls. Meg had tried three times, left messages, and even asked if she could stay with her for a while. Meg was discouraged. She was sure she was ready to leave. She'd have to go through her phone book. With all the close friends she had, surely someone would put her up for a couple of weeks.

A month later, as Meg sat in her room contemplating her fate, one of the counselors came into her room. "Megan, you have a visitor."

Meg ran down the long winding stairs, figuring it was Liz. Thank God! She could leave today! As she turned the corner of the first landing, there stood Jimmy. Meg stopped in the middle of the stairwell.

"Jimmy, what are you doing here? How did you know where I was? Liz promised not to tell a soul."

"I threatened her," said Jimmy with a big grin on his face. "Is there somewhere we can talk?"

"Let me get a pass for an hour," said Meg. "Maybe we can go walk on the beach."

He just smiled in response.

"So, why are you here?" asked Meg, as she bent down to pick up sea glass. The waves were pounding on the beach, loud crashes against the sand.

"I've been doing a lot of thinking, Meg. Since I last saw you, I realized you mean something to me. I was so afraid — you know, afraid to commit. I didn't want to be hurt, have someone leave me, like my dad." He hesitated. "His death shattered me, you know, and the only way I could respond was not to respond or get involved. Now I know I'm missing out. I can't get you out of my mind."

"Jimmy, I'm pretty fragile here. I can't afford to be hurt. I don't know if a relationship is right for me now. I'm supposed to concentrate on staying off drugs, get to know myself before I get involved. That's what they tell me, anyway! Besides, I was so rude to you the last time I saw you. I owe you an apology; I know that. You're nothing like my father."

"I knew you didn't mean it," said Jimmy with a grin on his face. "Sure, I was mad at you, but I knew it was the drugs that were talking and I've pretty much forgotten that incident. What I can't forget is you, Megan. I really want you in my life."

Meg took off her sweatshirt and placed it on the sand, sitting down with her face in her hands, deep in thought. She finally responded. "My counselor, Annie, said not to have a relationship for a year after you're sober — to go slow, give it time. I need to get to know myself or I could slip, do drugs again, and believe me, you don't want me, Jimmy, not like this. I need to get strong first; plus, you wouldn't want me if you saw me the last day before I came here. I was hallucinating, seeing friends who weren't there! Jimmy, I had flashbacks and they could come back. You don't want a girlfriend who you will have to take care of emotionally, a high maintenance girlfriend." She took a deep breath and then told Jimmy about Katie O'Toole, hoping that would turn him off and he would run away.

But Jimmy had another person inside, similar to Meg's Katie O'Toole, and he knew the feeling all too well. He loved Meg even more for opening up, sharing that part of her with him. A level of trust was beginning between them.

Jim reached over, placed his hand on her head, feeling her warmth, her silky strands of hair. He bent down and lifted her to her feet.

"Can I kiss you, Megan Flaherty?"

"If it's anything like the kiss before, I don't know. That kind of knocked me for a loop."

But he smiled, leaned over and tenderly kissed her, not like before, a slow gentle tender gesture, a kiss of simplicity, showing her he cared.

"Oh, Meg, I've missed you. Please just be with me, we've played games long enough. I want a relationship. Let's try; let's get strong together. I know what you were like and I don't care, we'll take it one day at a time, love each other one day at a time, Meggie."

"I don't know. I'll give it a lot of thought tonight. I know I'm ready to leave, but I'm not sure it should be with you."

Jimmy spent the night in a hotel room. Meg went back to the rehab and knew a few hours later that she would leave with Jimmy. She was in love with him, was sick of playing games, and although it wasn't the safest decision she felt right about it.

She had told Jimmy that evening she was fragile, could use drugs again, but Meg knew she would not, she felt strongly about that and only said those things to Jimmy so he could back out, walk away from her if he wanted an out. But he didn't walk, he stayed and wanted to be with her and was ready to face any difficulties that may arise. This was destiny and she believed God wanted them together for a reason.

Around midnight she called Annie and told her she was leaving in the morning.

"With Jimmy, Meg?"

"Yes, with Jimmy. We're going to try and make a go of a relationship. I'm going to stay with him for a few weeks, hopefully get a job, find my own place, and then we'll see."

"It's dangerous territory, Megan. Jimmy used drugs, too, you said. You could both end up in a rehab again."

Megan paused, and then asked, "Did you ever read *Gone With The Wind*, Ann?"

"Sure," she replied "Why?"

"Remember Scarlett O'Hara, how she stood on her land and declared, 'I'll never lose Tara,' which was her home, her place?

She was determined never to weaken. Well, that's how I feel. I will never, never use drugs again. I will never put myself in that position — just like Scarlett O'Hara!"

"What an analogy!" said Ann.

The next morning Meg called Jimmy and an hour later, he was waiting for her in the lobby of The Way Back. His hands were in his pockets and he was pacing back and forth, waiting for Meg. He was introduced to Ann, who looked at him tentatively.

"You both take care of yourselves. Keep in touch, Meggie. Call me anytime." Annie said as they hugged one another good-bye.

"I'll never forget all the help and support you gave me, Annie. You're like a sister, to me. I've even started to learn to trust again." Meg took one last long look at the rehab center as they drove away. She had meant what she said to Ann. She would never do drugs again, she would never be back to this center again, and she had the same constitution as Scarlett O'Hara. End of story.

Jimmy and Meg drove slowly down the Maine coast. It took them a week to get back to Newport. They stopped at quaint bed & breakfasts, hotels, and friends' houses in Maine and New Hampshire. They went to Wells Beach, took long walks, jogged around Perkins Cove in Ogunquit and treated themselves to an expensive dinner overlooking the Harbor in York, Maine, staying at the beautiful Cliff House overlooking the ocean. Meg had been to her girlfriend Arlene's wedding there several years before and had always loved the view, the ocean and rocks. Not once did either of them think of drinking or drugs. Simply being together was enough. Their lovemaking seemed natural, like it was always meant to be. The chemistry was just there and after the week together, Meg and Jimmy made the decision to live together.

Meg, at first, was hesitant, "I don't know, Jimmy. Maybe we're moving too fast."

"For Chrissake, Meggie, we're almost twenty-eight years old. Let's just go for it. I love you!"

So, it was an instant honeymoon. When they returned to Massachusetts, they stayed at Jimmy's apartment in Newport until they found a larger place. Jimmy worked while Meg stayed home, fixed the apartment up, cleaned, cooked (even though that was one of her least favorite tasks!) and waited for Jim to arrive home each evening. They were settling in. Meg was looking for a job, and resolved to call her old boss and explain what had happened. Eventually. She had virtually just disappeared from work. Liz had told them very little, only that her sister was not emotionally stable and needed time off. She would look for jobs elsewhere if she couldn't get her old one back. Something, she was sure, would materialize. In the meantime, she was basking in their contentment; she couldn't remember when she had been so happy.

CHAPTER TEN

May — 1978

It was a hippie wedding of sorts, despite the fact that the long hair, bandanas and love beads of the sixties and seventies were giving way to disco dancing, permed hair and straight legged jeans and the Saturday Night Fever craze.

Meg and Jimmy were married at Our Lady's Church by a priest who was a friend of the Romano's. Colleen, Meg's best friend, sang *In My Life* by the Beatles as the couple walked down the aisle. The reception that followed was at the Romano's family estate at Charlton Pond, with over two hundred people attending.

Meg wore her grandmother's 1900's wedding dress that her father had restored; she had her hair done with ringlets and flowers throughout the long black tresses.

Jimmy had cut his hair shoulder-length and wore a tuxedo jacket, but he refused to wear the pants and shoes. "I won't be caught dead in those goony slacks and Fred Astaire shoes!" he exclaimed. "It's my wedding, too, and I refuse to be dressed like a monkey in a three piece suit!"

There was a band and a disc jockey, free booze and plenty of marijuana floating around. Mr. Flaherty was anything but pleased. He held his feelings in, but it was clear that he hated Italians, the Romano's, and most especially Jimmy. When Meg told him she was getting married, he wouldn't respond with anything positive.

"So, Dad, what do you think of Jimmy?" Meg asked him tentatively two weeks before the wedding.

"What do I think?" he said angrily. "I think your future husband's hands are too clean."

"And what does that mean, Dad?"

"It means he doesn't have a job. It's an old Irish saying."

"He works!" Meg exclaimed.

"You call bartending and doing construction work? You can do better than him, Meg. You're marrying beneath you."

Meg had stormed out of the house, furious with her father. He had never liked any of her boyfriends. What made her think that would change? And he refused to contribute any money for the wedding.

"Don't worry," said Jimmy. "I'll pay." He hated Mr. Flaherty, and it gave him great pleasure to show him he could afford a wedding. Besides, the Romano's weren't exactly poor! His father had made money, invested well. They had the insurance settlement from the accident, too. They weren't quite multi-millionaires, but each kid had a trust fund they could dip into. And Jimmy did just that, with his mother's blessing. He spent over fifteen thousand dollars on the wedding.

"To hell with Old Man Flaherty. I'll take care of Meg," Jimmy said.

Besides, he was working, still bartending and taking college courses. And Meg didn't have to work. She had gone back to school full time to get her master's degree. She was going to teach in a nursing program someday.

The wedding ended up making the papers. Of course, John Flaherty had called the media, pretending he had dished out the money for it all. What the papers missed were the joints being smoked, the lines of cocaine being snorted in the guest room on the main house's complex at Charlton Estate. And thank God for that! The last thing she wanted was the newspaper getting wind of drugs at her wedding. Meg had walked into the reception not expecting people to be as stoned as they were.

And she also saw Jimmy, joint in hand, getting high with one of his buddies from high school. What was he thinking? Later that night, when everyone had left, Megan confronted him.

"I didn't know you still got high, Jimmy," she said, tentatively.

He reacted at once. "Lighten up, Meg. I only smoke pot occasionally. Don't make a mountain out of a molehill, honey. Okay?"

Maybe I am overreacting, she thought. *Hell, what's pot, anyway? No big deal.*

They honeymooned for one week in Bermuda. The weather was perfect with long, lazy days on the beach and cozy nights together spent at a quiet Oceanside restaurant or calling room service and making love all night.

"Before we leave, Jimmy, I just have to go on a glass bottom boat tour like my parents did on their wedding. My mother told us stories about that boat since I was a little girl, how you could see the fish right through the glass!" exclaimed Megan excitedly.

"You sound like a little kid, too," Jimmy said laughingly, "like you're five years old again." But Jimmy made sure she got her wish and rented a small glass bottomed boat for just the two of them on their last day there. Meg pictured her parents on their honeymoon over forty years before, wondering if her mother was as much in love with her father as she was with Jimmy.

A month after the wedding, Jimmy came storming into the house, kicked his boots off, and exclaimed, "My job sucks, Meg! Newport sucks! We got to get out of here. I want to move to Florida."

"Florida? Why on earth? What's wrong?"

"I want to go to the Keys. Key West, actually. I can get a construction job there with some guys I know, ex-bartenders, who are living there already. There's plenty of work."

"I don't understand," said Megan. "What about school, Jimmy? You're smart. You've only got another year to go. You're so close! And then you can get a real job."

"You sound like your old man, Megan. Isn't construction work good enough for the Flahertys?"

"That wasn't fair to say Jimmy; you took that the wrong way. Besides, I'm in school. I have two months before I graduate. Where will I find work in the Florida Keys?"

"Come on, Meggie! This is a break for me, a business opportunity. If I invest in this new project, I'll be all set in the construction company. I need to do this, honey."

He came up behind her, arms around her waist, kissing her neck, caressing her all over. Why did he have this effect on her all the time? She was always giving in to him. She'd weaken. He knew her vulnerabilities.

She pushed him away half-heartedly, giggling at his touch. "Okay, okay! Look, Jimmy, you go. I'll finish school here and meet you in a few months if you're so anxious to go right now, but I need to finish school. I need to do that for me!"

To her surprise, he agreed immediately. "I'll make arrangements and leave in a week or two, then, if you're sure that's what you want," Jimmy said. "The opportunity is now, and I want to take it. I'll find us a nice place, and you can fly down and be with me every weekend."

Jimmy found an apartment right near the water in Key West. *Jeez, there's still a lot of hippie looking people here,* he thought, as he started to unload his truck full of furniture. *Volkswagen buses, long hair, love beads … and everyone looks pretty stoned.*

Jimmy had even gotten his hair all chopped off a year before. Long hair was becoming unfashionable at home. *Guess not in Key West,* he thought.

His friends, John and Tony, helped him unload the furniture. He had bought a few things to tide him over until Meg could arrive with the rest. When they were done, all three men went to a local bar for a couple of beers and some burgers.

"Work is great here," said Tony.

Tony's dad, Frank Johnson, owned the construction company. It originated in Newport, and he was offered a big contract in the Keys. If his son, Tony, and two friends could get this job off the ground and show they were hard workers, he was planning on letting them become partners in the company. He knew all three needed a break, especially the Romano kid. He remembered him from high school, a fantastic football player, full boat to Northeastern, and then the injury ruining any hopes of a career in football. Then his father's accident! What a tragedy! He had known Eddie Romano, even had a few pieces of furniture he had made. He had been a good man, well respected. The least Frank could do was help these kids out.

As they each ordered a second beer, Tony told them the plan. "My dad says if we show we can work in the construction business, do the labor, and eventually the business end of it, then he's going to let us be partners. His company is really branching out in the Keys. There are lots of hotels going up. We could be millionaires in ten years."

And that was what Jimmy needed to hear. He wanted to show the almighty Flaherty family that he could support Meg, that he wasn't useless. That's what John Flaherty had said to him, totally insulting Jimmy when Meg first introduced them. Two weeks after they'd arrived home, old man Flaherty had come to their apartment trying to convince "his Meggie" to go back home. His home, that was.

Right in front of Jimmy, he'd said, "He's useless, Meg, a lazy bartender who will never make anything of himself. The only thing he was good for was football and he even screwed that up."

Jimmy had charged at Mr. Flaherty. "Get outta my apartment. At least I won't cheat on my wife like you've been doing your whole life, Mr. Ex-senator!"

Meg had to break the two of them up or they would have duked it out. Jimmy couldn't wait to show the old man that he wasn't useless.

Jim, John, and Tony worked from morning till night. All three put their hearts and souls into Johnson's Construction Company. They had contracts with two big hotels going up, and Jimmy was in charge of hiring. He spent half the days interviewing and hiring, and the other half building. He felt as if he died and went to heaven. His self-worth was returning and he truly felt alive again.

But he missed Meg. He'd call a few times a week. She promised she'd be there soon, as soon as school ended. She would have her master's degree in nursing, and she wanted to teach, to find a university that would hire her in Florida. Jimmy felt he and Meg were on the way up.

He had told her a white lie about moving to Florida. Back in Newport, he was starting to get tempted to use drugs again. He had run into some old high school buddies and they kept frequenting the bar, encouraging Jimmy to try some new heroin that had arrived recently in Newport. Jimmy came close to caving in — getting high — but something always stopped him. It was probably thinking of the consequences, of Meg's reaction.

Fortunately, he heard of the opportunity in Florida and Jimmy knew he had to act quickly.

And as he drove back to his apartment he thought of his life now and he had made the right decision to leave. The geographical cure might work after all! Soon they could start a family, maybe have a beautiful daughter, just like his wife. He couldn't wait for her arrival.

Two weeks later, Meg called to say one of her classes — in which she needed to do community service — had been extended. She thought she'd had enough credits but she didn't. She wouldn't be through until after September.

"Quit school, Meg," Jimmy said grandly, "I'm doing great here! I miss you!"

"Are you crazy, Jimmy? I'm almost done. I'll fly down for the long weekend and we can talk. Okay?"

Meg arrived on a hot, muggy August day. Jimmy picked her up at the Marathon Airport on the Keys. "God, its hot here, Jimmy! Hot, but beautiful. Oh, wow! Look at that ocean."

Meg glanced over at Jimmy. He was so tanned and handsome. *Here I am, white as a ghost, exhausted from school,* she thought.

As they got out of his truck in front of the apartment, Jimmy scooped Meg up into his arms and said, "Okay, Mrs. Romano, over the threshold." A bunch of little kids standing around started clapping as Jimmy started singing *Crazy Love* by Van Morrison.

"I can hear her heart beat for a thousand miles/when I come to her when the sun goes down/She gives me love, love, love, love, crazy love …"

Meg laughed. "You got the words right but in the wrong order, Romano."

The kids yelled, "Hey, you two in love?"

When they got upstairs, Jimmy yelled out the window to the ten-year-old kids, "Hey, do you little smart asses know what making babies means?"

"Sure, mister. Whatta ya think, we're five or something?"

"Well, that's what we're gonna go do: make babies!"

Meg pulled him away, "God, Jimmy, they're going to run home and tell their parents!"

"So what?" he said, as he put the tape of Van Morrison on. "Dance with me, Meggie."

As they slow-danced around the living room to the music, Meg said, "You know, Jimmy, we don't have a song of our own. You know, like *I Got You, Babe* or *Unchained Melody.*"

Jimmy said, "Gag time, Meg," as he stuck his finger down his throat. Those sounds are old news. Sonny Bono — forget it!"

She laughed. "Well, what do you like then, Jimmy? What about *Can't Find the Time to Tell You?*"

"Now you're really going back in time, Meg! I remember seeing Orpheus at the Hampton Beach Casino in '68!"

She put her arms around him. "It's a great love song. What do you think, Jimmy?"

"I think picking our song is so dippy, hon."

"It's not dippy," she replied, "its romantic. Come on … get into it. Let's pick one of Van Morrison's."

"I wanna rock your gypsy soul/way back to the days of old," Jimmy sang in Meg's ear. "Okay, okay, then this'll be our album, not just our song. You can remember me when I'm dead and gone. I can see you now, sitting and crying while you listen to *Crazy Love*."

That evening they went out to a quiet restaurant overlooking the water. A few waitresses came over to say hi to Jimmy.

"Should I be jealous?" asked Meg, jokingly.

"Hell, no. There's no one like you in this world, Meggie. Don't ever worry. I will never, ever cheat on you. I can't believe I waited so long to be with you. I was such an asshole, a real screwed-up mental case."

Meg said, "Remember the time at the Grog; the first-kiss night? Why did you say that to me about Steve? You made it sound like I left him because of his injuries in Vietnam."

"I was being my usual shithead self, darlin', trying to make you mad at me. I didn't mean it. I didn't know anything about your relationship except you were going out with someone that was hurt in 'Nam. Do you really want to talk about it?"

She shrugged. "I guess so. But it was a high school thing, like you and Amy. My father hated him, too, but he had reason. He was mean to me sometimes. He put me down a lot. To this day, I don't know why I dated him. He probably feels the same way.

"I wouldn't have sex with him in high school so he always cheated on me with girls that would."

"Wow! You didn't have sex in high school?"

Meg rolled her eyes, "God, Jimmy, I can tell it's hard for you to believe, but, no, I didn't. Lizzy got pregnant when I was sixteen. She was only nineteen and she had to quit college to have her son. I didn't want that to be me. I saw how hard it was for her. So, I promised myself I wouldn't fool around. Besides, at Westbridge High, if a girl slept around she'd get a reputation. The most I did with Steve was go to second base, heavy-duty making out at the

Fresh Pond drive-in watching steamy sex flicks!" She laughed. "So, your turn. How old were you when you first had sex?"

"Thirteen" Jimmy said calmly.

"Come on, honey, stop fooling around! How old really?"

"Seriously Meg, thirteen!"

"God Jimmy, I was still wearing a snowsuit at thirteen! Who with?"

"Now you're getting too personal, Meg" he said with a grin. "Okay, I'll play fair. She was older, a friend of my sister's. She had this thing for younger guys, but I looked old for my age anyway. Hell, I was buying booze in liquor stores without an ID when I was fifteen!"

Meg shook her head, "Ye old double standard," she said knowingly. "If a girl sleeps around, she's a slut; if a boy does, he's a stud!"

Jimmy decided not to go there. Time to change the conversation, he thought. "So, how did you break up with Steve?"

Meg allowed herself to be deterred off-topic. "I didn't break up with him. It sort of just happened. You know? When he went to Vietnam, I was heartbroken. I remember the day he left. God, he looked about fifteen. So, anyway, I was driving to the airport with him and his brother. *Leaving on a Jet Plane* was playing on the radio, and I just cried my eyes out. I was sure he'd get hurt or killed."

She sighed, a little restless. "Four months later we got word that he stepped on a mine. Shrapnel was imbedded all over his body. I guess he was lucky to be alive, but ..." She hesitated. "They sent him home and I went to see him and — he just wasn't the same guy anymore. You know? He was all angry and bitter ... so full of hate. And I was the most convenient person to take it all out on. And I let him do it for longer than I should have, because I kind of felt sorry for him."

They had been sitting in the restaurant for four hours. The lights were dimming and the wait staff was cleaning up all around them as they kept sitting and talking.

"What about you and Amy?" Meg asked, relieved to change the subject.

"There's nothing much to say. I feel guilty the way I hurt her toward the end of our relationship. She was trying to be so kind when my dad had his accident and I totally blocked her out. I wouldn't let her inside my head. I was so messed up and pissed off; I didn't want to get hurt anymore." He hesitated, tracing the outline of Meg's hand that he was holding across the table. "Well, that's not exactly true. She wanted to get married. She was talking about getting married all the time, and I wasn't ready. I was twenty-one and unhappy and couldn't even face myself, much less another human being. So I guess I was a little like your Steve; I took it out on her. I wish that I hadn't."

Meg stroked his hand with her thumb. "She loved you, Jimmy. She didn't want to lose you. When I first met you, I was just over eighteen myself. I think I loved you the minute I saw you. I would have married you then, too."

Jimmy laughed. "I remember that first day. I hadn't seen a chick with rollers in her hair in years. I first thought, who's the flake?" He turned serious again. "But your eyes got to me. You know? Your green cat's eyes. And even though I couldn't let myself feel then, even though I was so angry about my football injury and was walking around feeling sorry for myself, angry at the world, well, even then, you got to me."

The lights in the restaurant blinked twice. It was time to leave.

Jimmy said, "Let's go have a beer with John and Tony. It's not too late."

As they were climbing the stairs to Tony's apartment, Meg could smell the marijuana. And when they got inside a joint was passed around. Meg just handed it back. She wanted nothing to do with that world. Katie O'Toole was dead! But Jimmy took a couple of hits and became giggly, like the rest of the people. And when they went home, Meg wanted to address the issue with Jimmy but didn't want to ruin the intimate mood they had been sharing in the restaurant. She wondered why Jimmy hadn't wanted to go straight home and make love with her after that closeness, why he had wanted to go see his friends instead. She hoped that it wasn't because of the pot.

"Do you get high a lot, Jimmy?" she asked hesitantly once they were in bed.

"Now and then," he said, defensively.

"I guess I worry. It's illegal, it can be addictive."

"Chill out, Megan. I only smoke it a couple of times a week. It's better than drinking."

Meg felt that way, too. She knew Jimmy wasn't much of a drinker, but why did he have to do anything? Wasn't she enough? Why did he have to get high when he was with her?

"Is that all you do?" Meg asked, hoping the answer was going to be yes. She had remembered the stories of his heroin use and wanted to make sure that really was firmly in the past.

"If you're worried about smack, honey, please don't. I haven't touched that stuff in over a year. Forget about it … I was a dumb, immature shit who was experimenting. It's over with."

Still, Meg had an uneasy feeling a few days later when she had to leave. Her flight was going back to Boston in an hour and, as she was packing her things, she opened a dresser drawer and saw an ounce of pot, rolling papers, and some other paraphernalia.

Forget about it, she thought, Jimmy said he wasn't doing anything more. She needed to believe that. Besides, like he said, "It's only pot. No big deal."

CHAPTER ELEVEN

November — 1978

It was about the third morning in a row that Megan had thrown up. She knew she was pregnant. Her breasts were sore and she had missed her period for three full months.

She hadn't thought much about that part, because she had never been regular with her periods. But this was different.

Without even going to an obstetrician, she knew the rabbit would die!

She felt more surprise than joy. Even with Jimmy's inappropriate shouted assertion in Florida that they were going to "make a baby," she hadn't really expected it to happen. And she wasn't at all sure that she would have chosen this moment for it to happen, had she really thought about things. She had wanted to wait another year, be able to get a job, work for a while and take a leave of absence and go back to work. She had it planned perfectly in her head.

"Damn! Why didn't I bring my diaphragm down here when I visited in August?"

She was living in the Keys now, and had been since the end of September. She was waiting for her reciprocity certification from the state nursing board so that she could work as a registered nurse in Florida.

So, in a sense, it wasn't as though she had been working, anyway …

But as she touched her stomach, picturing bringing a new life into the world, she started to hum out of sheer pleasure.

And Jimmy was ecstatic! When she told him she thought she was pregnant, he picked her up and started dancing around the living room with her, singing, "Isn't she lovely … isn't she wonderful. God, I'm so happy … only one minute old," a Stevie Wonder melody.

"Jimmy," Meg laughed, "I haven't been confirmed pregnant and you don't know it's a girl."

"I know it's a girl. I feel it," he said. "A daughter, Meggie. She'll look just like you, I know she will."

Jimmy was doing well in his work. He wasn't a laborer anymore, but rather was part of the business end of the construction work, getting new accounts, making sales for the company. Business was booming and he told Meg she didn't have to work. It was her choice, but financially they were set.

"Tell your old man that, will ya, hon? How I'm not so useless after all."

"Why is it all about money with you, Jimmy? Who cares? Who cares about what my father thinks?"

"I do. I want ex-Senator Flaherty to eat his words, baby."

She put down the dishcloth and turned to him, leaning against the kitchen counter. "You know, you really should give that topic a rest. Dad's mellowing out. He's almost seventy years old. The things that were important to him aren't so important now. He's semi-retired, works in the congressional office part-time, and spends much more time with my mother now. I think he's come to terms with things that have happened in his life and has made peace with himself. I even think he's beginning to like you, Jimmy."

"Oh, that makes me so happy, Meg," Jimmy said, sarcastically, "like who really gives a shit?"

Meg realized Jimmy had so much anger stored up, anger and resentments over the last ten years that he held in, let fester and fester and wouldn't talk about. Someday he'll boil over, she thought.

The doctor soon confirmed that, yes indeed, Meg was pregnant. The baby was due in April. Meg and Jimmy went to Miami for the weekend to celebrate their good news. They rented a hotel room on Biscayne Boulevard, where all the activity was going on. Jimmy had wanted to stay secluded, to have Meg all to himself.

"No," Meg said. "I want to party. I feel good. I want to go dancing!"

And that's what they did.

"Thank God these places have class," said Jimmy, "Not like the good old Grog. God, what a drug den that place was!"

"I'm sure this place has its fill," said Meg. "It's only higher class druggies. You know, druggies with money."

On their last night in Miami, about midnight, as they were walking back to their hotel, Jimmy spotted a couple of friends from high school. Their names were Dave Macalaster and John Toomey, guys that Meg had met only once, the night she had seen Jimmy at the Grog.

"Are you guys living here?" Jimmy asked.

Dave was full of plans. "Believe it or not, we're trying to open a restaurant, you know, bring Boston food to Miami. A really good Italian restaurant is just what Miami needs."

Jimmy laughed, "A Scotsman and Irishman are going to open an Italian restaurant!"

"I was brought up with an Italian mother," said John. "Just the same as you, Romano. I remember as well as you do all the pasta shoved down our throats. Anyway, she taught me to cook, and now we're ready to rock and roll."

"I'm going to run the lounge side," said Dave. "I know everything there is to know about bartending!"

Jimmy had worked with Dave for a while as a bartender in Brighton. But those were days best forgotten because the two of them got high much too often.

"Well, look," Jimmy said, "if you're ever in Key West, look us up. I'm a almost partner in Johnson Construction Company." He handed them his business cards. "And Meggie and me, we're having our first baby in April!"

They all shook hands, hugged, and congratulated one another. Jimmy wished them well on their new adventure.

Back at the hotel Meg said, "I hope they don't come to our house. I had an uneasy feeling about them. Plus, they looked high."

"Meg, everyone looks high to you. Since you left that friggin' rehab you think everyone is high or drunk. So, half the world is an alcoholic or a drug addict. Relax, baby. Stop worrying. They're okay. They just got a little mixed up for a while, like me. I'm normal now, right?"

"Romano, you'll never be normal, but I think that's why I'm attracted to you. I always hated normal." She made a face. "Besides, what's normal? My father always told us to act like a normal family — smile all the time; act as if you're happy. So, we were the perfect family, and just look at us! My father has cheated on my mother his whole life and pretends he didn't. I have a weird, schizophrenic brother that doesn't take his meds, walks around dressed up like Robin Hood, my sister's the meanest women on the planet, and my dad pretends we're normal!"

"Well, hon, lots of families are like that. It's not just yours. I knew a family in Newport whose two older kids had sex with each other all through high school. Everyone knew it and their mother walked around town, went to PTO meetings and school functions like her kids were perfect, like everything was normal. Either she was really out to lunch or was in major denial."

"What's that family doing now?" Meg asked curiously.

"Parents are divorced, the two who were having sex — well, let's see, the guy is a Newport cop and is married with a couple of kids. His sister moved out of state. I heard she was too jealous of her brother's relationship with his new wife."

"Weirdsville!" said Meg. "Regardless, do me a favor, if those guys call, please discourage them? It's a gut feeling. I don't want you mixed up with them."

Jimmy rolled his eyes, "You got to learn to trust me, hon, trust my decisions. You know? You can't control who I see and who I don't see, that's my business." He yawned and stretched. "Besides, I bet that's the end of them. I don't know if a Boston type restaurant would take off down here. There are too many foreigners who probably haven't even heard of Boston or the North End! I bet I'll hear those two are back home in a couple of month's bartending again."

But that wasn't the case. Two months later John and Dave walked onto the construction site where Jimmy was working in Marathon.

"What are you guys doing here," he asked, "looking for work?"

"No," said John. "We have a proposition for you. How about meeting us after work for a beer?"

"No harm in that," Jimmy said.

"Meet us about six at the Roadside Café; we noticed it on our way over here."

On his lunch hour, Jimmy called Meg. "I'm gonna work late, honey, maybe have a beer after. I'll see you about nine. Okay?"

Fortunately, Meg didn't mind. She was working part-time at a nursing agency, picking up shifts here and there. She herself was actually going to be working until eleven.

Jimmy was fully aware of lying to Meg … or sort of lying, anyway. Okay, he wasn't working late, but he was going out for a beer. He just didn't want to worry Meg or have her get mad at him for seeing John and Dave. At worst, he reasoned, it was a sin of omission.

The two were on their third beer by the time Jimmy got there. "You guys are really pounding down the brewskies. Aren't you?" he asked, as he pulled up a stool next to them, ordering a beer himself.

"We're celebrating," said Dave. "We got a spot for our restaurant. We put money down on the building today. We're going to call it Boston's Best."

"Great, you guys!" Jimmy said, as he shook their hands. "Tell me more about it. How are you going to pay for all this? Loans?"

"We've taken out loans to get the place up and running," John explained. "Fortunately, my dad was willing to co-sign for us. He really thinks it will work. The thing is, we're short on cash. We need another partner or investor. We're short fifty grand."

They both stared at Jimmy.

Jimmy lifted his glass toward the bartender, signaling for another beer. He swallowed hard, looked up at them and said, "And you want me to be that fifty thousand dollar man. Right?"

Dave chimed in, "The place will be a gold mine, Jimmy. You'll make your money back in no time, or you can be partners with us."

"You guys, where do you think I'd be able to come up with that much cash?"

But they knew Jimmy had extra dough from his father's insurance settlement. Word around town was that Jimmy Romano and family had a trust fund.

"Come on, Jimmy, think about it!" exclaimed Dave. "Look at the layout. I have blueprints." He reached in his back pocket and unfolded a set of prints showing the design of the restaurant. There were pictures of the whole layout inside the place, as well as the extra land they would own in the back where they could have outdoor seating.

"I'm impressed, guys, but it's too risky," said Jimmy. "I'm going to be a father in three months and I know Meg wouldn't go along with it. I'm gonna pass."

"Oh, come on, Romano!" urged John, "Take a risk, for once! Look at the menu. It's like the best of the North End. This place could really do well. Think about it: with your partnership in the construction company and your investment in the restaurant, you could be a millionaire in a few years. We all could!"

"You're full of pipe dreams, boys," Jimmy said, as he slid off the stool. "Can't do it. Good to see you guys, but I have to pass. I wish you a lot of luck."

It was a little after eleven when Jimmy pulled up in front of their apartment. Meg was just unlocking the front door when he came up behind her and wrapped his arms around her blossoming belly, kissing her neck tenderly.

"Hey, you," she said. "A couple of beers under your belt?"

"Only two," he said, defensively.

"I didn't mean anything by it, babe. It's okay. I was just teasing."

They went inside and he found himself looking at her changing figure. She had put on a little too much weight and the doctors had told her to cut back on her food intake. She could only put on five more pounds in the next three months.

He said, trying to be funny. "God, Nurse Flaherty, you're looking a lot like your Auntie Theresa these days!"

"Was that supposed to be funny, Jimmy? If it was, you've failed. That hurt my feelings."

Meg's Aunt Theresa was a large, buxom woman in her sixties who lumbered around her house taking care of Meg's uncle. A nurse herself, the first time Jimmy met her she was coming from work and had her uniform and cap still on, looking larger than life.

"I'm sorry, Meg," he said laughing. "It just struck me funny, the way you turned to the side. Your belly … it looked like your aunt's."

And to make matters worse, he said (thinking he was helping the situation), "Look, she's still at least ten pounds heavier than you now."

Meg looked at him with daggers in her eyes.

"I'm going to take my fat body in the shower now, Mr. Asshole."

When Meg came out of the bathroom, Jimmy was passed out on the bed. She knew he hadn't wanted to hurt her feelings and she knew she was overly sensitive since her pregnancy.

Now, with him asleep, she couldn't discuss how their night had been. That had become one of their nightly rituals. When they went their separate ways and reunited, they couldn't wait to tell one another how their time apart had been. It was one of those silly romantic things. Meg was pulling the blanket over Jim when she noticed a card had fallen from his pocket. It said, "David Macalister." Underneath was the name, "Boston's Best."

He lied to me, she thought. *Jimmy was with Dave and John tonight.*

It was the first real fight they had.

"I hate lying," said Meg.

"It wasn't really a lie," said Jimmy. It was the next morning, and he was already late for work, sitting on the bed tying up his work boots.

"I didn't lie, Meggie. I omitted."

"Well, fuck you and your omission! Why couldn't you just be honest?"

"Because you would have flipped out, hon, just like you're doing right now! You think everyone in my past life is a drug dealer, a criminal, worthless people. You're starting to sound like your old man!"

"Oh, sure, bring my father into this!" shouted Meg.

Jimmy stood up, took a deep breath. "Look, baby, you're not yourself. You're close to your seventh month … you're emotional. Let this go, okay?"

Meg started to beat him over the head with a pillow, side to side, back and forth. "Ever since I told you I was pregnant you don't take anything I say seriously. You don't validate me, Jimmy!"

He grabbed her arms, kissed her as hard as he could. Then he looked in her eyes. "Meg, how can I validate you? You're trying to kill me with a pillow? Just stop!"

"Just leave!" she shouted.

And he did, walking abruptly out of the room. Meg heard the door slam.

Later in the day, Meg showed up as Jimmy was ending work. He was on the phone with a client and signaled her to sit down.

When he hung up, they just stood there staring at one another. They laughed.

"Okay, Mrs. Romano. Where do you want to go to dinner?"

"Well, since I can't eat anything fun, I don't know. How about Boston's Best?"

"Too bad it doesn't exist," Jimmy said. "Not with me, anyway."

They ended up at a sports bar and watched the Boston Celtics get killed by one of the new expansion teams in the league.

"I miss Boston," said Meg. "I'm here alone, without family, and I'm pregnant."

"Do you want to go back for a visit?"

"Maybe. We'll see. Lizzy might come here," Meg said, "when I have the baby. My mother, too."

She changed the subject. "So what's up with John and Dave that you couldn't tell me?"

Jimmy explained the whole scenario: the restaurant, bar, Boston's best Italian food in Miami.

"Sounds like they're still smoking too much dope," said Meg dismissively.

Jimmy felt that he had to defend his friends. "Maybe not. Maybe it will work. Those two need a break."

"But you're not going in on it. Right?"

God, he hated when she did that! Megan Flaherty had to control, always needed the upper hand. Like she knew what was best for him! And he swore, when he was about eleven years old, he'd never let a woman or anyone control him. He took a deep breath and responded evenly, "No, Meg. I won't do it."

But that night in bed, as soon as he heard Meg's regular breathing and knew she was asleep, he got up and looked in his trust fund account book. He could take the chance. Maybe he'd make millions, show Old Man Flaherty once again that he wasn't useless. As he lay wide awake, he thought he might go to Miami, do some investigating about restaurants, take a look and see if this one had any chance of succeeding. He'd have to lie again and tell Meg he was going on business. Why not? It was for business! It would only be for a couple of days. For crying out loud, it was for her, for the baby! Jimmy Romano needed to prove himself, needed to show he was worthwhile, a productive human being. He felt like he was the king on his chariot, going forth with a reckless energy. Nothing would stop him. He would prove himself once and for all!

CHAPTER TWELVE

April — 1979

"Welcome to the world, Isabella!" said the doctor.

"God, she's beautiful," Jimmy said, as he walked around the delivery room. He had on blue scrubs, a yellow sterile coat with blue booties. He looked like a crazed person, a crazed happy person, as he turned Isabella in circles.

"Can you believe we did this, Meg? Look at her, her pink little lips, rosy cheeks, black, black hair. What a friggin' miracle!"

Meg, tired but ecstatic, said, "Okay, my turn, honey! Let me see my daughter!"

It had been a long strenuous labor. Megan was pre-eclampsic. Her blood pressure was extremely elevated and her feet were swollen. She had called the doctor, knowing something was wrong. He admitted her to Miami General within a few hours of seeing her. She was only two weeks from her due date and was ripe and ready. She was started on Pitocin, a drug that induces labor by starting contractions. But Isabella's head wouldn't drop into the birth canal even after six hours of labor.

"We have to do a C-section, Mrs. Romano. I think there's a chance of fetal distress."

But within ten minutes of that decision, Isabella dropped and she came into the world on April 21, 1979.

Jimmy, who had been sure all along that it would be a girl, said, "We'll call her Bella. What do you think, hon? It'll be after my grandmother."

She gave in. "Okay. Isabella, and we can call her Bella, but I get to name our second kid."

Jimmy was beside himself. He left the hospital to let Meg sleep and went over to the construction site to pass out cigars. He actually did a cartwheel in front of the canteen truck as the guys were getting afternoon coffee. Everyone clapped. "Okay, Romano," they yelled. "Not bad work!"

Jimmy went to the apartment to shower and clean up before he went back to see Meg and the baby. He thought of the past few weeks and how tumultuous they had been. Meg had been angry, in a rage, when she found out about Jimmy's investment in Boston's Best. After going to Miami a few months back and finding out more about the restaurant, the land, the chances of its success, Jimmy decided to go in on the deal. It was a prime location in the heart of Miami. The restaurant would be different from all the others around; it would bring good Italian food at a reasonable price into the city. That area was lacking restaurants like Boston's Best. He felt it would be a gold mine.

Two days later, Jimmy had handed John Toomey and Dave Macalister a check for fifty thousand dollars. Jimmy felt his father would have wanted him to do this, to make an investment, take a chance. Hadn't his grandfather done that to get started when he had come to America? Life was all about chances, anyway. But he didn't tell Meg. He knew she'd be furious if she found out and he wanted to see some profit before he told her, so he took his chances by hiding the information.

And it was easy to hide. He had work in Miami. Construction was booming. He never needed an excuse as to why he was there. But the fateful phone call came two days before Isabella was born.

Anna Romano called to find out what Jimmy was up to. The lawyer in charge of Jimmy's trust fund had called her, concerned that Jimmy needed that much money. Anna didn't have any idea what her son was up to, needing that much money, and called Jimmy to find out. Of course, he wasn't at home, so Mrs. Romano questioned Meg, figuring she would know what Jimmy did with his money. Meg was furious. She knew immediately what he had done against her expressed wishes. When Jim got home she confronted him calmly, but she was so hurt, hurt that he lied or hid what he had done, that finally she lost it and started screaming at her husband. "It's a lot money Jimmy, a huge risk! I'm part of that risk! I should have been in on the decision."

And that was it; end of conversation. Meg refused to continue with any discussion. She was hurt beyond belief but she was too tired to argue. And Jimmy was right in that he was concerned that she never trusted his judgment about things. But she often felt he didn't make the right decisions. He was too impulsive. His anger often took over and he'd make the wrong choices. She knew he invested in this to get back at her father, to prove to him he wasn't useless.

For the next two days, Jimmy wondered why Meg ended the conversation so abruptly. Suddenly it was done, forgotten. Fifty thousand dollars later, and Meg refused to either argue with him or listen to his plans.

"It's over. Okay? I don't want to hear about the restaurant. It's your investment and yours alone."

Her medical problems began soon after. Her blood pressure was high, swelling in her feet and ankles. He felt that maybe their altercation had something to do with her physical status and that Meg would blame him for her physical problems.

But when Jimmy walked into her hospital room there was happiness written all over her. She was breast-feeding Bella and she smiled and waved him over to the bed.

"I love you so much, Meg," he said.

She reached over and placed her hands on his head, playing with his wavy hair.

"Me, too," she said. "I've always loved you, Jimmy."

The Romanos left the hospital three days later.

They were expecting company in another few days. Anna Romano was going to stay with them for a few weeks until Meg was on her feet and could take care of Bella alone. And the Flaherty's were going to arrive with Lizzy and stay in a hotel not far from them.

It had been over a year since Jimmy had seen his father-in-law and he was not looking forward to it. Meg had said he'd mellowed, was a kinder person, but Jimmy found that hard to believe. Once an asshole, always an asshole: that was his belief. But he was Bella's grandfather so he would try and be kind himself. Plus, he was doing so well! If he continued on the track he was on with Johnson Construction, he'd be one of the partners in another year.

And the restaurant! Even in its infancy, it was starting to flourish. Maybe it was the newness of the place, but they were busy every night. Even in the afternoon, with the daytime crowd, the bar was always filled and customers were happy with the food and service. Jimmy felt on top of the world. He'd show Mr. Flaherty — and even Meg — that he was no loser!

Anna Romano arrived first. She was now fifty-four and Jimmy and Meg almost fell over when they saw her. "What a babe you are, Ma!" Jimmy said as he went over and hugged his mother.

Anna had done a complete turnaround in the last year. Gwen had forced her to go to counseling, and she had immediately been put on anti-depressants. Six months later, she started to feel better emotionally, lost about twenty pounds, and had even started to date! She was thrilled to see her new granddaughter, the first girl — all the rest were boys. Anna squeezed Bella. "You look just like your Daddy!" she exclaimed.

Anna had never seen Jimmy and Meg look happier. Love spilled from their pores. *His hard days are over,* she thought.

Two days later, the Flahertys arrived. John Flaherty had definitely aged. Approaching seventy, he was now totally gray, a little heavier, and a little sadder. He hugged Meg, shook Jimmy's hand. "Congratulations, Jimmy. You have a beautiful daughter," he said it in such a rehearsed, congressional voice, Jimmy didn't know if he was sincere or not. And Mary Flaherty, holier than ever, proceeded to bless the baby with holy water.

"What are you doing?" Meg asked.

"I feel like I should baptize her. I don't know if you will."

"Of course, she'll be baptized, Mom. Put that stuff away!"

Mary Flaherty had become extremely matronly. Her once svelte body was twenty pounds overweight and she became short of breath with each step she took.

For two weeks, both families united and there were no altercations. But on the last evening before the Flaherty's were to leave, Jimmy took them out to dinner at Boston's Best. Mr. Flaherty immediately said, "Boston's best what?"

"It's a nice restaurant," said Jimmy. "I've actually invested in it. I helped get it up and running."

Once inside, Mr. Flaherty didn't have a kind word to say. He didn't even pretend. "This place is full of thugs, Jimmy. What were you thinking of? It has no class. There's so much smoke in here you could get cancer in one night."

Anna was shocked, and firmly said to John, "If Jimmy invested in this place then it's a good place. Think positive."

Meg was furious with her father. How dare he embarrass them both! But she felt the same way about the restaurant. The food was good, but the patrons were low-lifes, bottom of the barrel. Still, part of it belonged to her husband, and she had decided to get off his case about it once and for all. Things would work out.

That night in bed, Jimmy said, "Your father hasn't changed, Meg. He's still pompous, arrogant, and mean. The only difference is that he's all those things and old!"

"I'm sorry he said those things, darling, but I think he's afraid it won't work," said Meg.

"Yeah, well, he could have put it differently. My dad would never have embarrassed me like that. I'm glad he's leaving tomorrow."

On the plane home, John Flaherty felt more and more furious with what he had seen. He knew the place must have Mafia connections. He just felt it. The climate was terrible.

"You just don't like Italians, John," said his wife. "You're prejudiced and that's not fair. Give Jimmy a chance. He's trying."

But John Flaherty's feelings would never change toward Romano. His favorite daughter married a wop, a dago. That was something his Irish ancestors would not have tolerated … they were a different breed. He had a feeling the restaurant would fail.

He remembered those two loser friends of Jimmy's who owned the place. A lawyer friend of his from West Newport had been Davey Macalister's attorney when he was charged with drug possession two years before. Once a druggie, always a druggie: that was how John felt about it. He had a very bad feeling deep in his soul. Not that he cared about Romano, but he loved Meg deeply. She was sweeter and more beautiful then ever. And her little stint with drugs was simply that. She hadn't gotten involved for very long, and she had quietly cured herself.

His Meggie was on the right track: a nurse, and with a graduate degree, no less. How had she ended up with such a scumbag as Romano? He should have put a stop to it; he should have forbidden the marriage somehow. It was bound to end in tragedy. Sure, they were in love for now; you could tell by the way they looked at each other there was definite chemistry. But that would end … he was sure of it. And somehow, he wanted to get Meg back in Massachusetts. There was a teaching position at Boston College that he knew he could get her by pulling a few strings. Get her back home, John thought. Away from the seedy side of Florida and her husband!

Anna Romano stayed another week and had to get back home. Meg was doing great with the baby. She was breastfeeding, so there was little Anna could do. Jimmy drove his mother to the airport and although she had stuck up for Jimmy about the restaurant, she had her own reservations. She had seen a few of Jimmy's old friends in there from high school. She knew their backgrounds and they were drug-involved. It just didn't sit right with Anna. She put her hand on his shoulder as they were driving.

"Jim," she said, "you have a family now, a daughter. Those drug days are behind you. Right?"

Jimmy was insulted. "Of course, Ma! What do you think? I'm shootin' up every night?"

"Of course not!" she said. "But you have two other people to think of and I know the temptation might be there. Just, always think before you act. Don't make the same mistake twice."

"Ma, I don't do drugs. Don't worry. Okay? We'll be fine."

No one trusts me, Jimmy thought. *No one believes I'll succeed, even Meg. I'm so tired of trying to prove myself.*

CHAPTER THIRTEEN

November — 1979

The police cruiser had its flashing lights on, signaling Jimmy to pull over on the side of the road. He had been speeding. He was in a hurry to get home by eleven so Meg could go to work. It was his turn to watch Bella.

He had stopped by a friend's house after work to watch a football game, smoke a joint, and have some dinner. When he looked at the time, he flipped. "Shit! It's 10:30. Meg has to be at work in an hour."

He quickly called her and said he was on his way. Joey, his buddy, had also sold him an ounce of really good weed that he had on him. Fortunately, there was no booze on his breath when the police pulled him over. Jimmy had never been a big drinker. Pot was his thing if he was going to get high.

"Get out of the car," the larger of the two cops said to Jimmy.

The other policeman looked in the car with a flashlight.

"What's your hurry, buddy?" he asked as he moved the flashlight up and down his body. "Going to a fire?"

Jimmy rolled his eyes thinking, *Let's just get this over with! Give me my ticket and let me go.*

But the light had moved under the front seat and there was the marijuana. "What's this?" the cop said, as he flashed the light on the baggie full of pot.

"I think what you're doing is illegal, officers. I didn't give you permission to search my car," said Jimmy.

"Well, we'll talk about that down at the station, Mr. Romano," said the smaller of the two cops. He glanced at Jimmy's license and pulled out his handcuffs. Jimmy shook his head. *Oh, great,* he thought. *This is going to go over real well with Meg.*

Jimmy was brought to the police station and was allowed one phone call. When he got Meg on the line, he told her the story, how much bail would be and to locate a lawyer. The lawyer had to be there now, this minute, because what the police did was against the law. "It's called illegal search and seizure," he said. "Just do it, Meg."

Meg showed up at the police station at one o'clock with Bella in her arms. It was four o'clock before they left after locating a bail bondsman. On the ride home, Meg was silent.

"Why don't you just yell at me?" Jimmy asked. "I'd feel a lot better than having you give me the silent treatment."

She was looking out the window, and when she spoke, her voice was distant. "I'm too tired to yell. And Bella's had enough noise and disruption for one night."

"Oh, now I should feel guilty. Right, Meg?" he asked. He really wanted to start a fight, baby or no baby, to relieve the pressure that he was feeling inside.

"Yeah, you should," Meg said, still not looking at him. "For Bella, and for me, too. I missed work because of this shit."

"Well, this isn't my fault. The cops searched my car illegally. Did you find a lawyer?"

Meg looked over at Jimmy. He wasn't even remorseful, blaming the police, not looking at his part in the arrest.

"Yes," she replied tiredly. "He'll meet us in the morning at the courthouse; he said it wasn't necessary for him to be here tonight. He's going to find out what time your case will go before the judge. He agrees with you about the illegality of the search and says it'll get thrown out."

The next morning they sat before the judge, waiting to be called. Finally at eleven o'clock, Jimmy's case was called. The lawyer was top shelf. Within seconds, he had the case dropped because the police had no right searching Jimmy's car. He paid his speeding ticket and they left the courthouse.

"That was an easy five hundred for Mr. Scribner, eh?"

"Yes," said Meg. "An expensive lesson for you. When are you going to knock this shit off? You were guilty, no matter what they said back there. You did have pot!"

He was tired from no sleep and tired of her ceaseless pursuit of the subject. "Lighten up. Will you?"

"What, and smoke pot with you? Is that what you want? I've been there, done all that. It's over. I want a normal, drug-free life for us!"

"For Christ's sake, it's only pot. I don't drink much. I smoke once or twice a week. Is that so bad? Do you ever look at the positive stuff I do? I'm making a shit-load of money and I've gone back to school. Does any of that count?" Jimmy asked, angry and a little hurt.

Jimmy had gone back to school and was finishing up his last year in a business program at Miami University. He'd been taking two classes for the last year, every Wednesday night. He was committed and did well in them, Meg knew. What she didn't know was that Jimmy couldn't have cared less. He was doing it for her. For some reason, Meg wanted him to have a degree, so he would do it to make her happy. In his world, it was meaningless.

"Sure, all that counts," Meg replied, oblivious to his sensitivity to her in that area. "But I hate pot. I hate how you get when you're stoned. You become such a dreamer. You think you're in the same reality I am, and you're not."

"It helps me relax, babe. I work all the time. It simply helps me chill out. Please, stop making such a big deal about it."

"But you were arrested! You were wrong, and you can't see that, you're so willing to blame the police!" she said.

They didn't talk for the remainder of the ride home. There was simply no point.

They all went to bed early that night. Bella, only six months old and not knowing why she had been awakened in the middle of the night, gladly went to bed at six. Her parents followed soon after she was down. And for the next few days, things were quiet in the house. Neither Jimmy nor Meg wanted to discuss what had happened. Jimmy ended up apologizing and saying he would not smoke pot anymore, would give it a rest. And they considered the issue resolved.

A few weeks later, Meg was changing her clothes, getting ready for bed, when Jimmy came up behind her, put his arms around her waist and kissed her neck. Meg could never refuse his touch but soon after, lying in bed, she said, "Honey, sometimes our relationship is all about sex. We don't talk any more … communicate like we used to. Something is wrong, isn't it?"

Jimmy reflected, and then said, "Sex is a good thing, hon. It keeps us together, doesn't it?"

"Yes," she replied, "but I need more. I miss how we used to talk into the night, tell each other our secrets. I felt like I had a best friend and a husband. I'm starting not to feel that way anymore. We need to reconnect."

"As soon as school is over, Meg, I'll have more time," Jimmy said. "I'm exhausted. I need to study, work, help take care of Bella, plus help out at the restaurant."

Meg restrained herself. That damned restaurant again! She wished he'd stay away from it. Permanently.

Every Wednesday night after Jimmy finished his classes he'd go to the restaurant and bartend for four to five hours. Sometimes he'd close the place and end up sleeping at Davey or John's. Meg hated it when he did, but Jimmy told her it was his relaxation time. He needed time with his friends.

Time to smoke pot and whatever else you do, she thought.

But she decided not to go there tonight. "I just feel that I should be as important as all the other things in your life. I feel that somehow we need to pick up where we left off. You haven't even asked me how I am in over a month. Do you realize that? Not even a 'How's your day, hon?' Nothing, Jimmy … it's like I don't exist except to take care of Bella and as someone to have sex with."

"Oh, is Mrs. Romano feeling neglected?" Jimmy asked, turning toward her. "I love you, Meg. Things will get better as soon as school's out. We'll get back to normal. You'll see."

CHAPTER FOURTEEN

May — 1980

I'm glad that's friggin' over with, thought Jimmy as he left his last class. His last exam, for life! *I'm never going to school again.*

"Party time!" he said out loud, as he headed to Boston's Best. It was a beautiful May night and he was going to celebrate with his friends. He would soon be a college graduate. What the hell? He had always hated school, always felt claustrophobic within the four walls, even back in kindergarten. He remembered saying to his mother, "I'm not going to prison today."

But now he'd done it, once and for all. He'd done it as a gift to Meg, and also, he could admit it now, to prove to himself that he could. One more goal accomplished, one more place where old man Flaherty couldn't be better than him. And maybe it would turn out for the best in other ways, look good on a resume if he ever changed jobs; he'd get his diploma in the mail within the month.

Plus he needed to be even more responsible. He and Meg were expecting their second child in a few months. She had gotten pregnant a few nights after he had gone to court. And he had stayed straight since that time. Not even one hit off a joint. *Boring,* he thought. *I'm partying tonight!*

He had told Meg not to expect him home, that he was going to a business meeting at the restaurant, might have a drink or two to celebrate, might spend the night in Miami. Another little white lie wouldn't hurt her. He'd behave.

For a Wednesday night, Boston's Best certainly looked lively, Jimmy thought as he pulled into the parking lot. He was happy that the business was booming. He was close to making back his fifty thousand, even with interest, but Davey had approached him and wanted him to be part owner, to reinvest his money. He'd have to think about that one. Not that he needed money. The construction business was dynamite; he had a lot in savings, and would be a partner in another year or so. So why hang onto the restaurant if he didn't need to?

Because, he thought, *of the way I feel when I'm here.*

Jimmy walked in through the bar entrance. Dave and John were there to greet him.

"Party time, buddy," Dave said, as he handed him a beer.

Jimmy said, "Thanks, but I was thinking more along the lines of a big marijuana cigar to celebrate. Any good weed around?"

"Probably," said Dave, "but after we close we have some really good other shit you might want to try."

"Like what," asked Jimmy?

"Primo coke," said Davey. "Look who's here."

"Hey, Romano!" It was accompanied by a slap on his back. Jimmy turned and saw MacKinnas — Mac for short — another

Newport High graduate and now, from what he had heard, a successful drug dealer. "Long time, no see!"

Jimmy knew he should leave right then and there. Mac had sold him heroin in the past, and he knew this guy was not good news for him. I'll have a beer and leave, Jimmy thought.

But as the night progressed and had a couple of beers, a few joints, he was ready to party.

What the hell? he thought. *It's only one night, then back to reality.*

The restaurant closed and tables were pushed together as Mac got out the coke. "I'm gonna party while I'm in Miami," he announced to the place. "The coke's on me!" said Mac. The friends drank and did lines and lines of cocaine into the wee hours of the morning. Jimmy had never tried cocaine before, and after a couple of lines, he got hooked. It wasn't really the high as much as the energy, and with it the sense that he was being anesthetized into a state of not being, a state of euphoria that took away all emotions.

Jimmy went back to John's house about six in the morning to try to sleep. It had been quite a night. As he was finally drifting off, he felt someone next to him, someone wrapping her arms around him and kissing his chest.

Half-asleep, he said, "Meggie, what are you doing here?"

But when he turned, he saw it was the tall blonde that had been hanging on him all night. Her name was Gloria.

Jimmy jolted up in the bed. "What are you doing?" he asked, surprised.

"Let's do a few lines, Jimmy. It will turn you on," she said.

Oh, my God, he thought. *I gotta get outta here!* "No, thanks, Gloria. Really. No offense, but I'm married. And I do love my wife. Sorry," he said, getting his jeans on, clumsily backing out the door.

As high as he was, he still had boundaries. He promised himself he would never, ever cheat on Meg. He loved her passionately.

As he pulled out of John's driveway and took off down the street, he thought about the night. *Hell was that fun! I could do this every now and then, smoke a little pot, do a few lines. What's the big deal?*

He grabbed Meg as soon as he got in the door. "Hi, beautiful," he said. And she did look beautiful. Meg was glowing with this pregnancy. Her face was serene … her eyes were sparkly. "I love you so much," he said, as he cuddled her and Bella. "I can't believe how lucky I am."

Meg, however, was worried, and the next day she called Lizzy to talk about it. "Jimmy seemed so high, Liz. I never saw him like that, but he was so loving. He pounced on me the minute I put Bella down for a nap. I'm worried about his behavior."

"Maybe he just hung one on, seeing he finished school," Lizzy said. "Don't go projecting. See what happens."

But Meg had her doubts, especially in the next few months. Although Jimmy was through with school, he still spent every Wednesday night in Miami.

"What gives, babe? Why are you going into Miami, staying out all night?"

"I work there on Wednesday nights, Meg. I get out late, I'm tired, I stay at John's," he said irritably.

"Yeah, well, I'm seven months pregnant. What if I go into labor early?" she asked.

"Meg, you're the picture of health. That's not going to happen. I'll only do it for a couple of more weeks, then I'll stop. Okay?"

He said, "okay" like it was her fault, as though he were a little boy and she his mother, making him give up his fun, nagging him. Her attitude made him want to escape even more. And

Jimmy knew every Wednesday night meant some coke: some anesthesia, something to get him out of himself, freedom from responsibility. And he resented the fact, one month later that he had to hang around and give up his Wednesday nights.

"God, Jimmy, you seem so restless, so annoyed with me, that you have to be here," Meg said. "You're so self-centered these days. Talk to me, please! What's going on?"

But he didn't want to tell her, didn't want to let her in. She wouldn't have understood, anyway. Every time he told her how he felt, she told him his feelings were wrong. To hell with it. "Forget it, Meg. I'm okay. I'm just nervous about another kid, more responsibility."

But Meg knew that wasn't it. There was something more. She couldn't place it at first but then she realized he was acting like the addicts at the rehab she had been in. In fact, he was acting like herself a few years before.

It went on for two more months. Jimmy would be irritable, nasty, short-tempered. He'd go into the bathroom frequently and come out more loving and caring, rubbing her stomach, affectionate. The realization came slowly to Meg, and it finally hit her in the face two days before she delivered Michael. She was putting Jimmy's clothes away when she found a small baggie filled with white powder. *Heroin,* she thought. *He did heroin before. But he seems so jumpy, so irritable. Heroin is a downer. He wouldn't be acting like this if he was doing smack. So, what is it?*

Meg confronted him the next night. She had just put Bella to bed, walked into the living room, where Jimmy was sitting watching television with a blank expression on his face.

"Do you want to kiss Bella goodnight?" she asked.

"Later," Jimmy replied. "I'm going out for a walk."

Half an hour later, he came back. He was a different person, talkative, loveable and sweet, giving Bella a goodnight kiss.

"Okay, Jimmy. What's going on? You're high as a kite and it's more than pot," Meg said.

He came up behind her, kissing her neck. "Nothing is wrong. I'm not high. I'm excited about the baby coming."

"Yeah, right, Jimmy. You're full of shit. Be honest. Give me some credit. I'm not stupid!" She was raising her voice and finally Jimmy had had enough. Enough of being treated like a child … enough of being responsible to her all the time.

"Okay, fine, Ms. Perfect. Joe Gallucci's back!"

"Who's Joe Gallucci?" she asked.

"Joe's my other self. He's my Katie O'Toole. Remember when you told me about her? Joe's who I was when I was into drugs, before we got together, when I tried heroin. Anytime I wanted to get high, I'd give myself another name. It was Joe Gallucci."

"So he's back," Meg said. "You're doing drugs. You're doing something now. Right?"

"You want the truth? Okay, yeah, I've been doing some coke. I have a little habit but I have it under control, too. So you don't have to worry about me, Ms. Perfect."

Meg sat numbly. She knew that she had known all along, but hadn't wanted to really believe the evidence. *I'm about to have a baby and my husband is telling me he's a cocaine addict,* she thought. *Terrific! What do I do now, God*? She wanted so little: a normal life, a good husband, a beautiful daughter, and another baby on the way. Meg wanted to pretend everything was okay. But she looked at Jimmy's eyes, his railed look, and knew something had to be done. He needed help.

And then, in the middle of the night, her contractions started.

CHAPTER FIFTEEN

August — 1980

Michael James Romano was born at six in the morning on August twenty-fifth, and he was the picture of his father, with thick, black hair and deep-set brown eyes. He was precious.

And Jimmy hung in there. He called their neighbor to watch Bella when Meg's contractions started and Jimmy stayed with her through labor and delivery. Even in the four months that followed, Jimmy seemed fine, back to normal, as if his revelation of Joe Gallucci had never happened. Meg confronted him on more then one occasion, trying to find out more about his drug use, if there was any, if Joe Gallucci was hiding somewhere in Jimmy's consciousness. Each time, Jimmy refused to talk about it, said he was fine, stayed close to home, worked, and did his share with the kids. Meg mentioned counseling for him for them, even, but he adamantly refused. As Christmas approached, Meg noticed he started to get antsy and tense, that he was occasionally mean to her.

"I think I'll go to the restaurant tonight," Jimmy said to Meg one Friday night in December. "I haven't been there in a long time. Do you mind, sweetie?"

"Why don't I get a babysitter, and go with you? We haven't been out together in a long time."

"How can you do that? You're breastfeeding."

"It's okay, I'll pump my milk. That way the babysitter can give it to Michael when he wakes up. Or is it that you don't want me to go with you?"

"Why don't I go alone tonight, and see how things are? You sometimes say that the people there are a little rough, and who knows who's hanging out these days," he said, thinking quickly. "Then we can go together next week."

"That's bullshit, Jimmy, and you know it. You want to get high and you don't want me there. Right?" Meg didn't know whether to be angry or hurt. Or both.

"You're overreacting, Meg, as usual. Just give me a break. Okay? I'll be home later!" And he slammed the door.

On the ride to Miami, Jimmy knew he had been an asshole, but he didn't care. He had been good, really good for her, and he deserved some sort of reward for it. He simply wanted to get high. He had been straight for almost four months, with the exception of a joint here and there. Jimmy just wanted some space, have Meg get off his back about being a father, responsibility, and getting a better job now that he had his degree. Couldn't she just leave him alone?

Christmas decorations lit up Boston's Best. Everyone was in a holiday mood and a disc jockey was in the bar area for a wedding that was going on. Davey waved him over, introduced him to a few of his friends. As Jimmy shook hands with the new acquaintances, he looked around the room and saw Gloria, the blonde bombshell who had been all over him a few months before.

He knew she'd have some cocaine on her. She dealt the stuff and always had good connections for the best quality around. His intentions were simply to do a few lines, party hard before he had to go back home. But after a few lines, some beers, he started dancing with Gloria and forgetting totally in the process that he was a married man with two kids … or maybe not caring.

The last thing Jimmy remembered was dancing with Gloria and the next morning waking up in bed with her in a strange apartment.

What have I done? Jimmy thought as he pushed aside the sheet and pushed himself out of bed. He had a hangover the size of Chicago. Gloria was still sleeping and there were two lines of coke still on the vanity. Sitting in his car, Jimmy put his face in his hands and cried. He couldn't believe what he had done. He was no different than Meg's father. He'd cheated on his wife, and he had no idea how it was going to change things between them.

It was early Saturday morning and Bella was watching cartoons. Meg had Michael in her lap, nursing him, when Jimmy walked through the door.

"Daddy's home!" yelled Bella, and ran to give him a hug.

"Hi, beautiful," he said, swinging her around in the air.

"And how's my other beautiful girl?" as he bent down to kiss Meg.

She was exhausted. She'd been up the entire night worrying. "Not even a phone call, Jimmy," she said, tears stinging her eyes.

"I fell asleep at John's. I'm sorry, I should have called."

"No, you didn't," said Meg. "I called there, and I called Davey's, too, so don't lie to me. I'm going out for a while," said

Meg. "I called Lizzy and she's coming down for a week. I'm going to get her at the airport."

Meg put Mike down for a nap, got dressed, kissed Bella, and said to Jimmy, "I don't know when I'll be back. I pumped milk for the baby, it's in the fridge."

Jimmy was feeling so remorseful, and her reaction hadn't helped. Now he was once again in the role of little boy, apologizing to Mommy. But he had, in fact, done something wrong … His feelings were confused.

He also felt sick, physically sick. And when he put the children in for their afternoon naps, he rolled a joint and went out on the porch to get high. *I need help,* he thought mistily. *I better get some help before I destroy everything important to me.*

Lizzy and Meg were listening to Christmas carols at the bar in the airport. "It's so weird, being in eighty-degree weather during Christmas," Lizzy said.

"I know. It takes getting used to. I really miss Boston, Liz. I want to move back."

"Does Jimmy?"

"I don't know. And you know what? I don't care," said Meg. "I'm thinking of taking a break from Jimmy Romano and going back home for a while."

"Is it that bad, Meg?" Lizzy asked, as she took a sip of her eggnog. "To leave him now, with two small kids?"

"He's sick, Lizzy. He's a drug addict and I can't stand it. I'm walking on eggshells all the time. I'm afraid if I do something wrong or look at him the wrong way, he'll run out and get high. That's no way to live," Meg said, sadly.

She told Lizzy everything: the pot, the coke, his taking off to Boston's Best. How he told her he was Joe Gallucci when she was pregnant with Michael, then how he had been so good for a few months, and finally, the last twenty-four hours and what had happened, and how quickly he had decompensated.

"I think I'd be better off without him now. I just wish I didn't love him so much. I look at him and just melt, Lizzy, and he knows it. He'd never expect me to go," Meg said.

"Why don't you try going to Alanon or Nar-Anon meetings before you make a decision, Meggie?"

"What's that?" asked Meg.

"They're support groups for families who are affected by drugs or alcohol. It could help you a lot. Friends of mine go. You learn to detach from the addict, live your life happily regardless of what the alcoholic or addict does."

"Maybe," said Meg. "I'll think about it."

"Don't think about it. Just do it! This disease makes you sick, too."

"I'm not sick!" said Meg angrily, "I'm not the one doing drugs!"

"No, but you're the one who just left two little kids at home with a drug addict. Aren't you? That's sick thinking."

"Or not thinking at all," Meg said sadly. She hadn't looked at it that way.

Even with that in mind, she found she couldn't face her husband yet. From the airport, the two sisters went to a bar close to Meg's house where there was live music and dancing. They didn't get back to the apartment until well after midnight. Jimmy was sitting up waiting, wanting desperately to talk to Meg.

"How are the kids?" she asked.

"Fine. They've been sleeping for hours," Jimmy replied.

He reached over and hugged Lizzy. "How's my favorite sister-in-law?" he asked.

"Real tired, Jimmy. Think I better go to bed."

Meg showed her to her bedroom and they made plans for the next day. When Meg went back downstairs, Jimmy was sitting in the dark, had a candle lit, and held up her mug.

"Cup of tea, Meggie?" he asked.

"I'm all set, Jimmy." She lay down on the couch. "I might sleep right here tonight."

"Please don't do that. My parents used to do that and not talk for days, months even. Please come to bed with me, hon," Jimmy begged.

"Why should I? I still don't know where — or with whom — you spent the night last night. You're doing drugs. You're hiding things from me. Why should I want to sleep with you?"

Jimmy was so remorseful he put his face in his hands and cried for the second time in twenty-four hours. "I don't know what I ended up doing last night, Meg. I did get high, did some coke. I know I fucked up and I know I need help. Please, understand. Please don't leave," he begged.

Meg wished she could hate him, hate Jimmy Romano — or Joe Gallucci — whoever he was at that moment. But she couldn't. She loved the man sitting in front of her more than anything in the world and she knew he loved her. Jimmy was sick with drugs, like she had been. They were married and had kids. She wanted to give him another chance.

"So, where do we go from here?" Meg asked.

"Counseling," Jimmy replied. "We'll find a therapist, someone who can help me with my drug problem, and help us with our marriage. How does that sound, honey?"

Jimmy had walked over and sat on the floor next to the couch. He had leaned his head back onto Megan.

"Okay, Jimmy. It's a start. We'll give it a shot," Meg said, as she wiped tears from her eyes.

CHAPTER SIXTEEN

January — 1981

Christmas had come and gone in the warm climate of Florida. Lizzy had stayed for seven days, helped Meg and Jimmy with their kids, and even had some personal conversations with her brother-in-law. Lizzy saw how sick Jimmy was. He was an emotional basket case. She thought the root of his whole problem was not dealing with his father's death. And she was perfectly frank with him.

"Jimmy, I was close to Gwen when your dad died. I knew what you were going through and you simply escaped, never felt the grief you were supposed to feel, because you drowned yourself in drugs and alcohol. I remember you using heroin, Jimmy."

"I don't want to talk about my father," Jimmy said dully.

"Of course you don't, because it's painful. Death is painful, but you need to go through the process or you won't get better emotionally. You'll keep escaping through drugs, or sex, or something," Lizzy said.

***

In early January, Meg got a babysitter for their first counseling session. The therapist's name was Bill Cartstone. He was a gentle, kind man in his early fifties, originally from California. Meg fell in love with him that moment. She was sure he'd be able to help them.

Bill gave them a wide grin, shook Jimmy's hand, and gave Meg a little squeeze around the shoulder. He was sitting across from them with his feet up on his desk, drinking a cup of lukewarm coffee.

"Okay, kids. What's up? What's going on? You go first, Jimmy," Bill said, as he waited for a reply.

Jimmy was nervous. He was having second thoughts after his conversation with Lizzy. Perspiration was dripping down the side of his face. "I don't know what I want out of these meetings," he said, "but I do know that I don't want to talk about my father and his death. I'll leave right now if you make me."

"No one is going to make you do anything, Jimmy," Bill replied. "I'm here to help, not have you run out the door on your first visit. Okay, Meg. What about you?"

Meg had entered the room thinking they were going to solve Jimmy's drug problem and that's what she told him. "I want Jimmy to stop using drugs. He can go for one or two months straight, then he starts snorting coke and smoking pot. I'm sick of living like this; I need to watch every move I make because Jimmy may erupt. It's like walking on eggshells. He's been straight for one month now and he's ready to blow. I can tell. He starts getting irritable, cranky. The next thing I know he's off to the restaurant he part owns, and that's it! A bender for two weeks!"

"That's not fair!" Jimmy retorted. 'I contribute a lot to this relationship and, frankly, you make me sound like the devil and you're a perfect little angel. Don't forget who rescued you from the rehab you were in, Miss Queen of the Seconals!"

"Okay, okay," Bill, said. "Slow down. One rule: no yelling at each other. Respect and love, respect and love for one another. No one ever gets anywhere being hostile."

The first session lasted about forty-five minutes and there was only one more to follow. On the second meeting, Meg brought up his father's accident, his death, and Jimmy flipped. "I said not to bring that up, Meg. It doesn't matter. He's dead!"

As Jimmy said this, he stormed out of the room. When they got back to the apartment, a yelling match ensued. Their neighbor still had the kids, so Meg let her Irish temper go. "Do you want help or not? Instead, you keep bringing up me and when I was in rehab. This isn't just about me; it's about you, too!"

"You know, I thought this was going to work. But guess what? It's bullshit, sitting and talking about the past. It's history. It's like looking in the rearview mirror of my life. So, fuck it! I'm not going back there."

"Then I'm leaving. Maybe I will move back home!" shouted Meg.

"Go right ahead! I don't care anymore!"

Jimmy slammed the door as he left the house. She heard his tires squeal as he rounded the corner of the street.

Meg didn't leave. Not that week, anyway. Jimmy returned home two days after that terrible fight, very high, very mean to Meg and Bella.

"What's wrong, Daddy?" cried his daughter. "Are you sad?"

Jimmy had come home briefly to get a few things. He threw his clothes in a suitcase and told Meg he was staying near the construction site with his friend, Paul. "Here's my number if you need me," and he handed her a slip of paper.

"I won't need it. I'm going back to Boston in a few days. I guess you forgot about my sister Tara's wedding in February. I'm going back early to visit, maybe move back."

"Where are you staying? How can I get a hold of you?" Jimmy asked.

"You can't. As long as you're using drugs, I don't want you in my life or the kids' lives, Jimmy."

"Fuck you, Meg!" Jimmy shouted.

"Intelligent comeback, Jim," Meg said quietly, "especially in front of Bella."

He called Meg the next day. He was so drugged that he'd called in sick to work.

"You're gonna kill yourself, Jimmy, if you don't stop using," Meg said. "You need a rehab." It was becoming her stock answer to everything.

"I'm not Megan Flaherty," he said, sarcastically. "I don't need a rehab."

"You're right. You're not Megan Flaherty. You're Joe Gallucci, and I'm beginning to really hate that person," Meg said.

"But I'll always love you, Meg. I just need some time," Jimmy said, tearfully.

Meg hung up. She couldn't believe her marriage had come to this. Tears wouldn't come; she was emotionally spent and sat staring at the four walls in a daze until she heard Michael crying. It was dusk. The thought of spending the night by herself with two kids alone was beyond her comprehension. She fed Michael and Bella, packed a bag of clothes, not knowing where she was headed, sshe only knew she needed another adult.

She headed towards the sunset, the ocean. Her two children were sleeping quietly in their car seats in back. She looked at the water and listened to Bob Seger singing *Night Moves* on the tape player: "Working on the night moves, awkward teenage blues; we were so in love, not far from." Meg sang softly along with the words, and then the tears finally came. Jimmy had left her, the man she was so passionately in love with. What would become of them? Meg drove to her friend Carol's house. *I'll spend the night here with the kids,* she thought, *and in the morning, I'll be clearheaded. I'll know what I really need to do.*

At that point, Meg didn't know if she should leave Florida. As much as she hated her husband's actions, she didn't know if she should leave the state, worrying he might die of an overdose. She would discuss it with her friend Carol, she would help make sense of what had been transpired and help her with her decision to leave Florida, her life here — or not.

It was blistery and frigid as Meg's brother, Jack, picked up Meg, Bella, and Mike Romano at Logan Airport.

"God, it's cold," Meg said. "Not used to this snowy, below thirty degree weather."

Bella and Michael's cheeks were rosy red. Meg felt happy. For the first time in months, she almost felt worry-free. She had made the decision to stay in Boston indefinitely. Carol had helped her make up her mind to leave for a while, take a break from her marriage and life in the south.

Except for Lizzy, Jack was the only other member of her family who knew about Meg's marital problems. She was spending the time in Boston with Anna Romano so she wouldn't have to deal with her parents. She had told them, even her mother-in-law, that Jimmy was busy with work and couldn't make Tara's wedding. Everyone was so excited to see Bella and little Michael that Jimmy was barely mentioned, and Meg wanted it that way. She'd handle this herself … especially with her father. She didn't want to hear 'I told you so.'

Plus, everyone was so excited for Tara! She had graduated from Yale, gone to Harvard Law School, and was a practicing attorney in Seattle. But she wanted to come home for her wedding, be married in Boston. The wedding was to be held on Valentine's Day at Our Lady of Mercy Church and the reception to follow at the Harvard Club.

Meg's twin sisters had also really made something of themselves. Both Ivy League grads, their boyfriends, as well, had made Meg's parents feel they had done something right in the bringing up of the twins. Meg hadn't been too close to them growing up, especially Tara. She had always thought her sister was too brainy, because all she did was study. Not like the rest of the Flahertys! But as the years went on, Meg realized Tara was a compassionate and loving person. She had spent two years in Boston as a public defender, met her fiancé, Peter, who was also within the court system, and then moved to Washington where Peter was from.

Two evenings before the wedding, Meg spent time with Tara and her girlfriend, Regis. Regis was a schoolteacher. Somewhat of a granola-head, she was more Meg's age. Tara and Regis had met because Francis, Regis' ex-husband, was filing charges against her for physical abuse. Regis obtained Tara as her lawyer. "I absolutely don't know what he's talking about," Regis said. "Physical abuse! The worst thing that ever happened was a pillow fight."

Regis had been found not guilty — after spending about five thousand dollars. She and Tara became friends during this drama, and here she was, foot-loose and fancy free, in Boston for Tara's wedding. Regis had long, flowing, golden blonde hair and still wore love beads and long dresses, even though this attire was long gone in the eighties. She was a free spirit who didn't care about others' opinions. That's what Meg liked about her.

Regis was staying in the Flaherty household for the week she was in Boston. She had brought with her an ounce of marijuana and made marijuana brownies to bring to Tara's party after the reception at Courtney's house. The wedding itself went beautifully … friends from both sides of the family from all over the United States attended, and went to Courtney's party after the reception. With all the activity of people coming and going, Regis forgot to bring the brownies. They were left behind in the Flaherty's freezer.

Meg had slept late the morning after the wedding. Mrs. Romano had taken both kids to the Children's' Museum, so Meg could sleep. As she was waking up, she heard a pounding at her mother-in-law's door.

"Meggie, wake up! Are you there?"

It was her sister, Lizzy, frantically banging on the door. But by the time Meg got to it, Lizzy was gone, leaving a scribbled note behind. "Please call Mom and Dad. I stopped over there but I had to get the kids to their gym class. I think they're stoned."

What? Meg thought. *Stoned on what?*

She called her parents. Mary Flaherty answered, her voice slow and slurred. "Megan … I ate some of those brownies, and I think … I'm sick … or something." Long pause. "I feel like … I've been drinking … or something." Another pause. "Your father's worse." A short giggle, "You know how he likes chocolate!"

Oh, my God, Meg thought, half laughing. *Better go over.*

Fifteen minutes later, Meg barged into her parents' house. "Ma? Dad? Where are you?" as she searched in the den, living room, and kitchen. Meg noticed the brownies sitting on the table. Half the plate was gone! She ran upstairs to Regis' room and woke her up.

"Regis," she said, "was there any pot in those brownies?"

Sleepily, she replied, "Oh, my God! I forgot them. They were meant for the party. There's about an ounce in there."

Meg ran back downstairs. "Ma, where are you?" she called. Then she heard some background music … Van Morrison of all people, singing *Tupelo Honey*. And there, with headphones on was Mary Flaherty, sitting under the dining room table, listening to Van, grooving to his music.

Meg bent down. "You okay, Ma?"

"Oh, yes," she replied. "It was those brownies." Then she giggled again.

Meg ran upstairs. There was John Flaherty, lying in bed, stoned out of his mind.

"How many brownies did you eat, Dad?" Meg asked.

"Only seven, Meggie!" he said brightly.

"Seven! Dad, you and Ma used to be so weight conscious. Why the hell did you eat so many?"

Mary Flaherty appeared in the doorway, turned on the television. "Let's dance," she implored her husband. "Lawrence Welk is on!"

"Ma, Lawrence Welk is dead, I think," said Meg.

She called her mother-in-law to tell her she'd be home late, that her parents were sick. Meg stayed with them for a few more hours to make sure they were okay. Upon leaving, her father said, "Meg, I'm supposed to be drug-tested this week. All members of the congressional staff need drug testing."

Meg said, "Put it off, Dad. You won't pass. Call tomorrow, tell them you're sick."

They both laughed. For the first time in his life, John Flaherty was vulnerable, needed help, and they both knew it.

"High-five, Dad," as Meg walked by with her hand in the air, she said "We'll talk about it tomorrow."

Anna laughed hysterically when Meg told her the story of the wedding, her parents eating the brownies, and the outcome. Anna was fifteen years younger than Meg's parents and was a lot more hip.

The Flaherty's turned out to be fine. Meg's mother said she had felt "the ultimate experience of her life." There couldn't be anything better. Mr. Flaherty stated he was just happy he was alive. Meg realized how comical this was now that it was over and her parents were all right. It helped her get her mind off her real problems with Jimmy for a few days. And poor Regis! She was so apologetic, and quickly booked a flight back to Seattle wishing the event never happened!

***

It was now the middle of February, cold, snowy, and making Megan wonder what was next with her and Jimmy. She hadn't heard from him, nor did she care. She was happy to be back home, carefree. Laughing like she hadn't done in so long.

But she did miss Jimmy, the old Jimmy, not the Joe Gallucci Jimmy. And she knew her mother-in-law was starting to suspect something was wrong.

Then the phone rang. It was Davey in Miami. He, of all people, was concerned about Jimmy. Jimmy had come to him the day before, asking for all the money back that he had put into the company. Davey handed him over seventy-five thousand in cash.

"Why did he want it?" Meg asked.

"Said he needed it for the construction company. It was his. I gave it to him with the interest. Then I started to wonder, why cash? So I thought I'd better call you, Meg."

What had happened, of course, was that since Meg left, Jimmy had gotten more and more into cocaine. Nothing mattered, simply the high. Somehow, he managed to work every day, fooled people, but he couldn't wait and often times, didn't wait, to get high. He'd frequent Boston's Best, socialize, get his drugs and leave, always alone, back to his apartment. Nothing mattered except the high. Anytime he thought of Meg, the kids, he'd simply escape into the world of cocaine and alcohol.

Meg had no idea Jimmy was this bad. She had been burnt out; sick of his behavior, and this vacation — this reprieve — was a blessing for her and the kids. But now she needed help. What should she do? Meg called her brother Jack. Although he was ten years older than her, they had always been close. He was just what she needed now — a big, older, protective brother. She had to tell him the complete truth but didn't want her parents to know.

After hearing the story of the last year and a half, Jack said, "We have to get him to a rehab, Meg. We've got to get him back here before he kills himself. He's loose in Miami with seventy-five grand. I'm booking the next flight and finding him. You tell his mother. Between the two of you, find a detox center and I'll get him there."

Meg hesitated. "I'll go with you."

"Absolutely not!" said Jack. "You stay here with the kids. I'll call you in a day or two, when I find him. Then we'll take it from there."

Jack was a special person, a wonderful brother. He had always protected Meg when she was little, stuck up for her when their father had way too many expectations. He was a gift in Meg's life. And he never let her down, especially now.

Meg told her mother-in-law what was going on. As painful as it was, Anna understood. She always understood Jimmy, her youngest and most precious child. She had been so sick her whole pregnancy with him, almost miscarried twice. Then Jimmy was born with asthma, and Anna, still sick herself, needed help physically and emotionally, from her sisters-in-law. They brought Jimmy up for the first three months. Anna barely held him. Then as he got better and stronger, she wanted to resume the care of her youngest child, but her sisters-in-law were overpowering and Anna, still tired and weak, gave in to these strong-willed women. It wasn't until Jimmy was almost two that he realized who his real mother was. Anna felt she had let him down in his formative years and that was why he had so many problems.

"We'll get him better, Meggie," she said to her daughter-in-law that cold February morning. "I'm going to make some calls. I have a friend who works in a halfway house. He'll help us out. You take the kids out for a while. I'll find Jimmy a place."

Meg wrapped the kids up in snowsuits, mittens, and hats and headed for the train station. Bella, who was now two years old, and Michael, barely seven months, set out for Boston.

"We're going on an adventure, kids," Meg said, as the train swayed from side to side. 'Mommy's taking you somewhere you've never been before."

The snow was falling lightly; the wind was blowing, as Meg entered the Arch St. Church in downtown Boston with her two children. Bella, legwarmers to the top of her thighs, rosy– red cheeks, and freezing cold hands, was ready to just sit in one of the pews and wonder why her mother had taken them there. *Why was this an adventure?* Bella wondered.

Her two-year-old eyes scanned the church, the twelve Stations of the Cross. She got up and walked to each one, hesitating at the eleventh station where Jesus was dying on the cross. Her little eyes gazed sadly at the sight of Jesus bloody, with thorns on His head. Meg noticed her daughter staring intently and called to her, "Bella, come here, honey. I have a coloring book." Bella obeyed slowly, turning back, looking at Jesus as she walked away, glad to be interrupted.

As Bella picked up her crayons and coloring book, Meg placed a sleeping Michael in his stroller. She thought back to four years before. Sick with drugs herself, she had desperately come to this church, looking for some hope, some reason to live. Her father had taken her here as a child, and several times and as a teenager. All the Flahertys had come here to worship, pray, visit, especially on Good Friday. It was a ritual to visit seven churches and pray, and make a wish in each one on Good Friday. Go to confession, repent for your sins you had committed. Megan had remembered those days so vividly, especially when she was ten years old.

For some reason she became aware of her Catholicism and wanted to be a good Catholic, just like her mother. She watched her dad that day, leading each one of the smaller Flahertys into the confessional, making sure they got absolution from the priest, doing his duty as a good Christian father, leading his children down the right path.

Meg had felt so holy and worthy of God's love then, and over a decade later she had been here again, praying in one of these pews, praying that her addiction would go, her need for drugs would dissipate. She remembered kneeling in the pew, looking up at Jesus dying on the cross, and feeling so guilty about her life. She was hurting herself and everyone around her. Meg couldn't relate that day. The God she was brought up to believe in, she hated. Why wasn't he helping her? Why did he let her get attacked? He was a hypocrite, instilling beliefs in Catholics that they needed to live a certain way in order to obtain salvation. Meg remembered how angry and frightened she was that day. She wanted help from God but she despised him at the same time.

But today with her children at her side, she felt different; the shackles of guilt were gone. God had helped her, saw that she found sobriety; and it was then that Jimmy Romano had come back in her life and they had created two beautiful children. And now she was leaning on God again, hoping He could restore her husband to sanity.

If she could do it, get off drugs, so could Jimmy. Meg had thought her life was over at the time. She was weak, suffering from the effects of being attacked, almost raped and killed, and not being validated. She looked over at her sleeping son and at Bella, her princess, and knew at that moment that God was by her side, always. Even in her time of anguish and hopelessness He had never really left her side, she just needed to find her faith again.

She knew than that God would do the same for Jimmy. Her brother Jack must be there now, with her husband. Something positive would come out of all of this. She had to believe that.

Bella, in that instant, looked up at Meg and said, "I miss Daddy, too, Mommy. Don't be sad."

***

Jimmy had gone through ten thousand dollars in ten days. He had missed work, snorted coke for the last forty-eight hours straight. He was on his last legs. In his conscious, straight moments, he knew he was totally messed up. He had turned into Joe Gallucci full force and was out of control. He would feel remorseful, miss Meg and the kids, but the urge to get high was so great that he would give in, buy more cocaine, and sit in the apartment or on the beach and get high. Snorting a few lines, smoking a couple of joints, and drinking a few beers brought him to the altered state of consciousness that he wanted. Jimmy had been in his room, stoned, listening to an album of Bill Withers and singing along with him. "Wonder where she's gone/wonder why she went away."

Then the tears started. He missed his Meggie, his kids, but he was so high, so fucked up, he couldn't get a grasp of what to do. All he knew was that he had hit bottom, had gone downhill very quickly.

He grabbed a blanket — and a Heineken — and headed for the beach. He'd think, collect his thoughts. Maybe the fresh air would do him good. He'd decide how to get Meg and the kids back here.

Even though he was thin and worn-out, he was still Jimmy Romano, the handsome guy from Newport. His hair was getting long again, and he still had a lot of muscle. Women always looked twice. And as he approached the beach and put the blanket on the sand and continued to sing along with Bill Withers in his head, a beautiful, tall brunette approached him, put her hand on his shoulder and said, "Jimmy, is that you?"

***

It was easy for Anna Romano to find a bed for Jimmy at a local detox center in Cambridge, Massachusetts. Her friend had pulled through, told her he'd hold a spot for Jimmy for seventy-two hours. *Now we need to find him,* she thought.

Jack Flaherty had called her when he landed in Miami. He had gone to the restaurant, but nobody had heard from Jimmy. The last Davey saw of him he handed him the cash. After that, Jimmy was gone. Jack actually wanted to strangle Davey for doing such a thing. … *What an idiotic move that was*, he thought. "I'm driving down to Key West," he told Anna. "I just hope I find him."

Jack had gone first to the construction site where Jimmy worked. His boss, Mr. Johnson said, "He's gone downhill. He hasn't been here in two days. I'd do anything for that kid. He's a hard worker and basically good, so let me know when you find him or if you need help."

Jack continued his search for Jimmy for a full day with no luck. The apartment was empty — a couple of beer bottles out, a mirror placed on the sofa that Jack knew he used for cocaine. It was obvious Jimmy was still getting high. Jack asked all around about his brother-in-law. In bars and restaurants, he ran into people who had seen him, but said he had left pretty high. Finally, in the last bar he went to, a woman named Suzie overheard him asking about Jimmy Romano.

"I think I know where he might be," she said. "He might be with a girlfriend of mine."

Jack followed her in his own car to an isolated beach at about six o'clock on a Friday night. Volkswagen vans lined the street of the beach. Guys with long hair and girls, too, smoking pot freely. He felt like he was back in the sixties. He pulled behind Suzie's car and followed her to a van. She knocked on the door, and then banged on it.

"Michele, I know you're in there. Open up. It's me, Suzie."

They both heard shuffling as Michele came to the door and slowly opened it, groggy looking, clearly stoned.

"Who's that guy?" But Jack was already pushing his way in. He was on a mission to find his brother-in-law. And he was there, huddled in a corner, blanket around him, staring blankly, then trying to focus on who was barging in. Jimmy squinted from the unwanted sunlight, then finally focused on Jack Flaherty.

"Oh, my God! Jack, is Megan here, too?"

"No, Jimmy, but you need to come with me. I'm going to take you to Megan. I'm going to take you to see your kids."

CHAPTER SEVENTEEN

March — 1996

The Narcotics Anonymous meeting was packed, over seventy-five people filling the chairs and standing along the walls to listen to the speaker. Jimmy Romano stood in front of this large crowd and said, "Hi, I'm Jimmy. I'm a drug addict and an alcoholic."

The crowd responded with, "Hi, Jimmy!"

He was the speaker that night. It was an important night — he was getting a chip for celebrating his fifteenth year of sobriety, and he was there to tell his story. He was also celebrating his forty-fifth birthday. Megan was in the crowd with their two older children, Bella, now nineteen years old, and Michael, almost eighteen. Their youngest son, Mario, now twelve, had a hockey game and would meet his family afterward.

"I'm a grateful alcoholic and drug addict," Jimmy said, "and, by the grace of God and these meetings, I'm alive today."

And he meant it! His story, the complete story of his drug use, would take hours to tell in its entirety. But that night, Jimmy highlighted the events as he told the story that led to recovery. After the meeting, Bella and Mike hugged their dad. Both had tears in their eyes. "I'm so proud of you, Daddy," his daughter said. "You're just so strong."

Mike, who was turning out to look just like his father, had a big grin on his face. "Good work, old man," he said.

Each of his kids had weathered the stormy days of his addiction. With each adversity they faced, the family became stronger. Each of his children was way beyond their age emotionally. This disease made them tough — made them fighters. And Jimmy was so grateful for them.

His children left to go pick up Mario at the hockey game, so he and Megan could go out and celebrate Jimmy's birthday and fifteen years of sobriety. Their very good friends, Max and Lisa, would join them; go into the North End for a big Italian dinner.

Jimmy looked at his wife, Meggie. He loved her more now than ever. How her eyes crinkled as she laughed, that infectious giggle that made him remember the first time he met her over twenty-five years ago on the elevator. And to think he almost lost her because of his addiction!

Jimmy grabbed his wife's hand, telling her they'd be late meeting their friends if they didn't head out. Twenty minutes later they parked the car and walked to the European Restaurant. Mac and Lisa already had a table and waved them over. Mac, also in NA, hugged Jimmy.

"Fifteen years, man — what an accomplishment!" he said.

"Yeah, and I'm an old man," said Jimmy, "Forty-five today! Un-fucking-believable. I used to think that was so old. Now I'm there!"

Although Mac and Jimmy had been friends for those fifteen years, Mac had never heard the whole story of what happened, of what brought Jimmy Romano to his knees, how he hit bottom — in fact, hit bottom several times before he became sober. The disease of humiliation: addiction. And his good friend wanted to hear, and Lisa as well, what finally made Jimmy "see" the light. Over coffee and dessert, Jimmy Romano told his tale.

That February morning his brother-in-law found him in a van, with some young girl that had picked him up. They had gotten high for two days straight on cocaine and alcohol. She was as sick as Jimmy and they leaned on one another for comfort in those desperate hours. *I didn't even know her name,* Jimmy thought, with little surprise.

She was a convenient little fling. He was so high he couldn't remember if they had been intimate, but he knew they must have been. When Jack Flaherty found him, he was huddled in a corner, naked, with a blanket around him. He and the girl were waiting for more drugs to be delivered. Jimmy had the money, over sixty grand, on him. They could get high for a long time with that. A knock at the van door brought him back to reality. He thought the dealer was there. Instead, he was face to face with his brother-in-law.

"God, Jack. Why are you here? Is Meg with you?" he asked.

"I'm going to take you to her, Jimmy," Jack had said, knowing it was a lie. But if he told Jimmy he was going to a Boston detoxification center, he'd never have gone with him. Jack had helped Jimmy get dressed and brought him to a hotel in Miami where they spent the night. Jimmy was sick, feeling the effects of no drugs in his system. Jack finally took him to the bar in the hotel and the two of them had a few beers. And the next day, on the plane ride home, Jack had to do the same thing. Letting Jimmy drink would make it easier for him to leave his brother-in-law at the detox center. Jack thought Jimmy might resist, become combative. The beer sedated him.

"Where are Meg and the kids, Jack?" Jimmy asked on the cab ride to Cambridge, to the detox center.

"You'll see them later, Jimmy. You need some help first."

And Jimmy was too weak, too tired and sick to resist when Jack told him where he would be spending the next few weeks. Little did Jimmy know at the time those three weeks would turn into over a year of treatment for him.

Two weeks later, he wasn't too tired to resist. "I'm not staying here!" Jimmy shouted at his counselor, Rich Caruso. "I'm okay now. I need to find my wife and kids."

They had detoxified his system physically of all drugs. Now the real work had to begin, facing the truth about the addiction, why he was doing drugs. It would mean delving into the past, getting the ghosts out of the closet and dealing with his issues. Rich Caruso was a recovering addict himself. Sober over ten years, he knew what Jimmy was going through but he had to be tough. "You're not going anywhere, Romano. You're not ready to leave. Sit down!"

"No!" shouted Jimmy. "I need to find Megan."

'Megan doesn't want you, man. Don't you remember the incident two days ago? She doesn't want you back."

Meg had gone to the center when Rich asked her to come. He needed to have an idea of what was happening with Jim's wife, her mental status, and how she was going to cope with this addiction. It was to be sort of a family meeting.

But Meg had other ideas. She had heard from her brother when he returned home with her husband, and when he told her he had found Jimmy with another woman, she had flipped. "I'm getting a divorce!" Meg shouted. "How dare he! We're married! He betrayed me!"

Jack had almost left the part out about the other woman for two reasons: he liked his brother-in-law, and he knew how sick Jimmy was. Jack also felt it wasn't right to hide events or pretend they didn't happen. He believed in the truth so he told his sister everything. Now he was regretting it.

"Meg, I don't think Jimmy even knew he was with her, he was so out of it. Misery needs company."

But Meg felt differently and when she went to meet with Rich and Jimmy, she told him so. "Cheating on me is not acceptable, Jimmy. I don't care about our relationship anymore. You've betrayed me," Meg said, with tears in her eyes.

But Rich could tell that she still cared, still loved her husband. She only needed time.

Jimmy started to cry, begging her not to leave. "I'm so sorry, Meggie. Please, let's work things out. I'll stay straight. We'll have a new start. Just don't leave me."

But she did leave and, two weeks later, Jimmy was coming to the realization that Meg may have really meant what she said.

Jimmy was in Rich's office, had his face in his hands. "Rich, I just can't stay here. I won't leave and get high. I just feel so confined! I've always been like that. I can only take the four walls for so long."

Rich softened a bit, put his hand on Jimmy's shoulder and said, "You're just not ready, man. You're too vulnerable. The world out there will eat you up. You need counseling, a long-term rehab, maybe for a year. That's what I'm recommending."

"That's bullshit!" Jimmy yelled, pulling away from the other man. "That's like going to purgatory. I'm leaving, finding Meg, getting a job. I'll die if I stay here."

"You have no money, Jim, no place to stay, and your wife doesn't want you. Looks like you have no choice," Rich said calmly.

"Where's the seventy thou. I had?" Jimmy asked him.

"Jack gave it to Megan after he dropped you here. And don't delude yourself; it wasn't seventy thousand. You spent a hell of a lot of it on that shit."

"Then I'll stay with my mother. She'll help me out." Jimmy's voice was half-hearted. He knew he had very few options. His mother had told him he could live with her when, and only when, he was ready for discharge. It would be Rich's call. Now Rich was talking about a six — to twelve — month stint in rehab.

"Where's this place you want me to go to?" Jimmy asked finally.

"In Gloucester, a beautiful old Victorian home that was made into a halfway house. Two more weeks here, Jimmy. Then I'll see if I can get you over there. This is your life we're talking about, brother — your sanity."

Jimmy thought, *Maybe Meg will come back to me if I go there. Maybe I'll have another shot.* "I'll think about it, Rich," he said. "I just really don't think I need it."

"No one thinks they need it. That's why, in the beginning, it's important to listen to others. They know what's best for you. This is a horrible disease we have. You could have killed yourself in Florida — OD'd, spent all the money that should be for your life with your wife and kids. I really don't see a choice here, Jim. You need rehab. Your life has become unmanageable. So, before you end up killing yourself, I recommend your ass be put in a rehabilitation center for at least six months, maybe a year. So, get used to it." And Rich walked out the door, not giving Jimmy a chance to reply.

Lizzy's voice was nonchalant. "You need Alanon or Nar-Anon meetings, Meg. I told you this before!"

Meg and her kids moved into Lizzy's two-family house. Lizzy had separated from her husband, so Meg moved in to help with the cost of the house. Meg had just landed a great job at a community college in the nursing program, and working as an instructor on a surgical floor with the nursing students. She was thrilled. Meg was determined to leave the past behind, to move forward and forget Jimmy Romano.

"I don't need Alanon," Meg said, as she tossed a salad. "I don't live with Jimmy anymore, so I don't need Alanon."

"Oh, but you do," stated Lizzy. "The dysfunctional effects are still there."

Meg had been hurt beyond belief, betrayed, and lied to. It was all still close to the surface, too. Tears streamed down her face as she said, "I can't believe he kept doing drugs when I begged him not to. It was like I wasn't important. Only the drugs were."

Lizzy put her arm around her sister. "What makes you think you have control over someone else's addiction? What makes you think you're so important that you can control Jimmy? He's sick with a disease, Meg. Your anger and hatred isn't helping you or your kids."

But Meg didn't want to think about any of her problems. Her kids seemed fine, happy little children who barely missed their father. She'd work and see what would happen. She was too sick and tired, hurt and angry, to put any more thought into her husband. And her parents were no help.

"I knew he was no good from the start, Meg," her father said when he finally heard about Jimmy's problems. "I'll pay for the divorce; we'll get you all set. Maybe you can even get an annulment so you can get married in the church again."

But Meg wasn't ready for any of this. She only wanted to forget about Jimmy, go to work, and take care of her kids. She was thirty-one years old, still young. Her life was really just beginning. Meg didn't want to take legal action. She only wanted to be just left alone, to move on to a normal life.

She found a woman who did daycare. Her job was only part-time so she wouldn't be away that much. Meg had Jimmy's sixty thousand dollars in the bank under her name only, so Jimmy couldn't get at it. Plus, there was his trust fund, and her mother-in-law was willing to let Meg get at the money if she needed it. Finances didn't seem to be the problem. Only her marriage was out of control.

What the hell happened? she wondered? *Was any of this my fault? One minute we were so in love, happy, and the next, Jimmy is off getting high.* She went to sleep that night feeling it was her fault, that she was a failure.

Jimmy was sitting in an AA meeting for the fourth time in a week. He heard the woman next to him say, "Hi, I'm Bev. I'm a drug addict and an alcoholic."

Jimmy stretched his long legs out, breathed a big sigh, and rolled his eyes. The group was going around the room, giving introductions. It was his turn.

"Hi, everyone," he said. "I'm Jimmy and I'm really not an alcoholic or a drug addict, but I'm here because I've nowhere else to go. I got a little out of control for a few months with drugs and money, but I know I can control this."

And he was telling the truth. At first, he believed that. He was going through the motions, pretending he had a problem; but, it was certainly one he could control, not like the others at the rehabilitation center. He was only there because he was being forced to stay there. His ulterior motive was to stay the minimum time possible and prove he was worthy enough to get Megan and the kids back. Stay sober, leave, and never go to another AA or NA meeting again! He wasn't really like these people; he could control his drug use if he really tried.

After the meeting an older man approached him and said, "So, you don't think you have a problem, son?"

"No, not really," Jimmy replied.

John, the man who approached him, said, "So, when you were in detox, did you throw up, sweat, have drug dreams, and wake up in the morning wishing you could get high like nothing else in the world mattered?"

Jimmy didn't reply. The man put his hand on Jimmy's shoulder and said, "Until you know you have a problem and admit it to yourself, nothing is going to help. You have to learn to be honest."

At that point, Jimmy had been at the rehab one month. He hated it, hated every minute of the program. Each day he swore he would leave, but for some reason he'd stay. Rich said, "Ninety and ninety, Jimmy," meaning give yourself ninety days of sobriety and ninety days of meetings. And each day was a struggle. Each morning he'd wake up and pray to God to help him. He felt in limbo. He couldn't live in the outside world and he couldn't live, exist much longer, in the rehab.

As each day went by, his head would become clearer and he realized what he had done to himself, Meg, and the kids. Jimmy was ashamed. And for three months, he stayed in denial of his disease, pretending he wasn't a drug addict. But as the fourth month approached, the fog his brain was in started to lift. His thought processes became clearer and he knew, as painful as it was, he needed to get the ghost out of the closet.

Jimmy woke up on the ninety-ninth day of his sobriety, walked into Rich's office, and said, "I need to see my mother and I need to see my sister, Gwen."

Gwen and Anna arrived the next day for family therapy. Rich was curious why Jimmy wanted his mother and sister present. Jimmy explained he was having flashbacks of his father's accident in the shop, and he needed to know why his father was there so late at night, working. Why wasn't his Uncle Vinny there more? He had been part owner of the business, but he didn't seem to do his share of the work. He always left work for Jimmy's father that should have been done by him. Jimmy was angry, raging at his uncle for all these years.

"If Uncle Vinny did his part, Dad wouldn't have worked so hard, been there so late at night," Jimmy said tearfully. "And, Mom, if you made Dad happier and didn't fight with him, maybe he would have been home more."

Rich said, "So, you're blaming your uncle and your mother for your father's accident and death?"

"Well, I don't know if blame is the word, but maybe this wouldn't have happened if his life was happier. It just wasn't fair."

Anna went over and took Jimmy's hands. "Look," she said, "your dad and me, we had our problems, and, yes, we argued because he worked so much. I had the same issues with your uncle. I wanted your father to speak up to him. I used to tell him he needed to speak up more. But your dad wouldn't. He didn't want to create problems in the family. Plus he was a workaholic, Jim. No matter what I said, did, or planned, work came first."

Gwen just sat there crying and said, "Why didn't we all talk about this before? Instead, we all kept in our feelings, suffered alone. God, I miss Dad. I was his little princess."

Jimmy put his head in his mother's lap like he had when he was small and just cried his heart out. All the suppressed feelings he had about his father were finally coming out. There was nothing to hide behind, not anymore. "I just don't think I can handle these feelings. It's way too painful. It makes me want to get high," Jimmy said, pain in his voice.

Rich replied, "That's the most honest thing you've said in months, Jim."

"Honest and scary and I don't want to keep thinking about it. I had a good relationship with my father finally and he gets pulled out of my life, just when I needed him," Jimmy said angrily.

"You're not gonna get high, are you, Jim?" Gwen asked. "I mean, like, you're here. You're gonna stay here. Aren't you?"

But Jimmy didn't reply. He thought that all he wanted was to run out the front door and escape with a joint or a few lines of coke. These real feelings were scaring the hell out of him. But he didn't tell his sister that. If he left, he knew he'd never, ever get Meg back, and he knew the world out there scared him. He would end up dead. He had no option. He wasn't ready to set foot outside of the rehab. He wasn't even ready for a day pass.

He asked his sister to please talk to Meg, let the kids come and visit at least. His heart was aching … he missed them so much. When Gwen had said she missed her dad, remembered how she had been his little princess, her words brought back memories, because Bella was his little princess. He would sit her on his lap, read stories and tell her she was the princess and Meg was the queen. Did Bella remember that?

Does she even remember me? he wondered despondently.

Gwen agreed to go over and talk to Meg. She wouldn't guarantee anything, nor should Jimmy count on a visit, but she'd try. Maybe between her and Lizzy convincing Meg, things would work out.

A month later, Rich was making Jimmy do an autobiography. He finally admitted to himself, and in front of fifty people, that yes, he was an alcoholic and drug addict and this disease was ruining his life. Knowing this, he wasn't exactly anxious to start writing.

"Write a book about yourself. Include everything, all the good and negative things. Get to know yourself! You might find out there's something you like about James Romano."

Rich had said this lightheartedly, but he was serious. He made all his patients do it. Writing was a way of healing, self-expression. And it was a requirement of Rich Caruso before you left the rehab.

Jimmy was reluctantly writing his story in the day room. It was a beautiful, sunny room, filled with plants, candles, crystals hanging from the windows, reflecting a rainbow affect across the whole room. Novels filling the bookshelves gave the room a very comfortable and homey atmosphere. Jimmy looked up when he heard his name. It was Susan, one of the counselors.

"You've got visitors, Jim. Do you want them here or in your room?" she asked.

"Here's fine, Susan. But who is it?"

"Your wife and kids," she replied.

Jimmy was emotionally paralyzed as he watched his wife and children enter the day room. He was so overwhelmed that he couldn't speak. As he described it five years later, "It was the best gift — better than the best Christmas, birthday, or vacation I'd ever had, all rolled into one, when I saw my family for the first time in five months."

Bella broke the ice. She walked over and said, "I know you. You're Jimmy Romano."

Meg and Jimmy both laughed.

"I'm your Daddy, Princess," as he lifted her in the air. "My precious little girl."

"And this is my brother," Bella said as she grabbed his hand and pulled him towards Michael and Megan.

Jimmy lifted Mike out of Meg's arms and just couldn't believe what a miracle this was. Michael was fifteen months old, chubby as all get-out, and grinned from head to toe as Jimmy nestled him in his arms. Then he looked at Megan, at her sad, angry expression.

"Hi, Meg," he said. "You look beautiful."

But Meg didn't reply. She had gone to visit him reluctantly, only because she felt Jimmy and the kids should have a relationship. When Meg looked at Jimmy, she knew it was a mistake. The minute she saw his puppy-dog brown eyes, she wanted to melt. But her anger took over. He had betrayed her. He had cheated on her. That was unforgivable.

"Look, Jimmy, I'm here for the kids. Just because we're not together doesn't mean the kids shouldn't see you."

Jimmy explained to her that he was trying, staying straight, and getting his life together and that he still loved her, wanted her back.

"I can't, Jimmy. I can't go back with you. The drugs are one thing, but you cheated on me — cheated on me twice. That's unforgivable. I watched my father cheat on my mother my whole life and I won't let that happen to me."

"Oh, Meggie," he said, "I was so stoned, it meant nothing. I don't even remember it or why I did it. I'm sober now. It would never happen again. I can't stand the thought of losing you forever."

He took the back of his hand and rubbed it on her cheek. Tears welled up in her eyes.

"I better go, Jimmy. Gwen will bring the kids once a week to see you. I hope you get well."

With that, she took Michael from his arms and Bella by the hand and walked out the door with a tearful James Romano watching his wife walk out of his life, maybe forever.

When Jimmy had been in the rehab for nine months Rich thought he was ready to go out on a day pass. As frightened as Jimmy was, he knew he needed to straighten out two things. He needed to go see his old boss, Mr. Johnson, and apologize for his behavior in Florida. He also needed to try to see Megan alone. He had seen the kids weekly for the past three months. Either Gwen or Lizzy would bring them. He was feeling stronger emotionally and was determined to try to win Megan back.

It was early September. School buses were picking the children up for their first day back after a long hot summer. Jimmy had been able to sit on the porch of the rehab, look out on the ocean and reflect quite a bit during the month of August. He told Gwen about it as they headed south on Route 128 toward Boston. Gwen picked him up in Gloucester; she was letting him use her car for a couple of hours. It was his first pass, but she trusted her brother.

Jimmy told her how self-centered his addiction had made him, not caring about others … only his needs, his wants. And he knew he had to apologize to his sister for past behavior. He was working on the twelve steps in Alcoholics Anonymous and he was struggling getting through the steps. But when he read over all twelve he focused on the eight and ninth steps, knowing he wanted, that day, to skip over the others and focus on those two. The eighth step outlines making a list of all persons one had harmed, and becoming willing to make amends to them all. The ninth step outlines making direct amends to such people wherever possible, except when to do so would injure them or others.

"I have a lot of amends to make, Gwen, and I'll start with you. I'm so sorry if I hurt you in any way."

Gwen leaned over, put her hand on her brother's knee and said, "No need, Jim. You're okay now. The past is the past."

"No, it's not okay," Jimmy, said gently. I got out of control a few times with you, scared your whole family with my outbursts, so I apologize Gwen, for that and anything else I did to harm you."

When they got to Gwen's house in Cambridge, they had a light breakfast before Jimmy headed out to see Mr. Johnson. Jimmy had set up an appointment for nine o'clock with him and from there he'd show up at Meg's unexpectedly. As Jimmy backed the car out of the driveway, he started to get butterflies. What if everything falls through and I'm back where I started, he wondered nervously.

But as he headed through old familiar parts of Belmont and Westbridge, and entering Newport, he knew that wasn't true. He was sober and had been for nine months, and he would try, day-by-day, minute-by-minute if he had to, not to pick up a drug again.

Mr. Johnson shook his hand as Jimmy entered his office. "You look great. This is the Jimmy Romano I remember."

As they sat and talked in his office, Jimmy told his story, his fight for sobriety and how he was turning over a new leaf. He ended by apologizing for his behavior. But Mr. Johnson loved

Jimmy. He always knew he was a good kid, had watched him play football all through high school and thought he got a bum rap with the knee injury. Plus, he liked Ed Romano. That was such a tragedy; it had probably left scars on his kid!

Jimmy could only remember the last time he had seen Mr. Johnson. It was in Florida, at one of the construction sites. Jimmy was stoned, unshaven, blurry-eyed. His boss told him to leave, but Jimmy kept insisting he was fine, just hung over. But he had made a scene about staying at work and Mr. Johnson finally had to call security to get him off the grounds. And now, nine months later, this wonderful man was willing to forgive and forget. "When do you get out of rehab, Jim?" he asked.

"I don't know. My counselor, Rich, says when I'm ready. Hopefully by the first of the year."

"Have you plowed snow, Jim?"

Startled, Jimmy replied, "With my dad a few times in the building parking lot that he owned."

Mr. Johnson said, "Call me when you get out in January and I'll show you the ropes about plowing. We have a busy business in the winter and if all goes well with you, there'll be construction work in the spring."

Jimmy said, with tears in his eyes, "I can't thank you enough. I never expected this!" He was full of gratitude and couldn't believe his good luck. This was something, a beginning, a new start. And if Meg didn't take him back, he'd stay with his mother for a while.

With the butterflies returning to his stomach, he left Newport toward Westbridge Square. Meg was staying at Lizzy's house, which was right across the Charles River. Lizzy knew he was coming and was planning to take Bella and Michael out for a while around ten thirty. Jimmy watched them leave. His little

Bella, the chatterbox: he could hear her voice all the way across the street. God, how he missed his family … living with them. He wanted his old life back so badly!

Meg answered the door, startled to see Jimmy.

"I had a day pass, Meggie. I just thought I'd drop by. Is that okay?"

"The kids aren't here," she replied nervously.

"Yeah, I know. I saw them leave." Jimmy glanced down the street. "I just need to talk to you."

"I'll get my sweater," Meg replied. "We can walk along the river."

They crossed the street and entered the walkway along the Charles, both remembering their first real date. They had met beside the basketball court near where they were walking and had taken the trolley into Harvard Square to see *Rocky Horror Picture Show.*

Meg said, "Remember our first real date?"

"Yeah," Jimmy said, "*Rocky Horror.* What was that 'first-date thing' with you, Meg? We were actually living together and you needed a 'first date!'"

"Come on, people need a beginning to every relationship, and that was our real beginning."

"Yeah, I see what you mean." He took a deep breath. "Is this our end right now, Meg?"

Meg kicked a stone, watched it glide into the water. She pulled her sweater around her, steadied herself.

"You cheated on me twice. You spent our money. You were selfish. I know you were sick; I've been going to Alanon meetings and I'm beginning to really understand the addiction part, but it's the betrayal, the other women. I don't know if I can forgive that."

"Please, give me another chance," Jimmy pleaded. "I will never look at another woman. I've loved you since our first elevator ride, Meg. We have two kids. Please, forgive me."

Meg, somehow, could not give an answer. Her fear of his cheating again was too great. "I need time. You do, too. This is too overwhelming for me. For right now, anyway."

She had so much self-control. Meg simply wanted to hug Jimmy, forgive him for the moment so they could be together, but she knew that was wrong. She must be virtuous, true to herself. Jimmy had that letdown look, the "I've failed" expression, but he had started to learn patience. The twelve-step program had taught him that.

He walked Meg to the porch, she unlocked the door, they stepped inside, and there was total silence. The kids weren't home yet. The thought crossed both their minds of making love.

Meg reached, touched his face. "You'd better go. I'll be in touch, let you know when the kids will visit."

"One kiss, Meggie?" he asked.

She felt his hand on her head, the slow gentle pull of her hair as he tilted her head back. Their lips briefly met and within seconds, Jimmy was out the door, a silent figure walking away. Meg closed her eyes, imagined what could have been, and as reality returned, she saw his car disappear in the downtown traffic.

Jimmy had left quickly. He had wanted to make the kiss go on and on, but he knew Megan. She wouldn't give in, and it would have been torture to stay and not be able to make love. He glanced at her standing at the door as he pulled the car away from the curb, wondering if he'd ever have her in his life again.

CHAPTER EIGHTEEN

December — 1981

The Christmas traffic was brutal. Everyone was out doing last minute shopping, including Meg. She had resumed her life of mother and nurse, immersing herself into her work and trying to forget Jimmy — well, not forget him, just sort things out. She hadn't seen him since September but she knew he was doing well. Lizzy and Jack took Bella and Michael all through the fall to visit him. Only good reports came back.

"He's straight, sober, getting more and more passes." Jack had told her he had a weekend pass in mid-November, had gone back to Florida with Mr. Johnson, and cleaned out his belongings from the apartment that his friends were now renting. He was due to get out of rehab in early February and would start working right away.

"Where's he going to live?" Meg asked her brother.

"Probably at his mom's until he finds a place."

Just as well, Meg thought, I'm still so damn confused.

The Flaherty's celebrated Christmas at their house. Both John and Mary Flaherty were well into their seventies, and were starting to feel the effects of old age. Moreover, Meg's dad was starting to soften ever so subtly. He wasn't so quick to judge, and he just seemed more tolerant and kind. He had just been awarded the Man of the Year award from the Gridiron Club of Boston. This honor had made the holiday even more special for the Flaherty's.

Jimmy had a pass for Christmas Day. He asked Meg if he could take the kids to his mother's.

"Why don't you pick them up at my parents'? We'll all be there around three o'clock," she had told him.

At three forty-five, Jimmy showed up, nervous and shaky, expecting Mr. Flaherty to be the tyrant that he knew. But instead, he was greeted with open arms and shown into the den where Meg and the kids were. Bella clutched his thigh when she saw her father.

"Oh good, Daddy, you're here. Look what Santa brought me," as she dragged him into the living room where the tree was.

Meg followed. They laughed at Bella as she talked non-stop about her gifts and sat down to play with her new Cabbage Patch Doll.

Meg and Jimmy wandered over to the stairs that led to the second floor. The chandelier was sparkling, shimmering, as they sat together on the bottom step. A Jim Morrison song was blaring from one of the rooms where a teenage grandchild was.

"Into this life we're born/into this world we are torn.."

"And to think I almost ended up like that guy," Jimmy said.

"You've been straight almost a year. Right?" asked Meg.

"Eleven months," he replied. "Hard to believe." He hesitated. "Have you thought anymore about us?"

"Not now, Jimmy: not today. Let's not start. I guess I just need more time."

"Is there someone else, Meg?" Jimmy had heard, through the grapevine, that Meg had met and gone out with a doctor at work. Although true, Meg had no feelings for Bob Smith, an orthopedic surgeon. She simply had gone to a movie on two different occasions.

"I'm gonna forget you said that, Jimmy," Meg said, her voice hollow.

At that moment, Michael crawled onto his father's lap. Bella grabbed their coats and said, "Let's go. Time to see Grammy Romano!"

Meg felt relieved. For some reason, she couldn't take Jimmy back. Not yet, anyway.

"We need to finish this conversation sometime. You know," Jimmy said to his wife. "I'm not going away. I want to be with you, and I can give you what you need now." *Why wouldn't Meg own up to the fact that she was dating?* he wondered. His jealousy over it was almost overwhelming. But Bella was pulling at her father's arm, anxious to leave. Meg, without saying a word, simply walked them to the door, not willing to give an inch. She just wasn't ready.

CHAPTER NINETEEN

February — 1982

Jimmy shook hands with Rich, and then they hugged. "Good luck, man," Rich, said to Jimmy. "Let's keep in touch. Still call me once a week and if you need some man-to-man counseling, I'm here for you, pal!"

They both burst out laughing because they would tease one another about who was more macho! And real men don't need counseling.

Jimmy left the rehab on February twenty-first. Almost a whole year had passed and he was ready to move on. A job awaited him, maybe even that night if there was a snowstorm. He had gotten a full-time job back, was going to live with his mother until — until what? Then he caught himself. A day at a time: he had to remember that. A day at a time and patience, then maybe Megan would return.

"Romano, you have to learn to move the complete pile of snow over to the side of the road, not just half of it!"

Jimmy was getting on-the-job training from Frank, a thirty-year veteran and one of the best plowers, who also went overboard on his teaching skills. Jimmy was exhausted. It was one of the biggest storms of 1982, especially for the end of March. The weather had warmed up so much; no one thought it would snow again. But, typical of New England weather, a big Nor'easter hit Boston and people were out of work and off the streets for over forty-eight hours.

Jimmy had been doing well since his discharge from the rehab. He stayed with his mother for about two weeks, realized he needed his own place, and had rented a small apartment in Allston, not too far from work. And that was all Jimmy did: work, and go to AA or NA meetings. He knew he had a problem but he found it difficult to relate to AA members. Cocaine and pot was his problem. In the beginning, when first recovering, he couldn't understand why he couldn't have a beer, since alcohol had never been a problem for him. He didn't even like drinking that much. But his sponsor had said, "If you're addicted, you're addicted. Same disease, different drug."

"Why?" Jimmy asked, and it was explained to him, "You drink a beer, maybe two, you know how to stop but your mind is altered and you might pick up your drug of choice. The solution is, don't do anything! Don't put yourself in that predicament."

But when Jimmy went to AA meetings, it was different. These guys couldn't put down their bottle of booze. Jimmy could, so he mainly stuck with Narcotic Anonymous and finally started to meet people who were like him. When he frequented these meetings, Jimmy couldn't get over the amount of professionals he encountered … doctors, lawyers, ninety per cent with college degrees, computer freaks, scientists.

God, he thought, *this disease doesn't discriminate. We're from all walks of life, from the indigent to the presidents of companies!*

And that had made him feel better. Nestled between the four walls of NA he felt at home, his self-esteem improved and he was full of hope, strength, and courage to move on.

Two weeks later, the balmy spring weather had arrived. The snow melted quickly, tulips and crocuses were starting to appear and tree buds were blossoming. Construction work had begun and Jimmy liked that best. He was good at it. He worked too much, though: he was becoming like his father. Different women had approached him at his meetings, beautiful tall blondes, and petite brunettes, all of them trying to get to know Jimmy Romano. But he went home each night to a lonely apartment, wondering when the hell Meg would see him.

He knew she loved him. He could tell: the chemistry and feelings were there when he'd pick the kids up. But she continued to shut him out. Some day he'd give it one more try, and ask her to come back. If she didn't, he'd move on. He felt in Limbo, and Jimmy couldn't go on like that indefinitely. He wanted a resolution, at the very least, some closure. He'd give it a few more weeks, one last try to get Meg back, but he wasn't going to beg for her forgiveness forever. He had apologized way too many times: he needed to move on.

Jimmy stopped at a flower stand on Brookline Avenue in Boston, bought a dozen yellow roses, Meg's favorite, and walked from there to the community college where she was teaching. He peeked in every room, up and down the corridor, but no Meg! He charged up the stairs of the building, two steps at a time. He knew she was here today, teaching Anatomy and Physiology. The third door he looked into was Meg's room. The first-year students were dissecting frogs, as Jimmy knocked and entered.

A bunch of nineteen-year-olds stared, along with Meg, as Jimmy got down on his knees and started singing *Unchained Melody* to his wife.

The students looked at Meg, anxious for her response, as Jimmy bellowed away, "I need your love, I need your love, come to meeee …" But she was in shock, just looking around at her class. When Jimmy stopped, they all started to clap.

"How romantic!" yelled one of the girls. "I'd die for my boyfriend to do that."

Meg, finally able to speak, said, "The Righteous Brothers, you're not!" and started to giggle. Jimmy reached over, grabbed Megan, tipped her backwards, and kissed her.

"Way to go, Mrs. Romano!" yelled the only male student. "My kind of class!"

Ten minutes later, as the students left, Meg said, "I can't believe you did that!"

"Oh, yes you can. It was only a matter of time. Knock off this bullshit. I want to come home. I love you, and I love the kids. Stop torturing me."

"I can't believe you think you can walk in here, put on a great performance in front of my students, and embarrass me into going back to you!"

"Embarrass you, Meg? Embarrass you? It's called love. Have you heard of that? I've paid my dues. You've made me more than pay my dues, and I'm sick and tired of trying to get you back! My self-esteem is in my shoes, for Christ's sake. And every time I beg you to come back and you refuse, it makes me feel I am worthless to you. Enough's enough Meg, you've been putting off this decision for too long. I can't go on like this, as hard as it is, if you don't make a decision, then I'm gonna move on."

With that Jimmy left the classroom and was out the front door of the building before he started wondering if what he had just done helped or ended their almost non-existent relationship.

A week had gone by since her encounter in the classroom with Jimmy. Meg hadn't heard from him and she knew she wouldn't. After all, he did have *some* pride! Why would he keep begging? The next move, she knew, would have to be hers.

The yellow roses were dying as she removed them from the vase. The beautiful yellow petals were faded, brown-tinged as they fell to the floor. *Did she want that for her marriage?* she wondered. *A faded relationship, a beautiful love affair that would never be again?* She loved Jimmy, couldn't imagine life without him, knew there was nobody else in the world for her that could fulfill her needs and make her laugh. She knew what she needed to do.

Meg rang the doorbell to Jimmy's apartment at about ten o'clock that night. He had just gotten home from a meeting and was drinking a cup of tea while catching the end of the Red Sox game. Not knowing whom it was, narrowing it down to someone in one of his meetings; he just rang them in without asking who was at the door. When the knock came and he opened the door, he was in total shock to see Megan. He never expected to see her. He had, in fact, been preparing himself for his new chapter in life, that of a single man once again; a lonely single man.

"Aren't you going to ask me in?" Meg asked in a tentative voice. "At least for a cup of tea?"

"Come on in, I'll heat the water for another cup" Jimmy said nervously.

"The Red Sox are having a bad start this year," said Meg, gesturing at the television, making small talk. "Lots of injuries already."

Jimmy laughed. "Since when have you been following the Sox?"

"Since your daughter has turned three. She is so into baseball, she loves the sport! So I have been getting into the game myself."

"Bell likes baseball, at her age. What have we created?" Jimmy was still laughing. *He seems completely at ease,* thought Meg. *He is at peace with himself. Finally.*

He sat next to Meg on the sofa, handing her a cup of steaming tea. He looked at her intently and asked, directly, "So, what's up, Meggie? Here to tell me it's over or what?"

She swallowed nervously. "Three strikes and you're out, Romano."

"What?" exclaimed Jimmy. It wasn't what he had been expecting to hear.

Meg said, "Just like in baseball, three strikes and you're out. You've already had two strikes — you cheated on me twice. If it happens again, you're out of my life for good." She paused. "Come home, Jimmy. Just pack your things and come home. I can't get you out of my mind. I can't imagine life without you anymore."

"You're sure of this, Meg? Like, you're not going to rethink this and toss me out on my ass in a few days? I just couldn't deal with that rejection … make sure of your decision."

"I thought it over long and hard since you showed up in the classroom. I want you back, the kids want you back, Bella misses you, so does Michael in his own little way, I am willing to try if you are," said Meg.

Jimmy simply wrapped his arms around her, held her, breathed in the scent of her perfume, shampoo, could not believe he was actually holding her again. She still wanted him, after everything that had happened! It was almost too good to be true.

And Meg responded, hugging him tightly, feeling as if this was the first time they met, instant attraction.

"Can we spend the night here, alone, Meg, and go back tomorrow?" asked Jimmy.

"Lizzy is babysitting, she probably won't mind, I'll call her now."

Two weeks later, in June of 1982, the Romano's started their lives over. The leaf had turned. All four moved into a rental house in Newport, a big old Victorian with a huge front porch and flowers in the front. The yellow roses, although they were dead — withered away — were reborn. Meg let them dry, preserved them, and Jimmy made a frame and they were hung outside the front door as a sign of rebirth. Their relationship had been reborn and placing the roses at the front door was a sign of love, hope and forgiveness. It was a time to move on, stop looking in the rearview mirror.

As Jimmy ended the story, Lisa and Mac just shook their heads in amazement.

Lisa said, "You guys have been to hell and back but what a romantic story."

Mac agreed and stated, "A fifteen year chip for sobriety is all you get? You deserve a new Mercedes for fifteen years and what you have both been through."

They all laughed.

Jimmy said, "I'm here, I'm alive to tell the story. Nothing … absolutely nothing … else matters."

CHAPTER TWENTY

March — 1998

The funeral procession went for miles from the Flaherty's home in Westbridge to the church and to Mr. John Flaherty's final destination on this earth, Mt. Auburn Cemetery in Cambridge, Massachusetts.

He was buried near Mary Baker Eddy, the founder of the Christian Scientists. He was laid to rest under a big oak tree, near a babbling brook with rocks, stones, birds, and turtles surrounding the gravesite. One couldn't be any closer to nature.

Meg, staring down at the big hole in the ground suddenly glanced across the street at the supermarket, Star Market, where her dad had introduced her to shopping for groceries when she was a little girl. Every Friday night, Mr. Flaherty would take Meg and her sisters on an adventure, letting them help him buy food for Friday evening supper. It was exciting, as a small child, simply because she had time with him without her mother tagging along.

And she thought of Saturday night Bean Suppers, political rallies for all local candidates at the high school. Everyone from the town involved in politics would show up and there, among John Flaherty's many speeches she realized his passion for politics and his love for doing the right thing politically for all citizens. Tears came to Meg's eyes at these memories and at how his death had happened.

He had been in the stands at Boston College, watching his grandson, Mike Romano, score the third touchdown of the game. John Flaherty clutched his chest, looked at his son, Jack, and fell from the stands. The ambulance had come rushing, the sirens drawing everyone's attention, even the players'. Someone grabbed Meg, who was sitting at the other end of the stands.

"It's your father," the unknown man said.

Meg and Jimmy ran to her dad. Mike was signaled off the field. He hurried over to his grandfather but it was too late. Mr. Flaherty was pronounced dead at St. Elizabeth's Hospital on November fifteenth, during the biggest game of the year for Boston College and its rival, Holy Cross.

The wake was two days long. John Flaherty was a legend. Politicians, dignitaries, and many of his relatives from Ireland came to pay respects. He had lived a long life, eighty-eight years, and was healthy and vibrant, adding life to the community and the political world. The eight Flaherty children, accompanied by their mother in the long black limo, paid last respects to their father and husband. Each with their own thoughts, each feeling he had done his best, tried to be a good father, had always, always had their best interests at heart.

Jimmy hugged Megan at the graveside. They were almost the last ones there.

"Your dad mellowed, Meg," Jimmy said. "The last ten years, your dad and I made amends. He actually understood me, as I did him. It took me being a father myself, understanding where he was coming from, to really understand John Flaherty."

"How will my mother survive?" asked Meg, as she glanced at Mary Flaherty, placing one more flower on the coffin. Meg and her mother's relationship had always been so distant — Meg could never live up to her expectations of being a good Catholic girl. As tough as her father was, Meg was close to him. They understood one another and he would be missed. The tumultuous relationship she had shared with her dad in the seventies changed as they both matured and accepted one another for who they were, especially when Mr. Flaherty finally welcomed Jimmy into the family.

It was if her dad had grown up and stopped criticizing their relationship … maybe because of her kids. And, oh, how he loved her children! Bella could do no wrong in his eyes. He even helped her get into college, had written an incredible recommendation to Yale where Bella would soon be a junior. And Michael, the light of his life, the second of the Romano children, just a freshman at Boston College, he had made the varsity football team. He had taken after Jimmy, a great ballplayer.

Meg's father had never missed one of his grandson's games in high school. Mike could count on his grandfather being in the stands, smack in the middle with his feathered fedora hat on. They would connect halfway through the game; give each other the high-five sign. Mike was crushed at the funeral. The rocky relationship his father had with John Flaherty was the opposite for Mike. He loved the man, worshipped and respected him.

And Mario, the youngest Romano, was now fourteen years old and a tremendous hockey player. "He's the wild one. You have to watch out for him!" his grandfather would say. And it was true. Mario, although athletic, was a hellion, had been since he was two, full of piss and vinegar. He always kept Meg and Jimmy hopping. Although he also loved his grandparents, Mario didn't have that tight-knit feeling shared by his older siblings. He felt more connected to the Romano's. He was very athletic and had gotten a scholarship to a private high school because of that ability, but he had the passion for building, for making furniture, and showed little interest in the academic world.

All the grandchildren, nineteen total, were in a separate limousine behind their parents. They watched in awe as car after car entered the cemetery to watch their grandfather be put to rest.

On the way home, the eight Flaherty children stared at their mother as she started to sing *The Rose* by Bette Midler: "When the night becomes too lonely … just remember … in the spring becomes the rose."

"Your dad loved that song," she said, as she wiped tears from her eyes. And life would never be the same with her father gone, Meg thought. She had loved him unconditionally, through her anger, fear and resentments of him he was still her father, she his little girl, his favorite and his princess. His memory would live on.

Meg and Jimmy had bought a house in Cambridge, a beautiful large Colonial with a farmer's porch, a year after they got back together. Mario, unexpectedly, arrived a year later. They had thought two children would be enough but along came little Mario, screaming himself into the world.

Life had been good. Sobriety was a wonderful thing and for years, Jimmy and Meg would often forget those earlier, crazy years of addiction. Oh, their kids knew. They were always upfront about it, truthful to a fault. Jimmy even went to schools, gave talks on what had happened to him and how drugs take you down a dead-end street.

When they had first bought the house, they put the kids to bed, went outside after dark, dug a hole, and wrote the names "Joe Gallucci" and "Katie O'Toole" on a piece of paper and buried it. Their old drug names, which they had given themselves, were now dead and buried forever.

Meg had coached Bella's softball team and Jimmy had gotten very involved with Babe Ruth and the football program in Cambridge, coaching for many years. When Mario hit the age of six he wanted to try hockey and slowly, each year, improved. And in the last two years he had become so good, private high schools were looking at him.

"Do they know what they're in for?" Meg laughed.

Mario was always up to something. The kid needed excitement: he couldn't sit still. And at the age of fourteen, he was gorgeous and had the physique of an eighteen-year-old. Yet Meg couldn't forget all the trouble Mario had gotten into — minor scrapes, nothing serious — just enough to keep Meg and Jimmy on their toes.

Meg remembered three years before when Mario was eleven; she had taken him and two neighborhood friends to the beach. Meg had met her friend Judy there with her son and two more friends — a total of six eleven-year-old boys loose on Salisbury Beach.

The boys had walked down to the Arcade, playing games for two hours. They finally returned with their hands full of stuffed animals and cheap trinkets they had won, and silly bumper stickers were sticking out of all their pockets. A few hours later, they headed home, exhausted, needing a nap after a long day at the beach. Meg had looked in the rearview mirror as she was driving. Her hair was going every which way, she looked a mess. Beach-hair, she thought. All the salt water, wind blowing, and the sand had given her the look of a witch. The traffic had been fairly heavy, but moving along about fifty at a steady pace. She had to keep yelling at Mario and his friends because they were holding up the bumper stickers against the windows and distracting the other drivers on the road.

"Mario!" she yelled, "put that bumper sticker down. What does it say, anyway?"

"Nothin,' Ma," he responded, shoving it back in his pocket.

She had looked over at the car next to her and saw the man staring at her. Meg sped ahead in the passing lane. Two minutes later, a state police cruiser pulled up next to her. If Meg sped up, he sped up. If she slowed down, he slowed down.

"Are all your seatbelts on, kids?" she said, as she checked all three boys.

Two minutes later, police cruisers surrounded her. One pulled in front of her, one in back, and two on either side. The one next to her said through his loud speaker, "Pull over to the side of the road!"

Meg's heart was beating fast as she eased the car into the breakdown lane. All four policemen got out of their cruisers. The largest of the four went over to Mario's window and signaled for him to roll it down.

"Are you kids all right? Do you know this lady?"

"Ye — s," Mario stuttered nervously, "Sh — she's my Mom."

"Well, what are those signs you're holding up?" the policeman asked.

All three boys slowly pulled the bumper stickers from their pockets. They read, "Help! I've Been Abducted!" In small letters at the bottom, it added, "by aliens."

"We got them at the Arcade," Mario said. "We were only kidding around."

But the police didn't think it was funny. They lectured them for ten minutes.

"Sorry, officer," she said, as she pulled a brush out and tried desperately to tame her unruly hair. Her appearance was still bothering her. "I'll make sure this never happens again."

The cop looked at her strangely and said, "These kids should know better, other drivers were worried they were kidnapped and called from their cell phones. You boys need to be punished!"

As they pulled away, as scary as it was, Meg wanted to burst out laughing. But she couldn't — the kids would've thought the whole thing was a joke.

"Mario!" she said, "Will you ever learn?" Meg never told Jimmy the story. Unlike Meg, he would have taken it far more seriously. She decided to keep that event and many more to herself, simply because Jimmy often had an explosive temper. *Peace at any cost,* Meg thought.

"Hurry up, Mom! If I'm late I won't play," shouted Mario as he watched his mother weave in and out of traffic, trying to get Mario to his hockey game on time. *Oh, bull!* Meg thought. *It's only hockey, you're only fourteen, and these coaches are much too intense.*

Mario grabbed his equipment and headed to the locker room as Meg finally got to the rink and parked the car. All of this was too intense for her. Not only were the coaches too serious, her husband was, too. He was the loudest one in the stands. People would move if Jimmy got too loud. Meg took a deep breath and sat out in the car listening to WZLX, her favorite rock n' roll station, for about fifteen minutes. Being with Mario that long in the car, and in traffic, put her over the edge. She needed to relax before entering the rink; she didn't want her husband and friends to see her so frazzled.

Somehow, Mario could always do that. He was the youngest, the baby, and she knew she wasn't as firm with him as she had been with her other two. She was older, less patient, and gave Mario his way so they wouldn't argue. As she entered the rink, she could hear Jimmy right away yelling to Mario on the ice.

"Move your feet! Skate! Skate!" he was bellowing.

He was the biggest critic but also Mario's biggest fan. If he made a good play or scored a goal, Mario would look up in the stands and father and son would lock eyes. Jimmy would give a thumbs-up sign. *And today is no different,* Meg thought.

She waved to Jimmy, signaled that she was going to go sit with her girlfriend, Sarah.

When the third period started, Meg happened to glance over at Jimmy; he was sitting with some of the other fathers at the other end of the rink and noticed something different about him. His coloring was weird. She knew he was far away but his face looked yellow or jaundiced, even sallow and gaunt.

"Sarah, does Jimmy look yellow to you?" Meg asked, frowning.

Sarah looked for a moment. "Maybe it's the lighting in here."

"I don't think so," Meg said. "No one else looks jaundiced."

When they got home, Meg could clearly see that her husband's color had changed almost completely. They often wouldn't see each other for a day or two, but this seemed to have happened quickly. She told Jimmy he looked jaundiced.

"Oh, come on, Meg. I'm not one of your patients," he said.

"Go look in the mirror, Jimmy. You're yellow."

And he couldn't deny it: a dull, sallow look. Even the whites of his eyes were turning yellow.

"You need to see a doctor, sweetheart. Something is wrong."

"Give it a few days, hon. Maybe I just have the flu, or a virus. It might go away."

"No," Meg said firmly. "It could be your liver. I'm calling the doctor, setting up an appointment. We can't fool around with this."

"It's my life, Meg. I'm not going. I'm fine. If you set up an appointment, I won't go. Leave me alone!" With that, he stormed out of the house, refusing to comply with Megan's wishes.

He didn't return for several hours.

CHAPTER TWENTY-ONE

September — 1999

Jimmy sat on the examining table in the doctor's office with a hospital gown on, his back exposed to the cold air. Meg sat in the chair across from him.

"I feel stupid!" Jimmy said, as he hopped off the table, starting to get dressed.

The doctor walked in as Jimmy was zipping up his jeans. He signaled to him to get back on the table. "I need to examine you, Mr. Romano," he said in a stern voice. "Please, undress and get up on the table."

Jimmy rolled his eyes. *This is bullshit,* he thought to himself. *I've waited for over an hour. Now, he wants to examine me.* But he reluctantly got back on the table.

Meg noticed the ever-present yellow tinge of her husband's skin as the doctor did his examination. The dullness of his skin was evident: dry, flaking off because he was scratching so much. He was always itchy. She knew why. The bile in his body was getting into his blood stream.

How bad was the hepatitis, anyway? she wondered.

Initially, Jimmy had waited several weeks, even a month before he agreed to finally go to the doctor. When he did, after blood tests and exams they diagnosed him with hepatitis. The doctor told him to rest, eat properly, and let the virus run its course. But months later, his symptoms were worsening and Meg wondered if his liver might have gotten worse because he had waited so long after his symptoms appeared to get medical attention. And now, here they were, back to see the doctor after convincing Jimmy he wasn't getting better. The doctor pressed down on Jimmy's abdomen and he winced. His stomach was slightly distended and uncomfortable.

"Mr. Romano, I need to do a liver biopsy. We've got to see how bad the hepatitis is, indeed what kind of hepatitis you have. I have to say, I think it has advanced since the initial blood tests. We need to see if it's caused any liver damage."

The doctor said this without any affectation and without any feeling, but Meg knew he cared. It was Dr. Sanders' way. He was always to the point … all professional, with no personal involvement. Meg knew, from her work with him, that it must be bad. He only recommended biopsies in extreme cases. Dr. Sanders avoided invasive procedures at all costs. He was an alternative physician — he believed in herbs, acupuncture, was even seen giving Reiki, a hands-on healing technique, to his patients. Meg knew he must be worried.

"I thought the blood tests showed hepatitis A," Jimmy said.

"Blood tests can be wrong. A liver biopsy is more conclusive, and your symptoms are exhibiting that there is more going on in there, you could have Hepatitis C. I'm sorry, Mr. Romano, I strongly urge you to have a biopsy."

Jimmy reluctantly agreed to the biopsy and Dr. Sanders left the room saying he'd schedule the procedure. As soon as he left, Jimmy jumped off the table, "It's not happening, Meg. I'm not doing it!" he said angrily. "I feel fine."

Meg was furious. She immediately grabbed his shoulders and shook him. She'd had it and was fed up with watching her husband turn more and more jaundiced, not get treated, staying in denial for months. It reminded her a little too much of all the years when he had been in denial about his addiction. "Bullshit! You're having it. You're a selfish, selfish human being. You could friggin' die from this, and leave the kids and me!! Don't you ever think of us?"

Jimmy sat on the stool; put his head in his hands. "Meggie, I'm scared. I've never been this frightened. I feel it's better not to know. What can they do, anyway?"

"Tons of stuff," said Meg. "There's medication — meds that kill the virus. You could be well again. Please, Jimmy, at least do it for the family if you can't do it for yourself."

For the first time in fifteen years, Jimmy felt like getting high, really high. Sure, once in a while the thought of getting a buzz passed through his mind — it did to most addicts — but this was the first time he thought he might really go through with it … a nice big bone, a joint the size of a cigar, or a nice cold Margarita.

He was in his truck heading back to work. He and Meg had taken separate vehicles to his doctor's appointment and Jimmy was glad. He needed to be alone. He drove by the bar in Newport where he used to hang out. Lots of old friends would be in there. He could drown his troubles with a couple of pops.

But he couldn't and he knew he would not. The desire to get messed up would leave. Instead, he didn't go back to work. He headed for the nearest NA meeting, for support. Drinking and drugging would only add to his misery. Sure, the high would be nice for a few hours, but he knew he'd wake up in the morning and have to look at himself in the mirror. Reality has a way of coming up and smacking you right between the eyes.

And he would never forget those days, the hangovers, drug hangovers, getting up to go to the bathroom after a long night of using drugs and having to pass the mirror. Oh, he'd avoid it at first, and then glance furtively in it. And he always hated what he saw … pain, misery, and reality.

Jimmy knew he'd never go back to that. It was tempting at times, when things were rough, but he never gave in. He knew, if he did, he'd risk losing Meggie, the only thing that was important to him.

The meeting had already started as he pulled up a seat and listened to the speaker, a friend of his who was chairing the meeting.

"Narcotics Anonymous is a selfish program. We have to think of ourselves, our needs, in order to stay sober."

Jimmy thought about that statement. He was selfish, was thinking of his needs, his fears — his fears of not wanting treatment. His narcissism was affecting his whole family, Meg especially. He knew, if he didn't have a liver biopsy, find out what kind of hepatitis he had, there would be risks, huge risks that would affect himself and his wife and kids. Jimmy raised his hand to speak and his friend, Rory, leading the group, signaled for him to go ahead.

Jimmy said, "Hi, I'm Jim. I'm an alcoholic and drug addict."

"Hi, Jim!" everyone answered.

"I just came from the doctor's. My wife made me go for the second time because I'm turning jaundiced. But I really, really don't think I look that bad. Anyway, I went and now they want to do a liver biopsy and I am so sick of people, of doctors, even my wife, trying to control my life. I feel okay. I only want to be left alone."

The congregation of people looked at Jimmy, at his yellow-tinged skin, his swollen abdomen, the expression of fear on his face. The group fell silent and in that moment, at that very instant, James Romano knew he had no choice. He was amongst friends here, friends with the same disease of addiction he had, and they weren't rallying for him. He was hoping against hope that even one person would tell him not to rush into things, to get another opinion. But those words never came. He could tell by their expressions that he was a physically sick man and his wife and doctors were right.

Jimmy no longer had a choice. He could get treated and live. If he ignored all this, he could die. He grabbed his jacket off the chair in the smoke-filled room and realized this was the biggest decision of his life.

CHAPTER TWENTY-TWO

October — 1999

The needle was slowly inserted in the right upper quadrant of Jimmy's abdomen. The doctor had let Meg stay during the procedure — the liver biopsy — the test that would finally diagnose Jimmy's problem.

Meg looked in his eyes. He was so frightened, so angry, and she felt so much for him. He was so resentful that he had to go through this. It was demeaning for him. He had told Meg he hated God. He had been through enough in his life. Why this?

The procedure was painless and simple. Jimmy had to lie on his side for two hours afterward and then another four hours on his back. It was a precautionary measure in case there was any bleeding. It was uneventful except for a confused woman in the bed next to him. She kept screaming for her dead husband and was throwing all sorts of objects at the nurses.

"How do you do this, Meg?' Jimmy asked as they walked out of the day surgery room several hours later. "How do nurses stand this?"

Meg laughed. "It's life, Jimmy. You deal with it. That's someone's mother, someone's neighbor — you just help out."

"Yeah, I'd rather be plowing snow all night long than dealing with that! The woman's ninety-five years old! Why is the medical profession keeping her alive?"

Meg laughed. "So, what do we do — shoot her?"

"No, starve her to death!" Jimmy said jokingly.

They both started to laugh.

Two weeks went by before they heard from Dr. Sanders. Jimmy was at work, up on the eighteenth floor of a new apartment building going up in Boston when he heard his name.

"Hey, Romano! Telephone!"

Jimmy knew it was the doctor. No one else knew his number here except for Meg, and she was teaching a class, so he knew it wouldn't be her. He took his hard hat off, nervously running his fingers through his hair as he listened to the doctor's voice on the other end of the phone.

"Okay, I can get there around five o'clock. No, don't call Megan. I want to be alone for this appointment."

Ironically, Meg was teaching her class of nursing students about the function of the liver at the same time Jimmy received the call from the doctor. Her students were feverishly writing down the importance of this large organ, trying to keep up with Meg's fast-paced lecture.

"The liver, largest organ in the body, lies just below the diaphragm, with the lungs extending over its upper portion."

Meg was saying this with no feeling. She recited by rote the functions of the liver. "Bile production, carbohydrate and fat metabolism, detoxification. In fact … In fact …" Her voice trailed off. She took a deep breath and managed to continue, "In fact," she said again briskly, once more in control, "You can't live without your liver."

It had just hit her, like a bolt of lightning. You can't live without your liver. You can't live without your liver. Jimmy would die if his liver stopped functioning.

Her students were staring at her. She had no idea how much time had gone by while she was preoccupied with her internal thoughts. "Sorry, guys," she said. "I got a little carried away. Guess I'm tired. Think I'm going to let you all leave early today."

As the class exited the room, she started to pack up her own books, pencils, notepads. She finally sat in her chair, slumping forward and letting the tears flow. She had a feeling of impending doom, the sense of a dark cloud hanging over her, her family, and especially her husband. At forty-eight, a seasoned nurse and generally wiser person, Meg knew Jimmy was sick. All she had to do was look at his sunken yellow face, his slightly swollen abdomen. She knew it was serious. Meg put her face in her hands and cried, cried for the unfairness of life, for her kids, herself. She was so in love with her husband, she couldn't imagine one day without him.

There was a gentle knock on the door. It was another colleague and friend who Meg had confided in about Jimmy's health. She slowly opened the door and saw Meg's face in her hands and quietly walked over and whispered, "Meggie, you have a phone call. It's Dr. Rick Sanders. Jimmy's with him. They want you to go to his office."

The traffic was bumper to bumper as Meg slowly inched her Chevy Lumina along Storrow Drive. There was nothing she could do about the traffic. Dr. Sanders and Jimmy would just have to wait for her arrival. Meg glanced over at the Charles River and saw the crew team from Harvard University in their shells, swiftly making their way back to Cambridge. They looked so carefree, healthy and lean. *I'll bet none of them have liver problems,* she thought jealously.

Meg remembered the time when she and Jimmy had returned from Maine when she had been discharged from the rehabilitation center, over twenty years ago. He rented a canoe and took Meg out on a warm summer night onto the Charles River. Jimmy was such a romantic! He had packed a cooler full of expensive cheeses, grapes, cider wine and hors d'ouevres, even wine glasses. For four hours, they talked, ate, finished the bottle of wine, and enjoyed the balmy summer night. And when they headed back to return the boat, Jimmy decided they needed to "christen" the boat by making love.

Meg had laughed. "Jimmy, we'll get splinters!"

Jimmy had rowed over to a desolate area and they had made love, unaware of other people in their cabin cruisers, motorists observing the rocking boat going from side to side. After that night, Meg knew she was madly in love. Nothing, absolutely nothing else mattered in her life except Jimmy Romano. And twenty-five years later, she felt the same about him. And she was on her way to learn his fate — her own fate and her children's. Two years before, at her twenty-fifth high school reunion the president of the class asked the question, "What do you know now that you didn't know in high school but wished you had?"

At the time, Meg thought it a silly question, who cares, really, so many years later? But now she knew. The answer was that life is simply not fair. You don't know what is going to be handed to you from the universe, from God. Life was just that, not fair. Some people seemed to have everything fall their way — good jobs, promotions at work, great kids that appeared to be problem-free. Meg felt too much had been handed down to her from the gods.

Why me, why Jimmy, she thought? We seem to have one crisis after another in our lives.

But a saying went through her mind, an old saying from religion class and from her mother. God doesn't give you more then you can handle. So, suck it up, Meg thought, life will get better, just trust God, trust the doctor that he will save Jimmy's liver.

Meg pulled the car into the parking lot of Lorriat Clinic in Burlington where Jimmy's doctor had his office. A world-renowned facility, the Lorriat had started its clinic in Boston, affiliated with hospitals in the area, and then moved its site to Burlington, Massachusetts in 1981 where it was a clinic and hospital combined.

Meg walked through the front entrance, still noticing the hustle and bustle of the hospital lobby, even though it was after seven o'clock at night. She made her way to the elevator and pushed the button to the sixth floor. Meg was alone and leaned against the side of the elevator, head back, as tears started to seep from her eyes.

Be brave, she thought. Jimmy needed her strength and her ability to withstand the news she was going to receive.

Dr. Sanders was in his mid-forties. The head of the liver transplant unit in San Diego, he decided to move his entire practice, staff nurses, doctors, and secretaries to Boston, where his wife was from. Lorriat Clinic was thrilled. Meg had gotten to know him and his brilliance as a surgeon and physician with her schools affiliation with the hospital. Her students did clinical rotations there and had much respect for Dr. Sanders.

Meg walked down the long corridor to the doctor's office. Her legs were aching — arthritic pain — and she suddenly felt old. Facing adversity makes the heart and soul stronger, but it also has a way of aging youth before its time. It infuses the soul with wisdom, a wisdom that speaks to you in whispers from the depths of your heart, strengthening your emotions so you don't fall apart. Unfortunately, it also adds lines to your face, shadows under the eyes, and sadness to your demeanor. Meg caught a glimpse of herself as she passed a mirror in the hallway. Sure, she still had a youthful figure for forty-eight years old — running six miles a day did that for her, but she glanced at her aging, sad face, a face that once turned men's heads a second time, and she could see she had changed, aged too quickly in the last six months. Since Jimmy fell sick, her hair was grayer, and her worry lines increased: each day she felt she had another added line on her face, a new age spot. There was no denying it when you look in the mirror and those lines are staring back at you.

I need to smile more, Meg thought. *I'm Ms. Doom & Gloom. I already have Jimmy dead and buried, for Christ's sake. I have to get help. I have to have hope!*

Dr. Sanders and Jimmy were waiting for Meg inside the office.

"Sorry I'm late. The traffic was bumper to bumper," she said as Jimmy pulled up a chair for her. He looked into her beautiful green eyes and saw such sadness. And she hadn't even heard the atrocious news the doctor was about to give her.

Dr. Sanders got right to the point. "Meg, I just went over all the tests from the biopsy with Jimmy, and it doesn't look too good. He has Hepatitis C that is in stage four. And he has some fibrosis and cirrhosis that is in stage four. We have to act quickly, try to get the inflammation down with medication and see if that helps."

Meg was stunned. Despite being a nurse and knowing that Jim was sick, she'd had no idea it would be this devastating. "How did his liver get so bad so quickly?" asked Meg.

"It didn't," Dr. Sanders said. "I believe Jimmy was exposed to Hepatitis C in his early twenties when he shared needles with some friends. He told you about that, I know. Anyway, the virus has been causing damage all these years, though his symptoms didn't show up until just last year."

"Do you think the medicine will work?"

"Jimmy's agreed to give it a shot and, with his disease process, he has a twenty to forty percent chance of the virus being cured."

"Then we can't do it! With those low statistics? Why not get him a new liver? He's young … he could handle it. He's drug and alcohol free now!"

"Calm down, honey," Jimmy said as he stood up, hugged her and had her sit back down. "We already discussed that and it may be an option, but the last option. I want to give the medicine a shot."

Meg knew about the medication for Hepatitis C. She had taught this to her nursing students — Ribavirin and interferon, better known as Rebetron Combination Therapy. She knew of the horrendous side effects these could cause — constant flu-like symptoms, severe fatigue, depression, blood levels dropping causing anemia, and thyroid problems. She put her head in Jimmy's lap and cried. She cried because she knew it wouldn't work — she could feel it. She knew that they were taking the long road to an eventual liver transplant.

But Jimmy wanted to do it. It was his life, his body, ultimately she really didn't have a say.

"There are support groups for you, Meg, and for Jimmy and the children," Dr. Sanders said, compassionately. "I know this is a blow to you both. I also know that in time you will get used to it and not let it overwhelm your lives. But immediately we need you and the kids tested to make sure none of you are infected as well."

"I never used needles," Meg replied.

"I know, Meg," Dr. Sanders said, "But a small percentage of cases can be transmitted sexually. It's very rare, but it can happen. Also, sharing toothbrushes, razors — anything like that your children may have touched where blood was present."

Meg knew on road trips, vacations, someone always forgot a toothbrush or razor. And these items would be shared until the next day when they could be purchased.

"I've already set up appointments to have you and your children checked within the next few weeks. It'll give you all a chance to absorb the fact of Jimmy's illness and get used to it. But Jimmy needs to start on medication this week. We went over it and he'll see one of my nurses for further instructions."

"How expensive is it?" Jimmy asked.

"About eight hundred dollars a month, but I'm pretty certain your insurance will cover it. The HMO you have is good with preventive medicine and this kind of treatment."

"Swell," said Meg sarcastically. Her emotions were coming out quickly. She was worried, angry, hurt, pissed at God that this was happening. Meg had had enough. She stood up to leave.

"I'm sorry," she said to Dr. Sanders "This was way too much for me. I knew Jimmy was sick, but I didn't expect to hear all this. I hope I wasn't too rude."

Dr. Sanders replied, "You both need to get used to all this and not lose hope. I'll get Jimmy started on the program and in a few weeks, we'll do the first blood test: a complete blood count, liver function tests and kidney profiles. Just don't lose hope, Megan. This may work."

CHAPTER TWENTY-THREE

January 1, 2000

The new millennium was a time of rejoicing and partying. It was also a time of fear. All over the country people kept their eyes on their televisions, wondering if the world would end, computers would stop functioning, and life would come to a crashing halt.

The Boston area was feeling the effects, as well. Jimmy had been called to be on alert for the town of Newport in case there were power outages, buildings falling down, and electrical wires short-circuiting. The company he worked for needed available hands to help with disasters, and snow was expected and Jimmy would be out all night plowing as well.

Jimmy left the house at eleven that night with a party going on and snow falling heavily. All three children had friends over and neighbors had dropped by; but when midnight hit, he needed to be at the Town Hall, just in case.

He grabbed Megan, hugged her, and whispered, "Show up at one o'clock and go plowing with me."

Meg could feel the nervousness in Jimmy as he hugged her. He was actually trembling, not because he was worried about the year two thousand, but because of the medication he was on. Every time he injected himself with interferon, his body shook, chills ran through him for half an hour. Then he would be fine.

The mild reaction he had would dissipate and Jim would feel good except for tiredness. But he fought that off, pretended nothing was wrong. Jimmy had been on the medication for two full months, his liver function tests were dropping to a more normal level and overall he seemed better. The yellow of his eyes were turning white again, the abdominal swelling was going down. Both Meg and Jimmy were thrilled. He was going to get well again; they were facing the New Year with confidence.

The company left about one o'clock. Her two older kids went to party elsewhere, and when Mario was sound asleep, she headed out to spend some time with Jimmy. She didn't have long. Snow was falling and she knew Jimmy would have to plow fairly soon. As she headed north to see her husband, she realized nothing had changed. The year 2000 brought only a new hour, a new day. The world didn't end and life continued.

So, be it! Meg said to herself. *A lot of panic for nothing.*

Meg spotted Jimmy at the Newport Town Barns as he was placing chains on the wheels of the truck he needed to drive. The snow was falling harder and she knew she only had about an hour with her husband. Jimmy had started to let his hair grow longer — one of the side effects of the medication was hair loss, so he decided to do nothing, simply not go to the barber, let his hair grow just in case it started to thin.

But it had gotten long, close to shoulder length, and his beard and mustache had gotten even thicker. His older son, Mike, commented one night, "God, Dad, are you going through a midlife crisis, reliving your hippie days or something? You're close to having a ponytail."

"Live and let live," he had said to Mike. "Who really cares about my hair? I've learned to not sweat the small stuff."

And Meg realized he was at that point and not caring, nor did she. Taking it one day at a time was the easiest thing to do. It kept her from worrying. She had been so angry — especially when she had to be tested for Hepatitis C, HIV, and communicable diseases. Even her kids had to go through the process of being tested for HIV and hepatitis, and it was more degrading than she had imagined.

But then she realized she needed to learn to be humble. Humility was important and nobody was really looking at her! It was only her paranoia, a learning experience for Meg and her kids. All three children never gave it a second thought. But, then again, they didn't realize the seriousness. Only Bella had a clue.

"Is Dad going to be okay?" she asked one night. 'Is he going to live? See his grandchildren?"

"Of course," said Meg.

And Bella had walked away, a look of skepticism on her face; yet accepting what her mother said must be gospel truth.

Jimmy had to go check his plowing route, make sure the roads were pretty clear of vehicles, and that he met with all his workers and let them know when they would be starting. Meg went with Jimmy on this rendezvous. It wasn't new to her. She had climbed into the tall yellow truck many times, happy, a complacent wife, in the past ten years.

This time, though, she felt different. Meg was angry for no particular reason other than seeing her husband putting chains on a truck, looking thirty instead of almost fifty, with his long hair and beard. It had brought back memories — memories of his earlier days when he was in his hippie era, days that had probably contributed to his present day health problems. As they drove up and down each side street, Jimmy could feel the tension.

"What's wrong, Meg?" he asked.

"Nothing!" Meg said in a stilted angry voice — a voice Jimmy remembered all too well, the Flaherty voice, full of condemnation and snobbism, a voice that reminded him of the old days of John Flaherty and their prestigious family.

But Jimmy was beyond that. He had become full of wisdom and acceptance he had learned through the twelve-step program. Even though he felt slightly annoyed at Meg's attitude, he tried to convince her she needed to talk.

Meg remained silent, not giving in to his request right away then finally blurted out, "You got Hepatitis C because of those hippie chicks you slept with and shot up dope with, Jimmy, those girls you met twenty-five years ago. You shared needles with them … and now I'm suffering the consequences!" She was practically incoherent with fury.

Jimmy, tired and frustrated, yet trying to understand her feelings attempted to make light of what she had said. "Hippie chicks, Meg? Where did that saying come from?"

"Don't laugh at me, Jimmy. How could you have done that, acted so recklessly?"

Jimmy, finally unable to hold in his temper at Meg's better-than-thou attitude said, "Oh, really, Miss Perfect? Remember the guys you snorted coke with? You could have gotten Hepatitis C from them … or that asshole you went out with, slept with, the one who used you for your apartment and car — he could have had AIDS, Meg. You're lucky that through the grace of God you're not sick. I'm the one dying a slow death because of past mistakes. Yes, I used drugs. I mainlined with those so-called 'hippie chicks,' but you're no different. You're simply luckier than me. You did the same things I did. You just had different results!"

Meg was so angry she hopped out of the truck and ran as fast as she could, away from her husband, away from reality. She could no longer bear the pain, anger and rage she was feeling. *It's his fault,* she thought. *He's trying to blame it on me!*

Jimmy had pulled the truck to the side of the road. It was now snowing hard; the white flakes were blinding his vision as he tried to chase after Meg. His boot became untied and he tripped and fell on the grass, grabbing his knee in pain. His joints, muscles, were feeling the effects of the medication. "Damn!" he shouted, as he stood, tying his boot and resuming his pursuit of Meg. He found her on a park bench, sobbing.

Jimmy came up from behind, hugged her. "Megan, stop this craziness. I love you. We have to stop fighting — learn to deal with this together."

He took her hand and led her back to the truck. Somehow, Jimmy knew she would accept this disease. The argument was a turning point. His own anger, his vicious words, were necessary for his own emotional healing. In the truck, Meg laid her head on his lap. His jeans were wet with tears and snow. Meg sobbed, long shaking sobs that she had no control over.

Jimmy simply placed his hands on her head and just let her cry, praying that this would be the turning point and the acceptance of Jimmy's illness for Meg. And when they arrived back to her car, Meg was more composed, a look of defeat and yet a new source of strength appearing on her face. When she was calmer, she told Jimmy she had been storing all this pent-up anger. Even though he was doing better physically and his blood tests were improving, she was simply sick of not being able to carry on a normal existence. Jimmy was too tired to go to movies, out to dinner. This disease was only allowing his body to go to work each day, barely at times, and he was too weak to have a social life. Meg missed it, all the fun they had been having, especially since the kids were older. They'd had more freedom — and now this … this disease that held no promise of recovery.

And Meg felt so helpless. As a nurse, she had been taught to help heal patients, to provide answers, and she could do nothing for her husband physically, give him no answers at all. But she felt better — better than she had in months — for getting all her anger and resentment out.

Yet as Jimmy watched her drive away into the night, neither of them knew that the biggest snowstorm of their lives was just beginning.

CHAPTER TWENTY-FOUR

April – 2000

"So, my father was a junkie … that's how he got Hepatitis C?" Mario's words had such anger in them. Meg was making him breakfast. Her fifteen-year-old son suddenly started to ask questions. As Meg cracked two eggs into the frying pan, checked on the bacon, she turned her head, looking at her youngest child, ready to answer his questions. At fifteen, Mario was developed beyond his years, a hulking two hundred pound football and hockey player. She could no longer recognize any youthful and childish ways with Mario. He wanted answers, and he wanted them that minute.

Meg placed the plate of food in front of him, grabbed her cup of coffee, and decided there was no time like the present to begin to tell Mario about his father's past, her past. She'd do it in increments. Start small and reveal little details of his parents' lives, events that may have led up to Jimmy's present illness.

Why not? She had told Bella and Mike about them. Why wouldn't she tell Mario? But she knew why — she didn't want to.

He was an angry kid to begin with, full of an animosity towards the Flaherty's, including Meg. For some reason, Mario wanted to blame her for Jimmy's illness. She could feel it, sense that feeling in her youngest child. The Romanos did no wrong in his eyes. It had to be Meg and Meg's family that caused this.

But as Meg unveiled the story, Mario knew he couldn't blame his mother any longer. His father did this to himself and now they were all suffering the effects of his illness — the hacking cough, the increased weakness, the constant scratching of his body because it had become incredibly itchy over the last two months; no one could stand hearing his nails against his dry skin.

Now, as Mario sat there, breakfast untouched, he listened to his mother's words. "Things you've done in your life, events you've regretted sometime come back to you, haunt you, and you have no choice but to deal with them. Life, Mario, is simply not kind."

As Meg was cleaning up from breakfast, she could hear Jimmy's cough, his wheezing. She went upstairs to check on him. He had become worse in the last two months. The medication he was taking was making him sick and short of breath. His resistance was low and he was catching every virus that went around. But worse of all, he was becoming more and more jaundiced with each day. For two months, he had done well on the medication and then it stopped working. Although Jimmy claimed the "scratching" was dry skin. She knew it was the bile creeping into his blood stream and causing the itchiness. Meg knew his liver was failing, not functioning like it should. Edema was starting: she saw the slow signs of swelling in his ankles, around his abdomen; the sallow look in his eyes.

Meg picked up the phone to call the doctor, make an appointment for blood work. She sensed, and clinically knew, her husband needed to be re–evaluated. Intuitively Meg knew Jimmy would need a new liver. She quickly took an appointment for that day; there had been a cancellation and she was thrilled.

"You're going to the doctor today, Jim, about twelve-thirty," she hollered from the other room. Surprisingly, Jimmy didn't fight her this time — he knew he had to go. He simply nodded his head in acceptance as Meg watched his jaundiced eyes flicker and his body relax into a state of non-being.

"The medication isn't working anymore, Jim. We're going to have to try something else." Dr. Sanders was sitting at his desk across from Jimmy and Meg. He looked as sad as they did as he uttered those words.

"What else can you try?" asked Jimmy nervously.

"There are a few other medications that might help, but I need to consult with another specialist, a friend and colleague of mine at Mass General. In the meantime, Jim, just to be on the safe side — and we'll use this as a last resort — I'm going to have you evaluated for a liver transplant, get you on the transplant list. And I'm going to take you off the present medication."

Jimmy said, "Is this absolutely necessary? Let me stay on the medication a little longer. It's only been four months!"

"I can't do that. Your blood tests are way out of whack, way too high. Your bilirubin is high, causing bile in your bloodstream, making you itchy and jaundiced, and your creatinine and BUN, which are your kidney function tests, are sky high. You could go into kidney failure. I know this is hard, Jim — for you and Meg — but let's proceed. I'm going to have my secretary schedule an appointment to get the transplant process going. You may never need it, but let's get the ball rolling."

Outside of Dr. Sanders' office, Jimmy kicked the wall. "This is pissa! I'm forty-nine years old and I'm going to friggin' die!"

Meg grabbed his hand and headed towards the elevator. "Let's go, Jimmy. Let's go get something to eat. You're not dead yet! Besides, liver transplants work. I've seen great results in some of my patients!"

Meg said this convincingly and it was true — to a degree. But there was a lot to be concerned with when you get someone else's organ. Sometimes the liver you receive isn't in great shape. If the liver is outside the donor's body for too long, it may not work as well and not help the patient. Or the organ might be damaged during recovery from the donor or in transit to the transplant center. There could be too much fatty tissue or badly formed blood vessels. Rejection after the transplant from unknown incompatibilities is a possibility. But Megan knew she was jumping way ahead, projecting the worst-case scenario in her head. Besides, Dr. Sanders said there were more medications he could try.

Be hopeful, she thought as they exited the elevator. *There are certainly other avenues to take.*

"Maybe I should try acupuncture," Jimmy said suddenly. "You mentioned it before. I don't know that much about it, but I'll give it a shot."

"That's great!" she wasn't sure about how much she trusted alternative medicines, but Meg was willing to try anything. "Do you want me to find an acupuncturist or do you want to do it?"

"I'll take care of it. A guy at work goes to one in Westbridge for his back pain and has had good results, I'll get his name tomorrow."

"You're suddenly taking this pretty well. You know? it's not like you to go seeking out other doctors," Meg said.

"I'm angry, Meg, but I don't want to die. There has to be some treatment out there for me! Besides, acupuncture is becoming more and more popular; it certainly can't hurt to try it."

When they got home, there was loud music coming from the basement and hockey equipment all over the living room floor. Mario and his friends were blaring the music and having a party before hockey practice. The season was over, but Mario played on a spring league and was waiting for his parents to come home to give him a ride. Mario was getting older looking by the day, he looked much older then Michael who was twenty-one, and he was shaving on a regular basis. He was letting his hair grow and looked more like Jimmy every day. Meg opened the cellar door to the sound of Bob Dylan singing *"Like a Rolling Stone."*

"God," she said, "we listened to this music in the sixties."

"So what?" Mario said as he pushed his way past her by the door. "Who really gives a shit, Ma?"

Mario was becoming increasingly angry and unmanageable. He was angry at his father's illness, angry that he had to deal with seeing his dad become progressively sicker over the last few months. As he passed Meg, she could smell alcohol. They had been drinking downstairs and now all four boys were going to play hockey! Mario grabbed the keys and said, "Dad, I'll drive. I know how."

"Don't think so, Mario. No way!" Jimmy said, as he grabbed the keys back from him. He knew, as well, that Mario had had a few beers — his eyes were bloodshot and he was acting rude, on the verge of going out of control. But Jimmy knew he was okay to skate and he'd address the drinking later. "Come on, guys … get your equipment in the car. I'll give you a ride."

One of Mario's friends, Ted Esterbrook, looked at Jimmy and said, "Hey, Mr. Romano, did you know you were really like … yellow?"

Before Jimmy could respond, Mario said sarcastically, "My old man was a druggie, and now it's coming back on him. He has Hep C. That's what he gets!"

Megan lost her temper. "Have some respect, Mario! What the hell is the matter with you?"

Jimmy eyeballed her to be cool and mouthed the words, "I'll take care of this."

When Jimmy dropped all the kids off after practice, he took Mario to Juan's, a Mexican restaurant, for dinner.

"I'll have a Margarita," Mario said to the waitress.

"He'll have a Coke," Jimmy chimed in. "Two Cokes, please."

When the waitress walked away, Jimmy said, "Okay, talk to me. What are you so angry about? And don't deny it. You're drinking away your anger."

"Fuck off, Dad!" And Mario started to get up from the table.

But Jimmy still overpowered him and pushed him back in his seat. "Don't run, Mario. That's what I did. I ran. I escaped because I couldn't deal with my feelings. I lost my father. He died when I was only a little older than you. I escaped into a world of drugs so I wouldn't have to deal with your grandfather's death. And look where it got me — twenty-five years later, I'm a sick man because of my mistakes. I wish I had talked to someone, dealt with my feelings, instead of escaping. Please, don't let history repeat itself. Don't do what I did, Mario. Talk to me or talk to someone! Don't let your anger fester, build up, and especially, don't drink over it! I know you were half in the bag today. You may think you are, but you're not fooling anyone!"

Tears started to stream down Mario's cheeks. "It hurts, Dad — it hurts to see you sick. And Mom is so quick-tempered and yells a lot … our house isn't the most peaceful place. All I see pasted all over the refrigerator is your doctor appointments."

"Don't let my past become your past, Mario. I see some of your behavior and it reminds me of myself thirty years ago. That's what kills me — it's like watching me all over again."

"I'm okay, Dad. I don't drink a lot. I'm under control."

But Jimmy knew he wasn't. There were too many nights when he heard him stumbling into bed or throwing up in the bathroom. And there were too many girls. He knew Mario was sexually active, had found condoms in his coat, and even confronted him over it. But he had to let that go, pray that what he and Meg had taught him would sink in.

"You have hockey to think about, Mario. Colleges are starting to look at you. You're a Division One natural. Can't you see that?"

Mario knew he was a good player and was passionate about hockey and did want to play in college. He had his heart set on Boston University. Playing for the Terriers had been his dream since he was about seven years old. But he was so tired of always playing, missing out on parties and dates, drinking — he didn't feel like a normal teenager. And watching his father so sick just made him want to drink even more. He couldn't stand the emotions he was having and simply wanted to escape into a different world … even the world of sex. He had been having sex for over a year with different girls, no one special. He was usually careful. But being with girls, having sex, helped him erase all the problems in his life.

He looked at his dad and didn't dare tell him that his latest girlfriend, Shawna, thought she might be pregnant. The condom broke during sex over two months ago, and she was two weeks late with her period. Shawna was a senior, applying to colleges. Being pregnant was neither in her plans nor Mario's. He was only a sophomore in high school! The week before Mario almost told his mother. Being a nurse, he thought she could help, refer them to a clinic.

But Shawna had flipped. "Don't tell your mother! Are you crazy? Let's just wait it out."

But Mario knew that she was in denial, refused to do a pregnancy test, and said it was just nerves. If she didn't get her period by the next week, Mario was going to approach his mother. He didn't know what else to do.

Mario looked at his dad. He loved him so much, loved his mother, as well, and was grateful that he had parents who were so much in love. When he was little his mother used to tell him stories of their relationship, how they met and how Jimmy chased her until she finally said yes. And he knew how much in love they were still. The way his father would walk by Meg, brush his hand on her cheek as she was making dinner. She'd look up and smile, a smile that said, "There is nobody else in this world but you."

Mario knew they had a special relationship, unlike his friends parents', divorced or fighting. He felt bad he had yelled at his parents earlier. He knew it was the alcohol and pot he had smoked that made him be so harsh with words. He would never say those things sober. Mario knew he should stop drinking and smoking pot, even cut down on sex. Once Shawna was okay he'd break up with her, concentrate on hockey — he would try anyway, get his life back in order and talk about his problems like his dad said to do.

CHAPTER TWENTY-FIVE

July — 2000

Jimmy had started seeing an acupuncturist in Westbridge named Steve Jackson who had been practicing for over ten years. He was a fairly young man, in his thirties but full of knowledge and hope for Jimmy and his disease. He didn't promise miracles but felt he could relieve Jimmy of some of his symptoms.

"What does acupuncture do, anyway?" asked Jimmy.

"Acupuncture is one of the oldest, most commonly used systems of healing in the world that originated in China some thirty-five hundred years ago." said Steve. "There are more then two hundred acupuncture points on the human body, which are connected by twenty pathways called meridians.

These meridians conduct energy or qi,(pronounced "chi"), between the surface of the body and its internal organs. Each point has a different energy that passes through it and it is believed to help regulate the balance in the body."

"I still plan on seeing my medical doctor even though I'm doing acupuncture, you know," said Jimmy.

"And you should!" emphasized Steve. "Your liver is pretty damaged, I can't cure the hepatitis or cirrhosis, but I can help your symptoms, so I am hoping you continue with both methods of treatment."

Dr. Sanders had taken Jimmy off the Rebertron and started him on Ribitol tablets twice a day and peginterferon weekly injections three months before. It wasn't working. His white blood count dropped after one month and his hematocrit as well. Meg explained to Jimmy that with a low white blood count he was more susceptible to illness: his immune system had very little defense against infection and if his blood levels stayed low he would need blood transfusions.

"Your hematocrit measures the percent of red blood cells in the blood. Red blood cells carry oxygen to all parts of the body — that's why you're so sick, pale and weak: your hematocrit is low and not carrying the oxygen," Meg explained to Jimmy.

So Jimmy had to go off the new medication and what they had dreaded finally became reality: only a liver transplant would save his life. Jimmy was getting weaker and weaker. His symptoms were worsening. His whole body was jaundiced; his liver was enlarged which caused his abdomen to swell. Twice a month he needed fluid drained from his abdomen so he wouldn't be so uncomfortable. And through all this, he continued to work. Mr. Johnson had him in the office working, no longer doing construction, but every day was a struggle. Nevertheless, he made himself go to work.

The Romano family went in and out of accepting Jimmy's disease and understanding why the treatment wasn't working. Weeks would go by where their household would be normal, activities of daily living would go along smoothly, but ultimately something or some event would trigger one of them into going into rages and periods of intense anger. Meg and Bella attended support groups for families of hepatitis patients and occasionally Michael would go. Mario refused. He was the angriest at this injustice and continued to refuse counseling and talking out his anger as his father had suggested.

Meg tried to explain to him that Jimmy had to have a transplant for survival and was hopeful when she explained the situation to Mario. Yet it didn't help, her explanations only made Mario more furious and gave him an excuse to drink and do drugs.

Dr. Sanders told Jimmy he was high-priority for a transplant but it could still take months … even a year or so! He was registered with the United Network for Organ Sharing, which oversees the patient waiting list, so now Jimmy just had to wait.

"I have to wait for someone to die so I can live," Jimmy said to Megan. "That sounds so crazy!"

"Organs are taken from car accident victims every day," said Meg "and others live because of they donated their organs. I guess we need to be grateful."

At the end of August, Dr. Sanders gave Jimmy a beeper to wear. If it went off, that meant there was a potential donor. The doctor explained that the liver transplant team has to decide quickly if it is a good match-up and sometimes it isn't because of different factors, such as the donor having had high blood pressure or some other illness that damaged the liver, or simple incompatibilities that would result in failure of the transplant.

But Jimmy was hopeful and he prayed like he had never prayed before. He started saying the Rosary, making Novenas, all the prayers he was taught as a child going to Catholic Christian

Doctrine. He continued with acupuncture. It relieved the abdominal pain and aided him in breathing. With his swollen abdomen, his breathing would become labored because the fluid in his stomach pressed on his diaphragm and ultimately assaulted his respiratory system. The acupuncture alleviated some of his symptoms.

Dr. Sanders, at first, wasn't crazy about Jimmy doing acupuncture. Not because he didn't believe it worked, but he was concerned about the needles and Jim's blood work. His platelets were low and Dr. Sanders was concerned that needles would puncture his skin and cause bleeding. But Steve called him and assured the doctor that the needles used are unlike hypodermic needles, and are solid and hair-thin, designed not to cut the skin. Satisfied, Dr. Sanders wanted him to continue both treatments, especially since the acupuncture relieved many of Jimmy's symptoms, so that there was no need for extra medication.

Over Labor Day weekend, the beeper went off. All the Romano's were sitting by the pool when the beep-beep sounded. Meg was first to grab it and look at the numbers it was showing. "It's the organ transplant center — I'll go call!" Jimmy was already packed, as they had told him to do. If he were to have the transplant, everyone needed to act quickly.

"I'm going with you!" Mario shouted.

"No," Jimmy said, firmly. "Only your mother and me. You kids can come later. It will be too confusing."

Meg drove to the hospital while Jimmy leaned his head back on the headrest, sweat pouring off of him. Meg thought he looked sicker than ever. *What if he's too ill to undergo the surgery?* she wondered.

But he had been worked up — chest x-ray, cardiogram, ultrasounds, CAT scans — only two months before. All was okay. When they arrived, they were told the liver was on its way from Arizona; someone was picking it up at the airport. More waiting! The nurses prepped Jimmy for surgery, redid tests, and started an intravenous line in his vein. Meg called the kids and told them to head over. Jimmy had even been pre-medicated by an anesthesiologist because he was so nervous, and then — the liver arrived and Dr. Sanders and the team examined it and they found badly formed blood vessels in it. It was a no-go.

Everyone was disappointed. Bella cried uncontrollably.

"This isn't fair … we all get psyched up, excited, only to be let down."

Michael, calm and collected, held his father's hand. "Next time, Dad," he said.

"You bet," Jimmy managed to say.

But Mario was beside himself. "This is bullshit!" he screamed and ran out of the hospital. Seeing his father decline was way too much for him. He was almost to a point of accepting that his father was going to die — each day he looked sicker to him. Then, the beeper goes off, he gets his hopes up, and they casually say "no-go"!

Mario put his fist through the passenger window of his parents' car when he got out to the parking lot. He couldn't stand the way he was feeling. There was way too much going on. He reached into the glove compartment of the car, searched for the phone, and frantically dialed Shawna's number. Fifteen minutes later, she was at the hospital with a fifth of vodka. Mario grabbed the bottle and downed half of it, chugging it as fast as he could.

"That's enough, Mario," she said, grabbing it from him. "You'll kill yourself."

Mario didn't care. He didn't care if he lived or died, he knew his drinking was out of control, he was doing poorly in school, hockey, and Shawna was pregnant and going to have the baby! He looked at her swollen belly and said, bitterly, "I'm going to be a father … a fifteen year-old fucking father."

Shawna started to cry. "You don't have to take care of us. I'm not even telling my parents who the father is. Plus, I won't ask for your help; you're only a kid yourself."

Mario could not believe how out of control his life was. The promises he made a few months before when he had dinner with his dad never happened. He stayed sober for two weeks, found out Shawna was definitely pregnant and that she was keeping the baby. He then started to decline, give up. And now, sitting outside of the hospital after a false alarm for his father's liver transplant, all he could think of was finishing the bottle of vodka so it would take away the pain. Then he realized he shouldn't have left his family. He wimped out and his dad needed him — all of them — to be strong. But with everything going on in his life, he couldn't be strong; he could only try to escape.

Two hours later, Jimmy and Meg walked out the hospital door to their car. They were both disappointed and let down, but they realized it wasn't meant to be. The beeper was given back to Jimmy for the next time. He was told to be ready for it to go off again. When they got to the car, they couldn't believe the smashed-in window.

"Vandals!" said Meg.

"No, it's Mario," Jimmy said sadly. "I know it was Mario."

And when they got home, there was their son, passed out on the couch, empty vodka bottle beside him. Jimmy and Meg knew Mario's drinking had gotten worse over the summer. It wasn't addressed because of Jimmy's illness — one more thing was just too much for them to handle. They hoped once he got back to school, in a regular routine with academics and hockey, he'd be okay. But now they knew that Mario was sick.

"He needs a rehab, Meg. We have to get him in somewhere, somewhere fast, while he's still intoxicated."

Meg knew what to do. Having first-hand knowledge of the medical profession, she felt getting Mario to a rehab pronto would require a trip to the emergency room. She called Mario's doctor, told him the story, and he agreed to meet them at the ER. Between Mike and one of his friends, they got Mario in the car.

"He reeks of booze and pot," Mike said angrily. He was sick of his teenaged brother's behavior and wanted to smack some sense into him, was tired of trying to understand. He couldn't believe the downward spiral of his brother in the last few months. *What's happening to this family?* he thought.

Once at the ER, Mario was monitored all night. In the morning, after a complete psychological evaluation, he was transferred to Gottlieb Treatment Center for detoxification and a six-week rehabilitation program. He was transported via ambulance to the center in Falmouth, Massachusetts. Jimmy and Meg had wanted to drive to Falmouth with Mario in their own car, but prior to leaving the emergency room, Mario told one of the resident doctors he wanted to kill himself. The psychiatrist thought he might be suicidal and didn't dare take the chance of Mario's parents being responsible for getting him to the rehab center. This had earned Mario a ride in the ambulance with his parents following behind in their car.

Meg and Jimmy helped get Mario settled in at the center, filling out paper work and meeting with Mario's counselor. Although angry, their son knew he needed help, needed to be there and detoxify from all the drugs and booze he had been on.

On the way home, Meg couldn't believe what had happened in a mere twenty-four hour period. The focus was off Jimmy and on Mario — for a while, anyway. Jimmy was so wiped out that he barely made it up the stairs. "If the beeper goes off, I'm not going."

They both started laughing for the first time in months, laughing at the craziness of their lives and couldn't imagine what would happen next. Jimmy fell asleep, knowing somehow that Mario would be okay. His son was going to get the emotional help that he never received. His addiction was one thing. Facing what was happening was another, and with time, Mario would realize it.

The Romano family had needed a wake-up call and this was it! He drifted off to sleep in complete acceptance of what was happening in his life. Liver or no liver, Jimmy Romano would survive!

CHAPTER TWENTY-SIX

November — 2000

The beeper had gone off twice since the initial sounding over Labor Day, both of them false alarms. The second liver had gone to someone else more compatible and the third time had been a false alarm, the liver of a thirty-five year-old drug addict whose liver looked worse than Jimmy's. So, he learned to wait. The Romano's learned the art of patience — even Mario. Since the day two months before that had landed him in rehab, he realized he needed to be there. His sixteenth birthday brought with it a new awareness of himself, facing problems head on — slowly, but head on, plus a new acceptance of his father's disease.

He had gone to detox for a week to rid himself of all the alcohol and drugs in his body, and then he was sent to the rehabilitation section of the hospital where his healing really began. He had been using a melting pot of drugs to escape his problems: alcohol, pot, Ecstasy, even heroin. Whether it be maturity, or him being sick and tired of being sick and tired, Mario was getting rid of the demons and dealing with the problems in his life. Facing adversity was actually making him stronger!

As he watched his parents enter the doors of the rehab, he knew he needed to tell them he was going to be a father in less than a month. He waited as his mother pushed his father in a wheelchair through the automatic doors. He hadn't seen his dad in two weeks, but in that time, he had gone from ambulatory to wheelchair-bound. His disease was killing him, but he wouldn't stop coming to see his son. He still carried the beeper in hopes of a liver becoming available.

Two months ago, Mario would have held his feelings in, his stories and the fact that he got his girlfriend pregnant. Simply because he was a pleaser, he didn't want to upset the household because his father was so sick and he didn't think his dad could handle it. But after two months of therapy, he knew this was wrong. He needed to be honest, let the chips fall where they may and wait for an outcome.

Mario walked over and met his parents. He shook his father's hand, felt the limpness, the weakness. He couldn't help but concentrate on the jaundice, sunken eyes, and swollen abdomen. Jimmy Romano looked like he was going to die any minute. He had sandals on because his ankles were so swollen. His hands and face were puffy. But his spirits were high. When Mario shook his hand his father, weakness and all, pulled his son towards his face and kissed his cheek. And Meg! His mother looked glowing, beautiful. For some reason, the stress she was under made her look radiant. Of course, she jogged six miles a day, kept her slim; but there was a look of acceptance, less heartache, in her eyes and gait.

"You still have the beeper, Dad?"

"Yes," replied Jimmy. "Any time now, my new liver's coming. But tell us about you, Mario. How are you?"

Although difficult, he finally told them what had happened in the last six months — the drugs, sex, Shawna's pregnancy, hockey, school, his father's disease. By the time he was through talking, all three were crying. The tears brought a healing of some sort. As Meg wiped her tears, she said," I heard that if you don't cry your organs cry out."

"So that's my problem!" Jimmy said laughingly.

But he looked at Mario and said, "I am so proud of you — proud you're facing your demons and proud you didn't desert Shawna. You're only sixteen and you hung in there. That was very mature."

Of course, Mario didn't expect to be congratulated for his behavior, so he was in a state of shock. And his mother agreed with his father!

"Bringing a child into the world isn't a mistake, Mario. Shawna made a brave decision and we'll support you both, no matter what."

"Shawna isn't sure if she wants to keep the baby, he might be put up for adoption". Mario said this with no hesitation. "It's a boy … she found out the other day. He could be a hockey player. I don't know if I want her to give him up, at first she wanted to keep the baby, now she's confused as to what to do."

"Let it unfold the way it's supposed to unfold, just like you, Mario. Your dad and I didn't push or pressure you after you got admitted to rehab and now things are unfolding. You're taking the year off, going to repeat your school year, the way God intended. Shawna has her parents, and they will help her deal. Just know that we are here for both of you!"

As Mario watched his parents leave, his feelings were incredibly mixed — all over the place. He still wanted to drink, get high, and have sex. The only difference was now he knew he couldn't. He was an addict: addicted to drugs, alcohol, and women. At sixteen, he knew this and would have to learn to deal. At least he had support, not apathetic parents like some of the kids in this joint. And he knew, as much as he was attracted to Shawna, he didn't love her. This is what he had to face, deal with in the next few months. And, no hockey! Not a tragedy exactly, but a major disappointment. But he would move on: he was strong, like his father. He would cope, face his problems, and the answers would come.

The beginning of December was the first snowfall and Jimmy was now totally homebound, wheelchair-bound, only going out for doctors' appointments and an occasional dinner with Meg. He knew he was dying. No livers available, this would be his last Christmas — if he made it to Christmas, three weeks away. Meg was decorating the tree, acting normal, as if it were just another day. But they both knew that if a liver didn't become available soon, he would die.

"Let's talk about my death, Meggie."

She was hanging tinsel and tying red bows on the tree. "No, Jimmy. I'm not going there."

"We have to, Meg. I'm dying. I want things said at my church service, my wake and funeral. I want someone to sing, *Amazing Grace* at the top of their lungs at my church service. Come on, Meggie. Support me here … I am really dying!"

Jimmy's hair was thin but shoulder length. His face was still so handsome amidst the swelling and jaundice. Meg put down the tinsel and bows and put her head in Jimmy's lap. The tears came — not uncontrollable tears, but sensible tears — as Meg put it; tears of necessity. They helped her face what she knew was inevitable.

"I can't let you die, Jimmy. I've never loved anyone so much in my life. I don't know if I can go on if you're not here. I loved you thirty years ago when I set eyes on you and I love you even more now. How am I to ever get over that?"

Jimmy put his hand on her hair, stroking her, not responding with words, simply because there was nothing to say. They had both said it all — all their lives they had loved and lost. Loved and lost a few times, but always came back because of their deep commitment.

Meg gathered her composure and said, "When my dad died, in the limo my mother looked at me and said, 'it is better to have loved and lost than never to have loved at all.' So, I guess I need — we need — to focus on that. God, Jimmy, I even loved the other you, the Joe Gallucci you, and I would take Joe Gallucci back again if it meant you living."

"No you wouldn't, Meg. Joe died over fifteen years ago. I don't want him and those painful days back again."

"Okay," Meg said with sadness but acceptance. "Tell me what you want and I will find the courage to do it, now and when you do die."

Jimmy looked in Meg's eyes and said with strength he didn't know he had, "I need to be cremated, have my ashes sprinkled down the Keys. Take me to Florida, Meg. I always loved it there … that's where I want my life to end."

CHAPTER TWENTY-SEVEN

January — 2001

The holidays were spent at home in Cambridge. They were somber days. Hopeless feelings dwelled in the Romano household. Jimmy was getting sicker and knew, if he didn't get to the Florida Keys soon, he wouldn't get there at all, except in a box or a bottle — wherever they put his remains when he died.

The one thing that kept Jimmy happy and the other members of the Romano family laughing was Jimmy's obsession with a fantasy football league. He would spend hours on the computer, getting statistics, picking offensive football players so he could win, pick players that would ultimately beat his opponents and he would be the champion! Meg was putting laundry away one morning, glancing in the computer room as she put the towels away and laughed as she saw her husband quickly typing in his line-up for the game.

"Okay, Jimmy. Explain this fantasy football thing to me. I don't get it. What's so important about it and how do you play?"

"You pick a player like this one I have just chosen, Marshall Faulk, who plays for the St. Louis Rams, plus six other offensive players and one defensive player, then I go against one of the guys I am on the league with, Brad for instance, who picked his players like I did … then hopefully I win! Like last year I won the whole thing!"

"Terrific," said Meg, wondering how a man's mind truly works, to enjoy something like this, a real fantasy all right. But it kept Jimmy busy and happy. Football had always been such a passion for her husband.

He also kept up his sense of humor that he was known for. His one-liners always made people laugh although he kept a straight face. He would watch reruns of the comedian Don Rickles, crack-up laughing as he listened to one joke after another.

The end of January, four of Jimmy's close friends, Meg, the children, and Jimmy's mother boarded a plane to Miami where they would stay one night and then head over to the Keys the next day. Jimmy had come to terms with his imminent death and could say things; show his feelings to his friends and family before he died. Mario was still struggling with his father's illness as well as his own. He was in a halfway house, trying to stay sober and drug-free. He was also a father: Shawna had given birth two weeks before and decided to keep their son, Sam. Mario was sixteen years old, couldn't even take care of himself, never mind a kid!

"You're not going to have to, Mario," Jimmy had said to him. "Shawna and her parents are helping out now. Eventually, when you're out of school, mature a little, you can pitch in."

Mario had to take his junior year off, a whole year off from high school to get better and to heal. That meant no hockey, either. He missed his old life, wanted to be a high school kid again with no worries and carefree days. He couldn't believe he was actually going to lose his father to this disease. He was so full of anger and resentment at the world; yet somehow he felt his dad would rally, get better. Maybe a liver would become available.

When they got to Key West, the group of friends and the Romano's stayed at Mr. Johnson's condo right on the water. Jimmy could barely make it up the steps into the apartment. His legs and abdomen were so swollen he could hardly walk, and he became short of breath at the slightest movement. They had arranged to take Mr. Johnson's boat out on the ocean. Jimmy wanted to show Megan where to throw his ashes — there was a special place Jimmy wanted to be laid to rest and be remembered. He always loved the ocean, the peacefulness. He thought back to all the days he and Meg would throw a blanket on the sand, lie there together, make love, and listen to the sound of the waves as they drifted off to sleep. Meg would tell him he loved the water so much because he was a Pisces, the water sign in Astrology.

A water sign, Jimmy smiled to himself at the memories. Meg would tell him that Pisces motto was "serve or suffer," with emotions very strong and deep but were very moody. She would say because her sign was Libra, which is the balance sign, she brought things into harmony in their relationship, and overall she was right. Although she had an Irish temper, she somehow had a calming effect on the family and would find solutions to problems. But this time, Jimmy knew, there was no solution, only the answer that he was dying and would die very soon.

The sun was shining brightly as the gang of them boarded the boat with coolers, food and suntan lotion. It was eighty-five degrees at nine in the morning and was going to reach the nineties by noon. But Jimmy was prepared and wanted to see the spot where he would end up. As the motor boat picked up speed,

Jimmy could feel the water spraying on his face and could see the vastness of the ocean, see the deep blue, and smell the salt air, as he looked around. "This reminds me of Van Morrisson's song *Into The Mystic*, and he started singing, "Smell the sea and feel the sky, as we go into the mystic."

"Do you think there's an ocean in Heaven, Meggie?"

She laughed and said, "What makes you think you're going to heaven, Mr. Romano?"

They had gotten to the point of being comical about his death. The crying and seriousness of the outcome was way too much for all of them, so they joked. Except for Jimmy's mother — it wasn't her style. She cried on end, chanting, "A mother isn't supposed to live longer than her children."

As the boat approached the middle of the ocean, there was a small island up ahead, sitting alone, a few trees and a small beach area.

"Stop there," Jimmy said to Frank, who was driving the boat. "This is where I want to be."

And Jimmy felt like an island … all alone. He would leave this world alone just like he came into it, remembering his days of catechism in the Catholic Church on Ash Wednesday. The priest would rub ashes on your forehead and say, "Dust to dust, ashes to ashes, from dust you came and to dust you shall return." And his mother would confirm that you arrive in the world, screaming your way into this life, and you leave alone, sometimes fighting not to go, but you would return to God by yourself.

Jimmy lifted Meg's hand, put it to his lips and said, "After I'm gone, take my ashes and sprinkle them on the shore of the island; let me be washed out to sea, make my way to the middle of the ocean." He hugged Meg tightly. "I'm so sorry I have to leave you. I love you so much! I loved you the minute I saw you on that elevator and I love you ten times more today. I'll wait for you in Heaven."

Meg burst out crying. She sat on the floor of the boat and just cried. Tears were in everyone's eyes — they were losing their father, friend, and son, losing a wonderful human being who had added so much to this world.

"I'm tired," Jimmy said. "Let's head back to the condo."

It had been a long day; the sun was going down slowly as the boat was docked. Everyone was standing, stretching, most alone in his or her thoughts. Then it happened — the beep-beep-beep, the sound of the beeper the Romano's had learned to hate! It was the sound that gave them the feeling of getting your hopes up only to be let down. But somehow, Meg felt different this time. There was a ray of hope; a feeling that it wasn't over, that Jimmy still had another chance. Meg jumped out of the boat first, frantically searching for the keys to the condo as she ran down the pier. Jimmy, watching his wife, knowing that she wanted to call Dr. Sanders fast, thought to himself, I can't get my hopes up. I just can't.

The liver was in Georgia. There had been a serious car accident with two teenage deaths. One of the livers was going to Jimmy. Dr. Sanders instructed him to go to Miami General. He was going to meet him there, perform the surgery with the transplant team in Florida. It was too risky for Jimmy to come back to Boston. Time was of the essence and the liver could be at Miami General in an hour. Meg called the Key West Fire Department. Fifteen minutes later, they had an ambulance rushing Jimmy to Miami. Meg sat with him in the back of the ambulance as they went ninety miles an hour over the bridge, through small towns, siren howling. Meg looked at Jimmy, his jaundiced face, eyes, and fluid-filled belly. She thought he might be too sick to undergo surgery. *I'm not going to get my hopes up.*

But she prayed, prayed harder than she ever did in her life. *God, please, please let this happen — don't let us be let down again. I beg you. Please let this liver be the one, the one to keep my husband alive!*

Jimmy was rushed through the ER and up two flights to the pre-operative center at Miami General. The liver transplant team, including Dr. Sanders, who miraculously arrived two minutes before the Romano's via the hospital airplane, was waiting. The liver wasn't there yet. A nurse immediately transferred him onto a stretcher, wrapped a tourniquet around his left arm to draw blood.

"Jeeze," Jimmy said, "can't a guy get undressed, into his pajamas?"

'No," replied the middle-aged male nurse, with a smile, "This is serious business, Mr. Romano. Your liver awaits! The operating room just called, said the liver arrived and it's being examined."

All sorts of staff approached Jimmy: anesthesia nurses to check his vital signs and have him sign consent forms, start an I.V, and prep his abdomen for surgery. The anesthesiologist arrived, told him he was giving him general anesthesia, and explained the process, that an intubation tube would be put down his throat and he would be attached to a respirator that would do the breathing for him. The doctor asked more questions: "Do you have allergies? Do you drink alcohol … smoke cigarettes or pot, Mr. Romano?" asked Dr. Harkins, the chief of anesthesia.

The questions were way too much for Jimmy. Meg answered for him, gave his history. His blood tests came back within twenty minutes. His results looked good and were compatible with the liver he was to receive.

Dr. Sanders explained to Jimmy and Meg, "Once you're asleep from the anesthesia, I'm going to make an incision shaped like a boomerang on the upper part of the abdomen. My team of doctors will remove your old liver, leaving portions of your major blood vessels in place. The new liver will then be inserted and attached to the blood vessels and bile ducts. I'll also put a tube into you to help with bile drainage."

"Wow, this sounds like a go this time," said Jimmy.

'It's definitely a go," replied Dr. Sanders.

Medication was given to Jimmy to sedate him. He held Meg's hand. "It's possible I won't come out of this, Meg. I know how sick I am."

Dr. Sanders, overhearing Jimmy, said, "If we don't take the chance we'll never know. Your body is compromised but there is a good healthy liver here. I'm feeling positive."

With that, Jimmy was whisked away. Meg stood alone, watching her husband be taken away to the operating room. Everything had happened so quickly — she barely remembered the ride from Key West. Suddenly her kids were there, Michael, Bella, and Mario, hugging her, telling Meg it would be okay. In a trance, she was led away to the cafeteria for coffee and the long wait — several hours until she would hear anything. Meg followed her kids and friends into the coffee shop. She was in a daze, but relieved.

The waiting was over and his death sentence was put on hold, for a while anyway. She had to remain strong, help her kids, pray. She was powerless over the outcome and knew she had to turn Jimmy's life over to God and, at that point, knowing she had no control, she felt relieved for the first time in two years … she finally knew that it was God's decision if Jimmy would live or die.

***

Meg looked at Jimmy from the hockey stands, remembering the first time she noticed Jimmy's sunken, jaundiced face, knowing something was wrong with her husband.

Two and a half years later, same rink, Meg realized her husband was going to survive. His color was improving, day by day. The jaundice was gone, swelling diminishing, and she saw him laughing the familiar belly laugh, and deep from the soul that Jimmy was known for. Jimmy had lost weight, so much weight, which was all fluid. His hair was getting thick, so black with streaks of gray, and he was growing a beard once again.

And Meg was so in love, knowing she would spend many more years with her husband. They were grandparents together, a one year-old grandson. Jimmy had just turned fifty. Her husband looked over at her, they locked eyes, he smiled and winked … he knew her thoughts. Mario came flying out of the box onto the ice, caught a pass, a breakaway, and scored. Mario the Miracle, finally skating again, out of the rehab. It had been tough for him but he was on the road back.

Meg thought of the year before: the surgery and waiting for its outcome. It was hard to forget January twenty-first. From the coffee shop at Miami General, they had gone to the waiting room. Jimmy's mother had fainted, needed to go to the ER to be treated. She was okay, simply overwhelmed. Michael had paced back and forth, nervous for his Dad, and Bella, her sweet daughter, remained strong, held Meg's hand and they prayed together. Mario was somber, scared. Meg could see the red eyes from tears. She was hoping he wouldn't have a slip, use drugs again, and drink. But Mario knew better. He called his sponsor at AA and talked for over an hour. Meg realized how strong her children had become. They would survive.

The day Jimmy had surgery was almost surreal. Meg was waiting for another false alarm because that is how it was before. So, when they actually prepped Jimmy for surgery, drew blood and it matched the donor's, nothing seemed real. She was walking, talking, but felt in a daze. She watched as Jimmy was wheeled into the operating room, being transported in a rush by the liver transplant team. They all looked too young to be trying to save someone's life. But Meg prayed, trusted and waited for the outcome. It was a fifty-fifty chance of survival, Dr. Sanders had told her. Because of the severity of liver damage, it had caused a mild case of congestive heart failure and the beginning of kidney damage. "He may not make it, Meg, but if we do nothing he definitely will die."

Dr. Sanders had said these words so matter-of-factly, like there was no option, no choice. But it was Jimmy's life, not hers, and he gave the go ahead. And there were very few last words as they prepared him for the operation. The words they had were shared with the anesthesiologist as he started pushing meds into his I.V. line, the tech that was prepping him, the nurse taking his blood pressure, and the rest of the patients in the large pre-op area. Jimmy simply held her hand, told her not to be afraid and to hold her head up high, not to fear the unknown, to take one step at a time, one little moment and not look ahead, not project — especially not to project the worst.

Tears came to her eyes, she leaned over and kissed his cheek and simply said, "I love you," never knowing if she'd ever speak with him again.

At that time, Meg had thought the waiting was the hardest. Dealing with her emotions, her children's emotions, it was almost too much to bear.

Her sister Lizzy had flown in from Boston when she heard the news, her sister who was always there, weathered her storms right along with her. It was really the post-op period that was the most grueling. When Dr. Sanders came out of the O.R. ten hours later, he had the look of exhaustion, exultation, and fear.

"He made it, Meg. Jimmy survived round one. The next few days will be the real test, seeing if the liver doesn't reject Jimmy's body."

It is strange when an organ is donated. The family is simply told there is an organ available, not giving out too much information, any names, and addresses. Meg remembered wanting to send the family something, anything. Their family member had kept her husband alive. But there was no communication. She only knew it was a young, healthy seventeen-year-old liver from a car accident. God bless him or her.

Jimmy was in and out of reality for several days. He stayed in the recovery room for forty-eight hours to be monitored post-op, then to the intensive care unit for a few days until he was stable. But his stay in the ICU ended up being a few weeks. His liver function tests and kidney function tests were elevated. He spiked a high fever, hallucinated, and the chest pain he had was hard to evaluate because he was so confused. For one week, Jimmy went in and out of life and was close to death. He told one of the nurses he had spoken to his father. His dad told him he would live and not to give up, that there was more to be done on this earth. The doctor called it hallucinating. Meg and the nurses didn't.

"For God's sake, it's the new century! We've all heard of near-death experiences, seeing the other side, stated Angie, one of the outspoken Afro-American nurses on the night shift. "He probably met his old man down that long beautiful tunnel and brother, he sent him back!"

She had everyone laughing but she and Meg knew it was probably true, his time on this earth wasn't up, and Jimmy Romano had a ways to go before the heavenly tunnel would accept him!

Four days before he was discharged from the ICU, he started to feel better. The anti-rejection medication seemed to be working, his fever subsided, and blood tests started to drop, to fall within normal limits. All his cardiac tests and kidney tests were okay. It was as if Jimmy suddenly, miraculously responded to the treatment.

"What year is it?" he asked Meg. "I mean, are we in 2000 or 2001? Where are the kids? Is Mario okay, playing hockey yet?"

Reality was returning and he was soon transferred out of the Intensive Care Unit to a regular surgical floor for a week before his discharge from the hospital.

All family members were fearful when Jimmy returned home. He was on an anti-rejection medication that was powerful to his system. He needed frequent blood tests to avoid levels that were too high or too low. Elevated levels could lead to toxicity or over immunosuppression, and if levels were too low, they might lead to rejection. Many other tests were done, complete blood counts every few days and phosphate, magnesium, potassium levels, all monitored every week.

By June, Meg felt Jimmy would be okay. He was looking and feeling better.

It had been six months. All organs were functioning, and as the summer came and went, she watched Jimmy's strength return. October arrived and Jimmy went back to work, part time at first then a full schedule by the middle of November. Meg no longer worried that he wouldn't survive; she knew Jimmy would be around for a long time, and that they would grow old together.

Meg was wrapping Christmas gifts when there was a knock at the door. "Special delivery," said the mailman. It was addressed to "James Romano." There was no return address, but it was postmarked from Georgia. When Jimmy returned from work that evening, Meg handed him the envelope. Tears appeared in his eyes because he knew it must be from the donor's family.

He read the letter to Meg:

"Dear Mr. Romano,

"I was told it was not a good idea to write to you, to communicate. But it is Christmas time and Josh loved Christmas, and I was compelled to write as part of my healing process.

"You see Josh was my son and he died over a year ago in a car accident. His organs were donated and you sir received his liver, and I would like to tell you about my son.

"Josh, as you can see by the picture I sent, was a handsome boy. Considerate, loving and charitable, he loved his sister Denise and brother Danny. He coached little league baseball with his dad and loved basketball and swimming. He had millions of friends and his funeral procession was miles long. He laughed a lot, hated the dentist, loved strawberry ice cream and learned how to drive a two wheel bicycle before any of his friends, and was so proud of himself when he got his first A in math when he was a sophomore in high school. And he was healthy. Never drank alcohol or did drugs.

"He loved driving cars, fixing them and as soon as he had his license he bought his own red convertible and he was going to take a road trip with his friends for his senior graduation trip, and in the summer take off once again and drive cross country. Now he will never do that.

"The night of the accident, he got out of work late and was hurrying to go visit his grandmother in a nursing home before going to a dance at the high school with his girlfriend, Jennifer. He never missed a Friday night seeing his "Grammy" and this night was no different, except that he was running late. They say he never saw the truck coming and it was instantaneous for him and Jennifer. I thank GOD for that.

"I hope you don't mind that I found your address and that I didn't give a return address. It's best we don't communicate. But I needed to tell you about my Josh and the love he had for life, and I am grateful he will live on, in a way, through you.

"Sincerely,

"Josh's mother "

Meg remembered how speechless she and Jimmy had been after receiving the letter. Neither of them ever expected to hear from the family. The only information that was given was a seventeen-year-old accident victim. They didn't even know if the liver was from a male of female.

"I wish I could contact that family," Jimmy said sadly.

"Sounds like that wasn't the intent of the letter, Jimmy. Josh's mother needed to do it for her own healing process," Meg said sadly.

"And I will honor that, but it's hard to believe he died at seventeen and I'm alive because of him. God! He's Mario's age!"

"Guess we're not meant to understand God's purposes or intentions, maybe Josh is helping out on the other side if you can look at it that way. Maybe he's more helpful in heaven."

Jimmy had been very quiet and grateful after the letter and they never shared it with their own kids. The letter was tucked neatly away in Jimmy's desk, it was simply too personal to share with anyone else.

Now and then, when Meg would look at Jimmy, she would think of Josh and his young life and what he had contributed to this world — his beautiful smile and sparkly green eyes and how his death had saved her husband's life.

The screeching of jubilant onlookers in the stands as Mario scored another goal interrupted Megan's thoughts of the last year. He was clean and sober for more then a year; the worst was over. He was the father of a year-old son, was a great hockey player and a good student. Hockey scouts from the local colleges were waiting for their day, trying to recruit him to Boston College, Boston University, all the Northeast Division One schools. He had made a comeback in true form, like his father.

As Meg looked over at Jimmy and saw him yelling, "Go deep, Mario … move your feet!" she somehow knew all would be okay. The Romanos had survived once again. Megan Flaherty Romano relaxed — truly relaxed — for the first time in her life.